The

SECRETS
BENEATH

KIMBERLEY
WOODHOUSE

Faith
PERSEVERANCE
Joy

Kimberley Woodhouse

www.kimberleywoodhouse.com

Books by Kimberley Woodhouse

SECRETS OF THE CANYON

A Deep Divide
A Gem of Truth
A Mark of Grace

TREASURES OF THE EARTH

The Secrets Beneath

Books by Kimberley Woodhouse with Tracie Peterson

All Things Hidden
Beyond the Silence

THE HEART OF ALASKA

In the Shadow of Denali
Out of the Ashes
Under the Midnight Sun

THE TREASURES OF NOME

Forever Hidden
Endless Mercy
Ever Constant

JEWELS OF KALISPELL

The Heart's Choice

The
SECRETS BENEATH

KIMBERLEY WOODHOUSE

BETHANYHOUSE

a division of Baker Publishing Group

Minneapolis, Minnesota

© 2023 by Kimberley Woodhouse

Published by Bethany House Publishers
Minneapolis, Minnesota
www.bethanyhouse.com

Bethany House Publishers is a division of
Baker Publishing Group, Grand Rapids, Michigan

Printed in the United States of America

Library of Congress Cataloging-in-Publication Data
Names: Woodhouse, Kimberley, author.
Title: The secrets beneath / Kimberley Woodhouse.
Description: Minneapolis, Minnesota : Bethany House, a division of Baker
    Publishing Group, [2023] | Series: Treasures of the Earth ; 1
Identifiers: LCCN 2023012862 | ISBN 9780764241680 (paperback) | ISBN
    9780764242243 (casebound) | ISBN 9781493443765 (ebook)
Subjects: LCGFT: Christian fiction. | Romance fiction. | Novels.
Classification: LCC PS3623.O665 S43 2023 | DDC 813/.6—dc23/eng/20230327
LC record available at https://lccn.loc.gov/2023012862

This is a work of historical reconstruction; the appearances of certain historical
figures are therefore inevitable. All other characters, however, are products of the
author's imagination, and any resemblance to actual persons, living or dead, is co-
incidental.

Kimberley Woodhouse is represented by the Steve Laube Agency.

Baker Publishing Group publications use paper produced from sustainable forestry
practices and post-consumer waste whenever possible.

23 24 25 26 27 28 29   7 6 5 4 3 2 1

This book is lovingly dedicated to
Judy Hogan

My mom, avid reader, and cheerleader.

She chauffeured me around to piano and voice lessons, musical theater rehearsals, and hundreds of musical competitions. Always cheering me on.

Our home was filled with laughter and music thanks to this wonderful lady.

Now she's a grandma and a great-grandma, and her positive, cheerful enthusiasm for life oozes out at every corner.

Love you, Mom!!!!

And it's also dedicated in loving memory of
Donna Bell

She fought the good fight. She ran the race.

She finished well.

My beautiful aunt went home to be with her Savior while I was writing this book, and even though it was incredibly difficult (and I shed a lot of tears), we are rejoicing that she is no longer suffering in this world.

To God be the glory!

DEAR READER

To set the stage for this series, allow me to give you a little context. Dinosaur National Monument is in the northwest corner of Colorado and the northeast corner of Utah. Earl Douglass—a paleontologist for the Carnegie Museum in Pittsburgh—found the first bones (in 1909) that were the beginning of the dinosaur quarry, which is now famous around the world. Earl was a fascinating man and dreamed of having a place where people could see the bones in the actual rock for all time. His dream became reality.

It's because of him that Dinosaur National Monument is there. And it's amazing.

The idea for a series about women in paleontology and dinosaurs came because I threw out a question to my readers on my Facebook page about things/topics/people/historical events they would like to see next in my books. Laura Flint tossed out "The Bone Wars." Now, if you don't know anything about that, you'll learn about them through this series, but you can also look them up online. I'll give links in the Note from the Author at the end of the book. But through all of our chats, Laura connected me with Diane Douglass Iverson. Earl's *granddaughter*. Isn't that awesome?

Through this amazing friendship, I learned incredible things about Earl. That's why you'll see quotes from his personal journals (*Speak to the Earth and It Will Teach You: The Life and Times of Earl Douglass 1862–1931*. Book Surge Publishing, 2009) throughout the book. I hope they inspire and intrigue you as well. Diane has graciously given us permission to use Earl's words and poems and has helped me immeasurably throughout my research and writing of this book.

I spent almost two weeks out in Colorado, Wyoming, and Utah doing research. Meeting with real-life paleontologists like Dr. Sue Ann Bilbey, going to museum after museum, and visiting site after site. When it came down to figuring out the timeline for my novels, I wanted to show the progression in paleontology over the years. So I chose the southwest corner of Wyoming off of the Green River in what is now Flaming Gorge Reservoir. The area in this first story would now be flooded because of the Flaming Gorge dam. What is now Marsh Creek is the offshoot of the area where I imagine Walker Creek once thrived.

My research buddies, Renette Steele and Jeni Koch, were invaluable to me as I drove them all over God's creation to find the exact place to set *The Secrets Beneath*.

I intentionally placed this story there so I would not detract from the discoveries of the real paleontologists in history. Wyoming, Utah, and Colorado all have a wealth of dinosaur quarries filled with fossils, and many of the best discoveries in North America were found there.

This is a work of fiction, and while I did an enormous amount of research, any mistakes are my own and not a reflection of all the wonderful experts who helped me along the way.

I invite you to traipse along with me through history as we meet the people of Walker Creek and dig for dinosaurs.

Enjoy the journey,

Kimberley Woodhouse

"Go forth into nature and see what she has to show thee. Enter the silent wood and lose thyself in thoughts unthought before. Let fancy construct worlds unknown—fairy worlds of the mind. All this is wonderful, but the wonder is of thyself the mystery of the mind and that matter can arrange itself, know to perceive, to perceive other forms, other arrangements of matter and then to think beyond, to construct a new world of its own yet of fragments of the old."

~Earl Douglass—Saturday, January 28, 1888

PROLOGUE

"Our lives are books. Each day is a page written good or evil."

~Earl Douglass

The garden—*his* garden—was alive with color today, while the inside of him was black as death. Especially when he thought of his father.

The contrast of the lush vegetation, fragrant flowers, and colorful buds with the darkness that crept through his veins made him shiver.

Julian Walker tucked his chin tight to get rid of the thoughts. Damian was the one who embraced the darkness. Not him. His brother could handle it better than he could. Deep down, Julian's true yearning was for the light, to grow beautiful things, and to stay out of their father's fiery wrath.

He dug his fingers into the dirt. A rich, dark concoction of mud he'd dragged up from the river bottom mixed with lots of cattle manure. Wheelbarrow after wheelbarrow, he'd dragged the dark soil up to this place. It had taken him weeks. Mother

11

said it was work that would be worth it—her ploy to keep him away from his father. Randall Walker's violent temper was well-known throughout their little town and beyond. But he was a wealthy man with the largest cattle ranch in the whole territory. So mean ol' Walker—as everyone in town called him—did whatever he pleased, and people left him alone.

Julian hadn't missed the pitying glances cast at them. Especially his mother. But a kinder soul on the planet couldn't be found. She was an angel. *His* angel. Sent to protect him. To love him. To . . . fix him.

The more he grew, the more the blackness inside him grew. He hated it. Feared it would turn him into a man like his father. The past two years had been worse than ever.

"Julian . . ."

Mother's whisper washed over him in the garden. She tipped his face up to see her.

A single tear slipped down his cheek as the sun created a halo around her. "Yes, Mother?"

"Don't allow his ugliness to taint you, dear boy. I will fight for you. Fight for the good in you. I see it every day."

Plunging his fists back into the dirt, he fought the desire to hate his own father. "I don't want to be like him. Not ever."

"Oh, Julian." She knelt next to him. "You won't be. I'm here to help you be different. I promise. Now, you keep working out here while I go fix some supper."

Her soft footfalls faded as he studied the ground. It gave him the opportunity to swipe at his cheeks with his sleeve.

Julian shut his eyes and inhaled the sweet aromas of the garden around him. In those seconds, he took long breaths and time almost stood still. Everything else melted away. And a bright light in his mind made him smile. Just like Mother said . . . there was light to overcome the darkness. There was hope.

Time in the garden made the afternoon disappear. But

shouts and crashing from the house shattered the calm in his mind and the black fury inside him spread to every inch of his limbs once again.

"I hate him. I wish I was older. Then I'd show him." Damian stood there with his hands fisted at his sides, his face pinched and creased in a deep frown. He stomped off toward the trees.

Julian agreed. What he wouldn't give to be bigger than his father. To be able to show him the same pain he inflicted on a daily basis. Last time Julian stood up to the man, he hadn't been able to get out of bed for a week. At thirteen, he was puny compared to the hulk of his tough, rancher father.

So he dug in the dirt with a vengeance. One day. One day he'd be stronger than the old man.

The sounds from the house threatened to shatter the thin barrier that kept him from plunging headlong into the dark.

Mother's lilting voice echoed in his head. "Shut it out, Julian. Grab onto the light."

He was trying.

Clamping his jaw as tight as he could, he lifted his chin. He focused on the sun above him and allowed the warmth to cover him. The sun gave nourishment to the ground.

He was like the ground. Dark. Lifeless. But the light could change that.

Blocking out everything around him, he went back to work. Churning the soil as if it were his own soul. This morning, he'd killed three prairie dogs and five birds. All to bury in his garden. Funny how death made beautiful things grow.

Mother had taught him that.

Although she'd cried the first time he came home with an animal he'd killed. When he'd asked about her tears, she'd stated that she meant when things died *naturally* they fed the earth and the ground and helped things to grow. She didn't want him killing animals and birds.

13

But he'd continued. He couldn't help it. Not when his garden flourished like it did. He simply kept it from her. She had enough on her mind.

The voices inside the house grew in volume and shattered his barricade. Mother was screaming as his father yelled horrible words at her. Thuds and crashes followed. Mother's voice was full force now. Her anger evident.

But Father's was louder.

It drowned out any other sound.

FOUR MONTHS LATER

"This is why your mother left."

Julian's father poked a large finger in his face.

"You. If you weren't such a horrible, sorry excuse for a son, she would still be here. You made her life miserable."

The words sparked fire in him. How dare his father blame him? Usually Julian kept his mouth shut. Took the beatings. Took the yelling. Because there wasn't any way out. Damian was always there to comfort him, but it couldn't fix things. Couldn't fix him.

His father had been in a lousy mood for days. First it was because some of his cattle had gone missing. Then two horses carrying two of his hands had tumbled down a ravine. None survived. Not that his father cared much about the lives of the men who worked for him, but it did make him shorthanded. And he hated losing horses.

Mother's voice echoed in Julian's mind. *"Deep down, don't be afraid. You're a good person. You are. Don't let his words get to you. They're not true."*

Julian missed his mother. What he wouldn't give for her to come back.

"It's all your fault."

Father slapped him.

14

"She left because of you and you know it. Couldn't take it anymore. And now look what I have to put up with!"

Julian closed his eyes against the sharp sting in his face. Fought to grab onto something to keep him from plummeting into the depths. But he lost. Something inside him cracked. Like an earthquake splitting the earth in two, his battle between the dark and light tore at his soul.

Bolting forward, Julian roared and shoved his father. "It's not my fault your cattle have been stolen. And it's not my fault she left. *You're* the horrible one. Not me. She loved me." Tears sprang to his eyes. Hot and stinging. A sign of weakness to the man standing before him.

Damian never succumbed to them—Julian could hear his brother's disappointment in him now. The last thing his brother said to him before he left . . . "Don't cry."

Those large fists—like two hammers—pummeled him. Over and over. When he fell to the ground, his instincts kicked in. He curled into a ball and tried to protect his head from the assault. Closed his eyes and squeezed them as tight as he could.

In his mind, he pictured Mother's smiling face. He couldn't blame her for leaving. But why didn't she take him with her?

Julian eased his eyes open. How long had he been unconscious? He groaned as he uncurled. Everything hurt as he worked his way to his feet. His blood had dried on his arm and on the floor, so he'd been out longer than most times. Which meant his father could return at any moment. At least Damian would be gone for a while.

With soft steps, Julian made his way out the door to the well and lowered the bucket. He winced as pain shot through him, but he had to clean up the floor or there would be consequences.

And he'd had enough for one day.

It took half an hour to clean the floor and himself, but when it was complete, he headed out to the garden. The one place his father would never come. Mother said it was because he made her a promise. But then she also taught Julian everything to plant that made Father cough and sneeze. Well, she didn't say to plant it *intentionally*, but he understood it nonetheless.

The garden had been their safe haven. Their sanctuary. His mother could make anything grow. Now that she was gone, it was up to him.

In the months up to her departure, he'd been expanding the garden. Digging in the hard, dusty, rocky ground down a couple feet so that he could replace the inhospitable soil with thick river-bottom mud and manure. Every haul with the wheelbarrow made him a bit prouder. He'd almost doubled the area of the entire garden in size, which would be perfect to plant the precious bulbs his mother had ordered and kept hidden. If he could finish preparing the ground in the next few weeks, then he would be able to start planting the bulbs in fall which was when Mother said was the best time.

Maybe by the point he went back to school, he could tell Mary Ziegler about his plans and show her all his hard work.

She loved flowers too. Loved talking to him about his garden and the variety of plants. Just a couple years his junior, she was the only friend he'd ever had.

That is, with Mother gone, if Father allowed him to return to school. Even though mean ol' Walker prided himself on not having ignorant offspring, he often went on a rampage on a regular basis about how all the books were softening Julian's mind.

Julian kept quiet at school. Did his work. Learned what he could. But most of the other kids called him odd for wanting to talk about flowers and gardening or whispered behind their hands about how he was the son of mean ol' Walker and he must be as vile and hateful as his old man. Damian encouraged

Julian to stand up for himself, but he never did. He pretended not to hear and then read every book the teacher would allow. Mary was the one who invited him to play games with the others at recess. Or helped him when he struggled with the math work. She was the one who greeted him with a smile every day.

Oh, her friend Anna Lakeman said hello each morning to him too, but she wasn't as nice as Mary. He'd caught her staring at him and frowning on several occasions.

He couldn't blame her.

The sky darkened and Julian forced his focus away from his safe haven. He'd avoided the house as long as possible. After several hours digging in his garden, he was exhausted. Every inch of his body ached from his father's cruel lashing. If he could stay out of his father's way for the rest of the evening, it would be a miracle. But he'd have to do his best. Keep quiet. Hidden. He needed a bath. And a month of rest.

His stomach rumbled in a loud roar reminding him that he hadn't eaten. Another reason to sneak back into the house. With a groan, he got to his feet, cleaned up his tools, and took slow, agonizing steps toward the back door.

But the fierce hulk of his father stood there waiting for him, his arms crossed over his muscled midsection.

Julian's heart threatened to pound out of his chest. The instinct to run battled with his common sense to stay put and not risk another beating.

"I'm headed out in the morning. Gotta drive some cattle to Colorado. You'll have to fend for yourself. Scottie will be here taking care of the ranch."

At least the foreman treated Julian with kindness. Well, it *seemed* kind compared to the vicious blows from his father. Julian swallowed and blinked but held the older man's stare. A required response. Any words might rile the man again.

His father turned and walked away.

After he counted to ten, Julian released a huge breath. At least he wouldn't have to deal with his father's temper for a while. It put a bit of a spring into his sore and exhausted step. Perhaps he would even go into town and tell Mary. Her smile would make everything better.

Now if he could keep Damian away and avoid another altercation with their father before daybreak, the light might have a chance to chase the darkness away.

one

"I cannot tell what the years may bring, life is a scene of change."

~Earl Douglass

Home.

A seemingly innocuous word. A place she loved.

And yet, every time Anna Lakeman returned there, her insides begged to differ.

She could see it in the distance, just a few minutes away . . . the house where she grew up, where she learned to sketch and paint.

The wheels of the wagon bumped and rolled their way along the grass- and weed-covered lane. A testament to her absence.

What was it about coming home that made her want to run away?

With each return from a dig with her father, she pondered

19

the same questions. Never getting any answers. Or perhaps she'd been avoiding the answer for too long.

Memories of her mother were beautiful and made her feel warm and loved, so it wasn't the loss of the woman who gave her life that brought these feelings.

Then there was the loss of her best friend, Mary. It had been a decade since her friend went missing, but Anna felt the absence in her heart and soul every day. Some people said that grief lessened over time. And if she was honest, she could say that yes, the grief was less. But the loss . . . she knew that as keenly today as she had the day Mary didn't return.

Home was where she had the best memories of Mary and of Mama.

So why was it an uncomfortable place? This time she didn't silence the answer.

She knew why. Because *he* wasn't there.

It was best to face facts. Her struggle came down to the loss of her first and only love, Joshua Ziegler.

She drove her wagon up to the door and set the brake, her shoulders sagging with a long exhale. It exhausted her to deny that struggle over and over. The effort it took to shove it down so she wouldn't voice the words weighed heavier each day.

But that was the path of great loss.

And even though the loss wasn't in death, she felt it as such.

Three years had passed since he'd gone back east for medical school. Three years since their spat. Three years since they'd talked. Shared their hearts. Talked of dreams of the future. Until he left, she would've never dreamed of life without him. The community expected them to marry. Their families expected them to marry.

She'd expected them to marry.

The rumble of her father's wagon brought her thoughts around. This was no time for her pondering. She had work to do.

Every inch of Anna's body ached as she stepped from the

hub of the wheel into the tall, dry grass in front of her home. She stretched but it didn't help the soreness that seemed to scream from every muscle. With a glance around, she took mental notes of the scene. One she'd sketched a thousand times and would probably do a thousand times more. Other than the growth being too tall around the house, not much had changed in the months she'd been gone with her father.

"I don't know if it's me and my old age, but the road seems to get rougher every time we travel it." Dad's soft chuckle brought her gaze around.

"It's not you, I can promise you that." Turning on her heel, she stretched one more time and then stepped toward the supplies that needed to be unloaded.

A bone-jarring wagon ride over the rough Wyoming terrain for the past five hours had given her insides the impression she was eighty years old rather than a young twenty-one. But such was the life of a traveling paleontologist and his daughter. He went wherever the bones called. She tagged along to sketch and paint everything.

As they unloaded crates, bags, and fresh supplies they'd purchased from the large mercantile up in Green River, she longed to get back to all her sketches from the trip. The bones of the horse-like creature they'd found fossilized in the rock layer weren't the greatest find her father had ever had, but they *were* interesting. Quite exciting to draw too, since she'd never seen a bone structure quite like it.

As a child, she'd wanted to be a paleontologist just like her father. She'd hung on his every word, watched his every move, and read every tome written on the subject.

But over the years, she'd learned the harsh truth.

Women didn't pursue science like that. And they most certainly didn't dig in the dirt. That was unacceptable. And vulgar—according to the women of society who knew about such things.

Although, she had to admit that she'd always admired the work of Mary Anning from Lyme Regis, England. The woman had been a fossil collector pretty much her whole life, and even though she wasn't given the credit she deserved, her name was still well-known in paleontological discussions. Why couldn't Anna do the same?

If only she could have known the woman. But Mary Anning had been gone for thirty years and had lived half a world away. Besides, her fossil collecting had been her means of support after her father's death when she was eleven. Probably why it had been somewhat acceptable. The pity of the public gave allowances now and then.

Anna released her breath as she set down another satchel. Even though she longed to be the one to find the next great discovery in paleontology, her gifting truly was in the sketching. Oh, how she loved every little detail.

Now that they were home, Dad would sequester himself with all his notes and specimens, and she would need to put the house to order once again. After that, she could spend all the time she wanted going through the sketches and reliving their last dig.

They worked together hauling and sorting, enjoying the quiet camaraderie that had become habitual. It didn't take long to set things in their proper place since they'd left everything clean and in order. The one addition was the layer of dust, which Anna eliminated with the removal of the sheets covering the furniture and quick use of the broom.

"I'll be in my study, Anna." Dad's nose was in a book as he walked down the hall.

She'd figured as much, but unlike her usual desire to get back to her sketches, her insides swirled. The unsettled feeling called for something different from her usual routine. "I think I'll go see the Zieglers then, if that's all right with you?"

she called after him. "Louise will return tomorrow to help around the house."

"That's fine." His voice vanished as the door clicked behind him. Whether or not he'd heard what she said was the question of the hour, but he'd likely stay buried in his study for the rest of the afternoon anyway.

Anna hauled the tub into her bedroom and filled it with warm water. Washing away all the dirt from the travels made her feel a bit more like herself. She dunked her head to rinse the soap from her hair. She couldn't wait to see Mary's family. When her best friend disappeared ten years ago, Anna had spent days and weeks helping the community search for her.

When no trace of her friend had been found, she'd mourned with the family, begging her father to allow her to stay at their home for a few days. Each night, she'd cried herself to sleep in Mary's bed while Mrs. Ziegler sat in her rocking chair staring out the window at the dark.

It had taken the community months to recover from the loss. Mary's parents did their best to find joy in their faith and family, but the sorrow never left.

Over the years, Anna spent a lot of time at the Ziegler home. Martha and Joshua were older but had never seemed to mind when their little sister and her best friend tagged along. After Mary disappeared, Anna continued to spend a lot of time with the family. If she wasn't at school or out on a dig with her father, she could be found at the Ziegler home.

Then Martha got married, which left Joshua and Anna. They'd been comfortable with one another the entirety of their childhoods, but things changed. In the evenings they would read with his parents, she would show them her sketches, and he soon insisted on seeing her home each night.

It didn't take much for her to develop a deep crush on Joshua. For a long time, she thought it was mutual.

Anna shook those thoughts away along with the droplets

of water from her bath. There was no sense in pining for the man who hadn't even bothered to write.

After dressing and pinning up her hair, she grabbed her bonnet, went out to her horse, and saddled Misty for the short ride out to the Ziegler ranch. With the wind at her back, she hunched over the mare and gave her free rein to race along the trail they both knew so well.

The pounding of her horse's hooves shook the rest of her ill thoughts away. A chat with Mrs. Ziegler—who'd been like a mother to her—would certainly settle her down again and help Anna to get over this melancholy.

But the ranch yard was empty. No smoke rose from the chimney. The barn doors were shut. Animals corralled close to the house.

It was clear no one was home.

"Bother." Anna allowed her shoulders to slump. They must be in town.

The choice before her stretched. Go to town in search of her friends? Of course, she'd have to see other people as well. That made the option a bit less desirable. Or . . . head home?

Her shadow disappeared on the ground as she contemplated. A cloud must have covered the sun for the moment. As her gaze shifted upward, the sky darkened, and gray clouds staged themselves in the distance to roll in and cover the sun for the rest of the afternoon.

It might blow over and it might not. What to do?

A crack of thunder made the decision for her.

She'd have to head home. What had been a beautiful day now seemed downright gloomy. Sad how it matched her mood.

Turning her mount back to the trail they'd just ridden, she pulled her hat down and tightened the string. Fat drops of rain dotted the dusty road. "Time to go, Misty. Let's hope those clouds don't have much to spill."

She shouldn't have voiced the words. Because within minutes, the sky opened up, and a storm like she'd never seen before gushed from the heavens. The trail almost disappeared before her eyes and Misty's unease vibrated through Anna's knees and thighs as she held on. Slowing her horse to a trot so she could gain her bearings, she couldn't see anything but the downpour of water. Misty's head bobbed up and down with her discomfort with the thunder and lightning.

There was no shelter and no other choice than pray that her faithful mare could find her way home. Anna's dress, her underclothes, and every inch of her were now soaked.

Lightning struck a nearby tree and Misty reared. Anna held on with all her might and clung to her horse's neck. "Whoa. Easy, girl. We need to get home in one piece, all right?" She soothed the mare and rubbed her neck, keeping her words calm. Which grew increasingly difficult as the storm built.

Tension grew in her neck and shoulders as she gripped the reins. If she couldn't see where they were going, how would Misty? Her beautiful mare was getting up in years.

God, please help us to make it home. The prayer left her mind as the sky seemed to open its floodgates and dump oceans of water on top of them.

Misty's head was visible but not by much. Anna's bonnet was completely flattened from the deluge, and rivers of water raced down her face and body. Bending over her horse, she held the reins and hugged Misty's neck. "Get us home, girl. You can do it."

Misty whinnied and shook her head as thunder rumbled overhead in a constant rhythm. Then the mare trotted forward.

Anna counted each second in the minutes as they passed, hoping and praying they would reach shelter soon.

She had tallied eleven minutes when the roar sounded behind her. What was that? She sat up and looked around, but she couldn't see anything through the sheets and sheets of rain that continued to pour down from above.

The roaring grew. Accompanied by massive explosions—snapping and cracking. What was happening?

A wall of water barreled toward her.

"Giddyap, girl!" she yelled in Misty's ear.

Her mare didn't hesitate and raced into a furious pace.

But they were no match for the water.

Just as they crested a hill, Anna felt the horse underneath her lift with the wave.

God . . . help!

two

"But whatever may keep tomorrow know I not."

~Earl Douglass

SUNDAY, JUNE 2, 1878 ⁕ CHICAGO, ILLINOIS

The large stack of letters in Joshua Ziegler's hand were a reminder of his failings.

Failure to communicate with the woman he'd loved his whole life.

Failure to apologize for his blundering tongue.

Failure to rectify the situation and set things right.

Failure upon failure.

And now? He stood by his bed with a twine-tied stack of over one hundred twenty letters. Missives he'd been too apprehensive to mail over the past three years. What a fool he'd been!

On a whim, he tossed the packet into his small traveling trunk and slammed the lid closed. His train west left in an hour, and he *would* be on it.

With the packet.

Joshua left the small room he rented from Mrs. Greene near the university, his trunk in tow. He plopped his felt bowler hat onto his head. Back home, he wouldn't have need of such a thing, but as Professor Wright impressed upon him time and again, it was imperative that "he dress neat and clean for his patients."

Unwilling to spend the coin it would take to hire a cabby, Joshua walked the long way to the station, sweating in his summer suit and hat. Probably not the best idea but it was too late at this point. The Chicago summer was so different from his home back in Wyoming Territory.

Here, it was humid, sticky, sweltering. Whereas back home, it was hot but dry. Drier than old bones as his dad would say. Amazing how much heat a person could handle without humidity.

It had been one of an abundance of changes Joshua had to get used to.

It was worth it though, right? For the sake of his education? As long as he could remember, he'd wanted to be a doctor. But his family didn't have money for university. So he'd trained under the doc back in Green River for several years while still helping his family ranch.

Everything changed the day he received word from the university in Chicago that a benefactor had applied on Joshua's behalf and would pay all of his expenses. There were strict adherences to the terms that he had to agree to, but other than that, it had been a priceless gift.

His family had been behind him every step of the way. Even though the loss of his little sister, Mary, had devastated them all. But in the three years since he'd arrived at school, they'd done nothing but encourage him.

Noise in the busy streets of the Windy City threatened to overwhelm his senses. Whistles from the traffic cops, arguments between vendors, and everyone else trying to be heard over the same din crowded his ears.

With a shake of his head, he picked up his pace to the station. Not that it would be any less noisy, but the sooner he could settle himself on the train, the better.

His thoughts turned home. A couple months ago, letters from his mother changed. Not just expressing the fact that he was missed, but urging... pleading with him to come home. If only for a week. They had become harder and harder to ignore.

The station in view, Joshua lengthened his stride and took in the massive and beautiful three-story building. The Great Passenger Station of the Lake Shore and Michigan Southern Railroad. He hadn't been here since his arrival three years prior.

It was an odd feeling as he navigated his way inside and then studied the boards to find his platform. What decent son allowed all that time to pass without seeing his family? Especially a family such as his, fractured by the loss of sweet Mary. As his gaze shifted from departure board to departure board, the bile created by his own guilt crept up his throat. Swallowing it down, he blinked away the self-deprecation and headed for his train. At least he was on his way now. He couldn't change the past. All the what-ifs and should-haves of the three previous years were the choices he would have to live with. Face the consequences. And pray for a way to make things right and move on.

As Joshua stepped onto his train, he was glad to have had the push to go. Not wishing any disrespect for his benefactor— a Mr. Bricker, whom he'd never met in person—he'd written him and requested to take the break between terms to return home. The generous man had answered his letter right away and even paid his way. In first class! The gracious offering was given with a request and encouragement not to miss any of his schooling.

Professor Wright—who was his adviser in the medical program—told him it was a *decent enough* use of his two weeks off although the man had frowned the whole time. At least Joshua had approval to go. That had been quite the hurdle.

His professors had informed him more than once that their desire was for him to stay in the city. They needed more doctors of his caliber, they insisted. The first year, he didn't think there was any way he could stay out east. But then . . . the letters from his benefactor, the encouragement from his instructors, the awards he'd won . . . all of it added up to boost his confidence. He'd gotten used to the city, hadn't he? Besides, there wasn't much hope that he could go home and have what he wanted.

What he *wanted*.

In the past, his dreams had been to become a doctor. But not any high-falutin', big city doctor. A country doctor was what he aspired to be. Because he'd planned to stay in Walker Creek and marry Anna. Raise a family. Live happily ever after.

At the train, he shook away the thoughts. Things were different now.

A faint glimmer of hope spurred to life. This trip had the potential to change the outcome—put things to right again.

It was far-fetched. But God could still do miracles.

He showed the conductor his ticket and the man tipped his head and pointed. Joshua headed for the train car and then bolted up the steps. At the top, he showed another train worker his ticket.

"Allow me, sir." The man held out an arm.

Joshua followed the steward to his accommodations in the luxurious Pullman car. The porter stowed his small trunk and left with a nod. The trip west would be nothing like his trip out here.

That time, he'd been in third class. With a hard bench seat, and he'd had to bring his own food.

This time would be an experience that he wouldn't take for granted. Because he doubted he'd ever travel first class again.

It was good to be on his way home.

Family would be wonderful to see. Mom and Dad. His older sister and her family. His nephew Caleb had to be what? Nine or ten years old now? That was correct, the lad had been six when Joshua left. Precious boy, his nephew had followed him around for weeks before his train whisked him off east.

Goodness, so much time had passed. What else would be different?

His thoughts went back to the letters at the top of his trunk. To Anna Lakeman. The only woman he could ever imagine loving.

But three years was a long time. What if she was still mad at him? His apology was long overdue.

Then again, she could be off on some months-long expedition with her father digging for bones and might not even be home. What would he do then?

Or worse . . . what if she was married? Surely his parents would have mentioned that in their correspondence.

His stomach didn't like that thought one bit as it sank like a rock.

The train lurched forward and then started its way out of the city.

He leaned his head back and closed his eyes.

Anna. Her dark hair and dark eyes teased him with a smile in his mind's eye. Ever since they were young, she'd held him enraptured.

"Excuse me, sir."

The low voice pulled Joshua out of his thoughts. When he opened his eyes, the train was surging along through fields. Definitely not in Chicago anymore. "My apologies." He must have fallen asleep. Hopefully he hadn't drooled or snored. Heavens, he shouldn't be allowed in first class.

"Not a problem, sir." The steward clasped his hands in front of him. "The dining car is up ahead of you if you'd like to get dinner. Please let me know if there is anything else I can do for you." The man moved on to the passengers behind him.

Joshua swiped a hand down his face and blinked to clear the sleep away. Apparently, he'd slept longer than just a few minutes. Standing up, he straightened his suit jacket and headed toward the dining car.

As he made his way into the lavish area, it took everything in him to keep his mouth closed. Granted, he'd seen this kind of opulence in Chicago, but never thought he was deserving of the experience.

A waiter stepped toward him. "Allow me to seat you, sir."

"Thank you." Hopefully he didn't sound like the country bumpkin he was. Of course, if he chose to stay in Chicago after his medical training—which would only happen if Anna rejected him for good—he'd have to work on being acceptable to the upper classes.

Which held no appeal.

At all.

Who was he trying to kid? All the awards, encouragement, and education in the world didn't matter when his heart was back at home.

Once he was seated, a menu was placed in his hands. "Please let me know if there is anything I can get for you." The man gave a slight bow and walked toward another table.

Joshua took a moment to peruse the menu. Mr. Bricker had written that all of his meals were included on this journey. Luxury indeed.

A glance out the window and a deep breath helped to ground him back into reality.

This was his. If only for a while. Almost like his schooling opportunity, Joshua didn't want to take any of it for granted.

"Is this your first time headed out west, sir?" The waiter was back.

A smile lifted Joshua's lips. "No." How much should he say? What was the protocol for manners in such a situation?

"Splendid. I must say the mountains are glorious if you are journeying with us to the Rockies." He poured water into one of Joshua's glasses. "Would you like to order?"

"Yes, please." He glanced back down at the menu. "The chef's steak and potatoes sound perfect."

"Wonderful choice. I will return shortly." The waiter walked away and then a familiar face replaced him. She smiled at him from underneath a hat piled high with flowers and ribbons.

Joshua swallowed. When he'd met the young woman soon after his arrival in Chicago, she'd been a listening ear. Every few months, he'd see her at a fundraiser for the university or a social gathering he'd been obligated to attend. He'd even stumbled upon her once in the park, where he'd been stomping out his self-loathing after an unusually trying examination. But something had changed the last couple weeks. She'd become a bit . . . persistent. And had come to the university library every day, interrupting his studying. How she knew when and where to find him was a bit unnerving.

She walked toward him, an older gentleman behind her. "Why, Mr. Ziegler. What a surprise to see you here."

Joshua came to his feet. "Indeed a surprise, Miss Oppenheim." He pushed his negative thoughts aside and remembered his manners.

The man behind her frowned.

"Father, this is the man I was telling you about." Her voice was smooth and sweet.

One eyebrow lifted. "The doctor?" He pushed out a hand, a bit of the frown slid away. "Oswald Oppenheim."

Joshua shook the man's hand and gave a slight bow. "Nice to meet you, Mr. Oppenheim."

"My daughter has a fascination with medicine it seems." But he looked none too pleased. Bored was a better description.

"It is a fascinating subject. But I'm not a doctor quite yet, sir. I'm still studying at the university." He held the older man's gaze.

A quick flash of respect flickered in the man's eyes. "I admire your honesty, Mr. Ziegler. But according to my daughter, you are at the top of your class and should be finishing in the next year?"

"Yes, sir." Joshua darted a glance at Miss Oppenheim. While his recent wariness of her was at the forefront, he appreciated her praise.

She batted her eyelashes and his uneasiness returned. Why did women do that? He turned back to her father.

"Impressive. And what are your plans after that?"

Was that a glimmer of challenge?

Taking a moment to put his thoughts together, Joshua swallowed. Clarity hit him smack in the face. Rosemary Oppenheim must have hinted to her father that Joshua was interested in courtship or vice versa. Well, a life of opulence and riches wasn't what he was after. Nor was he interested in the beautiful woman before him although she'd been a good friend. Best to lay it out now. "I hope to serve the Lord with my work, sir. Perhaps in a small town that doesn't have a doctor already. Or even mission work, if that is where I am needed."

"Quite noble of you." The older man's eyes cleared, and he checked his pocket watch. "I'll look forward to hearing more about your accomplishments in the future."

"Thank you, sir." Obviously, he wasn't a threat to the plans for the man's daughter.

"Safe travels, young man." Mr. Oppenheim dipped his head at him. "Come along, Rosemary."

"It was nice to meet you, sir." Joshua sent them both a smile but didn't miss the downcast expression on Miss Oppenheim's face.

The father and daughter walked out of the dining car, and

it was only after they were gone that Joshua felt comfortable taking his seat again and relaxing his jaw.

Had he been too . . . abrupt? His thoughts took him back to his second meeting with the lovely young socialite. She'd found him out on a balcony outside a lavish ballroom brooding.

Back then, Rosemary was reserved. Concerned for him. Nothing more than a friend and sounding board. Perhaps he'd shared too much with her about Anna and how he'd left things. But at the time, he'd appreciated her calm demeanor and willingness to listen. Rosemary's words that evening had stuck with him. *"I know I wouldn't give up on someone I really care for."*

In his mind, she'd challenged him to not give up. Not that he wanted to. He cared for Anna. Loved her, in fact. And deep down, he knew that she loved him too. So he couldn't give up. And had prayed that Anna wouldn't either. Rosemary's words of encouragement had given him hope.

But then the weeks melted into months, the months into years. No word from his beloved. He'd continued to write letters but hesitated every time he thought of sending them. Coming up with excuse after excuse.

It had been too long.

It would be better if he delivered them in person.

Was all hope lost?

Joshua cringed as he replayed the conversation just now. The look he'd caught on Rosemary's face. She'd been a friend to him. They hadn't done anything wrong. All this time, she'd cheered him on at school and always inquired about Anna. And seemed to encourage him to keep on with his lost love . . .

Rosemary's demeanor might've changed in the last month, but he shouldn't rush to conclusions. Who knew what had brought about the change? Perhaps he should apologize to her later.

If he saw her again. The Oppenheims might not be on the train for long.

He reached for his water glass and tried to clear his thoughts with a drink but a rustle next to him made him shift in his chair. Miss Rosemary Oppenheim. Headed straight for him.

"I simply had to sneak away from Father and tell you how wonderful it is to see you again, Mr. Ziegler." She curtsied, her cheeks pink around a beaming grin.

He swallowed. But it didn't go down and he choked on it.

"Oh dear." She patted his back.

Joshua reached for a napkin and held up his hand. "That's quite all right. No harm done."

"I'm looking forward to catching up with you as we travel west together."

As they traveled west *together*? He coughed into his napkin again, hoping it covered the heat that rushed to his neck.

"I'll leave you to your dinner, but won't it be lovely to spend time together the next few days? You can tell me more about your dreams. And your family."

He lowered the napkin. "Um . . ." Then coughed again.

She dipped her lashes and scurried away right as his dinner was delivered.

What had just happened?

"Is everything to your liking, sir?" The waiter had a pristine white cloth draped over his arm as he waited at attention.

Joshua glanced at the food and then back at the man. "Yes, thank you."

"Enjoy your dinner."

As Joshua watched the waiter check on other tables around him, the chance of him following the waiter's instructions seemed dismal. *Uncomfortable* best described his predicament.

And he couldn't see any way out of it.

Three more days.

That's how long he would be on this train. The intent he'd seen in Miss Oppenheim's eyes had been clear.

How exactly did someone avoid another person on a train? The cars all of a sudden felt much smaller.

He glanced back out the window.

Jumping from the train was out of the question. At least for now.

three

"Alas, is not life only dreaming and death waking up?"

~Earl Douglass

The roar around her grew until her head was engulfed in the waters. All sound dulled as Anna gripped Misty's mane as tight as her fingers could squeeze. The water churned around her face, sucked at her torso, and swirled beneath her horse's strong hooves. The mare fought the flash flood with every kick and heave of her body.

Anna kicked her legs as well while her lungs burned, desperate for air. Several seconds passed and they found the top of the wave to ride. She gulped for a clear breath and reseated herself astride as best she could, keeping her chest low over Misty's back. This was no time for propriety. The terrain passed by in a blur of rain, uprooted trees, and waves of water crashing over them. Every second felt like an hour. They must have gone miles and miles past Walker Creek now. At this rate, they'd be in the Pacific Ocean by dawn.

Muscles aching, Anna spoke into Misty's ear every chance

she had. Keeping her voice strong, encouraging. Willing the horse to not give up their fight.

But as the evening faded, she wilted and thought of how easy it would be to slip into the raging depths. This nightmare couldn't go on much longer. Death was surely a better choice.

At least then . . . she'd see Mama again. And Mary.

And the ache for Joshua would be a distant memory.

Oh, God . . . please help!

She'd neglected her relationship with the Lord the past few years. Heartache had a way of wiggling its way in and taking up full-time residence. Not that she wanted it this way. But it had been easier not to feel.

As she laid her head against her mare's neck, Misty whinnied.

They'd been through a lot together. Did her horse sense Anna's mind to give up?

God, I'm tired. Weary of this ache in my chest that won't go away. Did You send this flash flood to bring me home? If so . . . take me now. I feel so useless to You anyway.

She closed her eyes and did her best to swallow the fear of drowning. Of death. It was inevitable after all. She should know. She spent her life sketching the bones of living things that had gone on before them.

And death should have no hold on her. She knew God. Had complete confidence that she would spend eternity in heaven.

But what about her father?

What about . . . Joshua?

"Joshua."

As soon as her heart allowed his name to be spoken, Anna couldn't give up. No matter how much her body ached, she had to keep fighting.

With a lift of her chin, she spoke into Misty's ear again. "We've got to find a way out of the water, girl. Just a little longer. You can do it. I know you can."

Up ahead, the water rushed around a large curve. The flow that had started out only a few yards wide when it first engulfed them was now at least an acre across. Flash flooding was common out in the dry territories. But the native Indians who'd lived there for generations warned them of the terrible flash floods that came through every hundred years or so, which were capable of completely changing the landscape. Anna just never expected to be caught in one.

As they approached the curve, Anna swiped at her eyes, searching for any way they could exit the rage of the rushing waters.

A jam of tree trunks gathered in the sharpness of the crook. But it seemed too dangerous to head straight for things that could spear right through their flesh.

Another wave slammed over her head and swirled them around under the water for several seconds.

Out of breath and strength, Anna's grip in her left hand weakened. Misty's mane slipped out of her grasp.

"Hold tight, my little one." Mama's voice drifted through the water to her.

"Mama?" Oh, if only her mother were really here.

"You must hold on. With your hands and with your legs." The memory of her mother teaching her to ride a horse without a saddle at the young age of four filled Anna's mind. At the time, she'd wanted to do everything like her mother. Even riding in the awkward sidesaddle that was much too large for her. But her mother was much too practical for that. The daughter of a rancher herself, she'd wanted Anna to learn by instinct. By feel.

As Anna's face breached the waters again, she gulped the thick air and grabbed onto Misty with her arms and legs. *I'm holding on, Mama.*

The water rammed them into a wall of something hard.

They fought against the tangled mass of debris for what

seemed like an eternity, but Misty finally found footing and surged up out of the water.

Collapsing onto the ground against her horse, Anna coughed up some of the liquid she'd swallowed. They needed to get home and dry.

Just as soon as she could move.

MONDAY, JUNE 3

Climbing out of bed, Anna groaned. She thought she'd been sore after the wagon ride back home. Today was a new kind of hurt.

While the flash flood hadn't swept her and Misty too far away, they were plenty bruised and banged up by debris and each other in the swirling waters.

Thankfully, Misty was still a strong swimmer, but by the time they'd reached home, Anna's horse was limping and slow.

She'd raced around getting the mare comfortable in the barn, tried to get her to eat, put liniment on all the open wounds. But Misty laid down in the hay and closed her eyes. It had taken every ounce of Anna's energy to get back to the house and undress so she wouldn't shiver herself to death.

As much as she longed for more sleep, Anna dressed as quickly as she could. The thought of finding her horse not breathing today was almost more than she could bear.

Whatever the outcome though, she *had* to know. She needed to see for herself.

"Anna?" Dad's voice stopped her as she tiptoed through the house.

"I didn't mean to wake you."

"You didn't wake me, dearest. How are you feeling this morning?"

She reached around him and kissed his cheek. "Quite battered, to be honest."

That brought his attention to full focus. "Should I fetch the doctor?"

"No. I don't think it's anything as serious as that. But I am worried about Misty and wanted to check on her."

"Me too." As much as her father seemed oblivious to everything around him when he was studying, he still cared. Last night he had comforted her in the barn, told her the sweet horse needed rest, and wrapped his arm around her. After he brought her back to the house, he'd ordered her to take a hot bath and proceeded to make a fresh pot of coffee. They'd chatted by the fire until her nerves calmed, the tears had stopped, and her body screamed for her bed.

"Let's go check on her now, shall we?" Dad wrapped an arm around her shoulder.

Side by side they walked to the barn. Words weren't necessary.

His presence gave her a bit of strength. She inhaled long and slow before opening the barn door.

Anna rushed back to Misty's stall and found her old horse standing and nibbling at the bucket of grain she'd left for her last night.

Dad stepped next to her. "Well, isn't that a beautiful sight?"

She hugged him and grinned. Her insides shuddered as tears slid down her cheeks. She'd braced herself for the worst, and now that it hadn't happened, her body didn't know whether to faint or jump for joy. "I was so worried . . ." She didn't even want to voice the words. Swallowing them back, she lifted her chin and breathed a prayer of thanksgiving to God.

"The Lord spared you two last night. I'm still amazed." Dad shook his head.

"Me too." She'd heard the stories of the hundred-year floods but had never seen one. Only the gullies they left behind. Reminders of last night prickled at her skin. But not just the physical wounds. It was time she came to grips with her feelings for Joshua and the fact that she'd kept God at arm's length for too long.

Her father took her elbow. "What say you and I get some breakfast and then take a walk. We can stretch our legs and see if anything has changed since we've been gone."

"You mean see if the flooding uncovered anything." She raised her eyebrows and crossed her arms over her chest. "I know you, Dad. Your eye is always looking for what you can dig up next."

"I love my work. What can I say?" With a shrug, he winked at her. "But if you're not feeling up to it, I understand. It can wait."

She wouldn't change her father for anything. "If I stay in bed all day, it will only hurt worse tomorrow. I'd love to take you up on that walk. As long as I get to bring my sketch pad."

"Deal."

"Let me leave a note for Louise. She'll be here in an hour or so." The sweet daughter of the Bowden family in Walker Creek was the oldest of twelve siblings. She'd worked for the Lakemans the last two years whenever they were home, and it helped provide for the Bowdens' large family. It would be good to have her around again. She was the closest thing Anna had to a friend her own age.

Thirty minutes later, she closed the door to her home and tied her bonnet under her chin. Dad stabbed the ground with his tall walking stick and held out his other arm. "Shall we?"

The air was crisp and clean after the rain. Wyoming was such a dry territory, it always intrigued Anna how much the air changed after a big thunderstorm. They didn't happen often, but oh, how she loved them.

Well . . . not getting stuck *out* in them.

Their steps were slow-going for the first thirty minutes. Debris littered their property. She directed Dad toward where the water had rushed through their south acreage and onto the Walker Ranch.

"Magnificent." Dad pointed to a new gulley that had been formed. "Look at those layers of rock."

At least forty feet deep. The difference in the landscape was astonishing.

They walked for an hour or so, following the fresh-cut gorge in the earth. Dad talked about the geology of the area, while she kept her eyes open for anything interesting.

The Green River was this whole region's source of water. It fed hundreds of creeks along its course and had carved what Mr. John Wesley Powell about ten years ago had named Flaming Gorge when he'd done an expedition down the river. The immense and beautiful red sandstone cliffs surrounded a good part of the river south of them. And when the sun set, it would set those rocks aflame. At least it appeared that way.

It was one of Anna's favorite places to visit. The beauty drew her eyes. Her father, on the other hand, was always on the lookout for fossils.

Today was no different.

"Over there, Anna." He pointed. "Do you see what I see?"

She squinted into the distance. "Um, no, I don't think so."

"Let's move closer." He tugged at her elbow, and she followed.

Even though the majority of the water had merged back with the Green River or been soaked up by the dry terrain, there was still a meandering creek at the center of the gulley.

"Hope you don't mind getting your boots wet."

She hiked up her skirt at the challenge. "I should have known," she mumbled under her breath. But the closer they crept to the forty-foot wall of rock exposed by the waters, the more her eyes widened.

"You see it now, don't you?" Dad stood with his hands on his hips.

She bit her lip and nodded. There, in the wall, was a clear outline of what appeared to be a curved spine. From an animal much larger than anything she'd ever seen. "It's . . . magnificent." Placing her hand on her father's arm, she inhaled a sharp breath. "Is it . . . is it a dinosaur?"

"I believe it is, my dear." His voice warbled and then he laughed. "A dinosaur!" He put his hand to his chest. "Thank You, God."

Her eyes widened. After all these years, could it be? To see her father's dream realized before her took her breath away. Every fossil bed they'd gone to, they found a large bone or two intermixed with other animals, but nothing like this. Why, the entire skeleton could quite possibly be here! For the first time that day, her injuries from last night no longer hurt. Instead, every bruised and sore spot was sizzling with energy and excitement. The Great Dinosaur Rush had picked up steam the last couple of years as fossil beds had been found and historic discoveries gave them insight into the great beasts of the past. The more she read about it, the more she longed to be in it.

"Could you sketch this for me?"

Dad's question broke through her thoughts. "Hm? Oh, yes. Of course."

"Just a quick one. I don't want to trespass on Walker's property for too long and invoke the man's wrath. But I will need it to contact my investors. That is, of course, if I can convince Mr. Walker to give us permission to dig on his land."

That would be quite the issue. Mean ol' Walker wasn't nice to *anybody*. Ever. And he probably wasn't happy about what the floodwaters did to his property.

Anna glanced toward the Walker ranch house. It now sat at least thirty feet above the gulley on the other side from where they stood. As she pulled her sketchpad and pencils from her satchel, she stared at what used to be the most beautiful garden in the whole area. Julian and his mother had worked tirelessly to make something gorgeous. Once his mother left, Julian did it all himself and made it even larger and more colorful. But he'd gone away a few years ago. No one could blame him. His father was not a pleasant man. The sad part was . . . the garden was now dead. Brown. Overgrown.

Situating herself on a large log the waters had deposited, she turned away and focused on the sight before her. Even though it was hard to ignore the moisture seeping through her skirts, she kept her eye on the bones. The more she studied, the more she saw the great beast come to life. It was there. Once it was etched in her mind, she touched her pencil to the page. The more she drew, the faster her hand flew over the paper.

She finished the sketch and held it up to her dad. "What do you think?"

He analyzed it. Then examined the rock wall. Then studied the picture again. "It's perfect." Holding out a hand to her, he grinned. "Let's get back to the house so I can search in my notes for what genus this might be."

His excitement was palpable. She stood up and had a hard time keeping up with him as they trekked their way back home.

The biggest hurdle standing in her father's way was Randall Walker. Would the man allow them to do a paleontological dig on his property? She glanced back over her shoulder, a slight chill making her shudder. Highly doubtful.

But she hated to rain on Dad's parade. He was such an optimist that he would think long and hard about how to approach the unfriendly ranch owner and find some way to sweeten the concept of granting them permission.

Of course, she had no clue how Dad would do it. But this could be the pinnacle of his career. Hers, too. Especially if she was allowed to do all the sketching for published papers. Which her father would insist on, as he always did. A fact she loved and appreciated more than she could ever express.

There was no harm in a father fighting for his daughter's chance at scientific recognition in paleontology. Especially since she'd become well regarded in their circles the last five years or so. It was the rest of the world they had to convince.

She glanced over her shoulder one more time. A lone figure watched them from Julian's garden.

"Dad." She stopped him. "I thought Julian left?"

"He did."

"Well then, who is that?" Tipping her head, she directed his gaze back in the direction of the Walkers' house.

Dad waved.

The man waved back.

Which made her dad rub his hands together. "This could help us accomplish our goal." He started his quick pace back home again.

"What could?" Her corset restricted her breathing as she ran to keep up.

"If Julian is back home, then maybe he's in charge. I'd heard rumors before we left that his father was sick. But no one knew for sure if it was true. I need to do a lot of research. Get a good plan together. Make sure the investors will help. Then I'll set up a meeting with Julian. Perhaps you should come with me. You went to school with him after all."

She bit her lip. "Yes, I did." But she'd never been proud of how she treated him. Nothing like Mary, who had been so kind to him. After her friend was gone, Anna had tried with Julian, but had only succeeded at being awkward at best.

Of course she would go with her father. This was too important. But the thought of seeing Julian Walker again after all these years made her nervous.

He'd been an odd boy. The other kids shunned him because of his father. All except Mary. She always had a soft spot for him. His face beamed whenever she was near.

Then she disappeared.

After that, Julian was quiet and reserved. Anna forced herself to speak to him every day. In honor of Mary. But he didn't respond to her like he had to her friend.

It was almost like he took Mary's loss even harder than her family. Because he never was the same after she was gone.

What would he be like now?

four

"... And there were wondrous stories
That never had been told,
Printed in rocky tablets—
Tales of the days of old ..."

~Earl Douglass,
from his poem *Nature's Noblemen*

Julian stared out across the gulley as the Lakemans walked away. What were they doing out here? From the house, he'd seen them studying the washout, but without going out there and speaking with them, he didn't know what had piqued their interest. So he'd come out to his garden area.

But Mr. Lakeman had waved, and then they left.

Which was good enough for Julian.

No one needed to watch what he did next. Cleaning up Damian's mess had become his lot in life. Although, since his brother had done plenty to keep him from harm, it was the least Julian could do.

Once the Lakemans were out of sight, he strode back to the house.

When his father had written last month to say he was sick and needed help, Julian wanted to burn the letter and never respond. But his mother's voice had been clear as day in his mind, telling him to go home. Back to Walker Creek. He didn't know why. But he obeyed. Besides, he hadn't set eyes on his brother since he left.

Nothing could have prepared him for his father. Skin and bones, the man was coughing up blood and could barely stand. But he was just as mean as ever. His eyes were pure evil. Full of hatred and anger.

Then today, it happened.

Father blamed him for everything bad that had ever happened. Again.

But this time, Julian scoffed at the old man. Even told him that his words couldn't hurt him anymore. Nor could his fists. He'd grown at least four inches taller than his father and had worked hard labor at ranches all these years. Probably outweighed his father by at least seventy-five pounds now.

When Father saw there wasn't any fear in him, he struck the devastating blow.

"I killed your mother. Rotten woman." He'd spat in Julian's face, then laughed as he confessed that he'd buried her out in the garden.

Julian's sanctuary.

He'd stared in horror at his father.

Father meant to hurt him. Always wanted the last word. The last strike. Like plunging a knife into Julian's chest.

Julian's mother was the most wonderful person to ever live on this earth.

His father, the worst.

That was when Damian stepped in and took care of their father. It hadn't taken much to squeeze the life out of the man.

"I killed her . . ." mean ol' Walker spat.

Julian didn't want to remember those words, but they were seared into his brain. Repeating over and over. He shuddered one more time as he stared at the lifeless heap.

"The distractions are gone, Julian," Damian hissed. "Don't let him have the last laugh. It's time to clear your mind."

He accepted his brother's words and went over to the pump to splash water on his face. All distractions *were* gone. The Lakemans had left. It was time to finish and clean up the mess. He grabbed the corners of the sheet wrapped around his father's body and dragged it out to the garden.

It was over. The years of torture and ugliness were over.

His father was over.

Gazing around at the overgrown mess that had once been his greatest joy, Julian dropped the sheet and picked up the shovel.

The garden was his biggest—and only—regret when he left Walker Creek years ago. But it couldn't be helped. He'd fought with his father one day—much worse than ever before—and they'd beaten each other bloody. Days later, when he was healed enough to go, he packed up his things and didn't look back.

Father found him all these years later because he was controlling and domineering. And every rancher in the country seemed to know him. But at least he'd let Julian be for a while.

Well, things would be different now. The ranch belonged to Julian. Damian wanted nothing to do with the place. Would he leave?

It didn't matter. Julian could do whatever he wanted. He could change everything. Clean up the place.

Starting with the garden.

With each plunge of the shovel, Julian imagined his life without Randall Walker. It made him smile. Something he hadn't done since . . .

Mary.

"I promise, Mary. It will be beautiful again. For you."

Eight long hours later, he surveyed the newly tilled up space. All the dead foliage, weeds, and grass were gone. What was left was the dark rich dirt he'd hauled up a decade ago. A clean slate. Ready for more good soil and plenty of manure.

Father was buried. Julian would have to plant something thorny atop him. Because that's what he deserved.

And Mother. Oh, sweet Mother. Tears burned his eyes. All these years, he had no idea she lay here as well.

In honor of her, he'd plant every possible flower he could get his hands on. Money was no object since his greedy father had hoarded away plenty of it. Wouldn't *that* make the man roll over in his grave? For Julian to spend tons of his accumulated wealth on flowers?

Julian laughed, the sound foreign to his ears. This day was shaping up to be the best of his life.

All he needed to do was get cleaned up and head into town. He'd order an entire railroad car full of plants and flowers. To-morrow, he'd meet with Scottie, who had managed to survive on this ranch longer than he had, and then with the clergyman in town. Tell them that his father died. They'd have a funeral service at the church, but the coffin would be full of rocks. Julian would see to that.

Randall Walker didn't deserve to be buried at the church cemetery.

Damian voiced the words Julian longed to say for the world to hear: "The man deserves to burn for all eternity."

~⁀꙰꙰◯

THURSDAY, JUNE 6—WALKER CREEK

Stepping off the stagecoach from Green River, Joshua eyed the small settlement he'd called home for the majority of his upbringing.

Not much had changed in the three years since he left. He hadn't warned his family of his arrival, so he'd have to walk out to the homestead. Or see if someone else was headed to that area.

As he made his way down the one street of their little town, a wagon came toward him. With a casket in the back.

Odd. Normally a funeral procession had lots of people with it. But there was one wagon. Nothing else.

Julian Walker sat next to the reverend on the seat.

Could mean ol' Walker be dead?

Men on each side of the street removed their hats. Everyone stopped moving. The singular sound was that of the wheels as the wagon rumbled by.

But no one followed to the church.

How sad that the richest man in their whole area—probably the entire territory—had no one to mourn him but Julian.

Once the wagon reached the church, people went back about their business.

Joshua headed toward home and then looked back over his shoulder. Mary had always talked about Julian, about how he had a sweet spirit even though his father was an awful man. For some reason, she'd wanted to reach out to him. She said it was the Christian thing to do.

The thought pricked Joshua's heart. His sister had portrayed the greatest commandments—to love God and love others— better than he ever did.

Turning on his heel, Joshua picked up his pace and headed to the church. Julian Walker wouldn't be alone today. Mary wouldn't want that.

When he reached the cemetery, Reverend Mills stood over an open grave with his Bible in his hands. Julian stood stiff as a tree trunk, his face a hard mask.

Reverend Mills spotted Joshua and raised his eyebrows.

"I don't mean to intrude. Simply wanted to pay my respects."

Julian's head snapped up. He blinked several times at him. Joshua swallowed. "I didn't want you to be alone, Julian. If that's all right?"

The other man nodded.

While the Reverend Mills continued, Joshua took a minute to study the man beside him. It had been several years since they'd seen one another. Julian left a couple years before Joshua went to medical school. In that time, he'd grown even larger than his father, who had been quite the imposing figure.

Psalm twenty-three was the only passage the Reverend read.

Joshua hated to think it, but there probably wasn't a lot anyone could say that was nice about the senior Walker.

Randall Walker had been on the same wagon train as the Zieglers, the Lakemans, and many of the other families that settled here. The Oregon Trail wasn't an easy journey, and their group—like so many others—endured much hardship and loss. Once they'd wound their way in between the Laramie and Bighorn Mountains in the eastern Rocky Mountain Range, Walker had seen the Green River and took his cattle south to settle. He didn't see the sense in risking the rest of the mountain crossings when there was good grass and water available right there. Several others followed.

Walker Creek was established not long after. Joshua had been a boy at the time, but he remembered that grueling journey across the country.

Randall Walker wasn't a leader. In fact, he wasn't a man who ever seemed to enjoy being around other people. But over the course of the trip, they'd all learned his skill with cattle. He was the one people had scoffed at when he brought a small herd with him—risking their lives and his own—on the grueling trail. When others were lightening their loads over the mountains and leaving animals behind, Walker continued on. His herd not only survived but multiplied under his care.

He was the first to build an actual house. The first to expand his ranch by purchasing more land. The first to have a successful cattle drive and sell a large part of his herd. Every year, the man added to his success.

But those were the entire sum of positives. In these parts, he was best known for his cruelty. Known for yelling at his hired hands every day. Had a reputation for a temper that flared at a moment's notice.

Joshua shook away the thoughts. He was here for Julian. Not to think awful things about the man's father.

The reverend was done speaking and he motioned to a man with a shovel. Without a word, the man started covering the wooden coffin with dirt.

Mills placed a hand on Julian's shoulder. "God has a plan for your life, Julian. He will direct your paths if you seek Him."

The big man nodded. Shook the reverend's hand and then turned to Joshua and studied him for a moment. Something flashed in his eyes, but Joshua couldn't decipher it.

As Julian walked past, Joshua reached for his arm. "I'm sorry about your father."

Blank eyes stared back at him. Julian blinked several times. "No one is sorry that he's gone. Least of all, me."

Not exactly what he expected to hear, but it was honest. "Well . . . I didn't want you to be alone."

"I've been alone most of my life. Other than Damian." With a shrug, Julian shoved his hat back onto his head.

Damian. The brother who rumors swirled around. People feared he was just as awful as his father. "Is your brother in town?" It was a shame the man wouldn't even come to his father's funeral, no matter how terrible Randall Walker had been.

"No. He left." Julian's feet shifted back toward the street.

Joshua stepped with him. "Does that mean you'll run the ranch by yourself?"

"Yep. For now."

Odd. Was there a rift between Julian and his brother? Or could the other man not stand to stay around what their father had built? No one knew much about Damian Walker. Thus the rumors.

Julian had been the one in school. Why he stuck it out, Joshua had no idea. Kids could be so cruel. Especially to a kid who was different. Julian's mother had rarely been seen in town. His brother, never.

Julian pointed to the small trunk Joshua carried. "Did you just get back to Walker Creek, or are you headed somewhere?"

"My train got into Green River too late last night to catch the stage, so I came in on it today."

"The railroad has done great things for this area."

"Sure has." Joshua nodded. Supplies were much easier to get, and building the railroad had boosted more than one family's income while the men worked on it. But it had been ten years since its completion.

The awkward conversation stalled.

Joshua turned toward the mercantile. "It was good to see you, Julian. I best be on my way."

The big man dipped his chin but kept on walking.

What heavy weight was the man carrying? Not grief over the loss of his father, but what about his brother? It couldn't be easy to deal with the ranch, what with his mother gone to who knows where, his brother abandoning him, and his father dead.

Another reminder for Joshua to be grateful for his loving family, although he should kick himself for not coming home sooner.

He shook off the thoughts and walked into the small mercantile and went to the counter.

"Why, Joshua Ziegler, as I live and breathe." Mrs. Jamison sent him a broad smile. "Are you done with your fancy schooling back East?"

"Not yet, ma'am. But I did have a break, so I came home to surprise my family."

She patted his hand. "That's right good of you. I know your mama has sure been pining for you." Pulling a pencil out from behind her ear, she was back to business. "What can I help you with?"

"Any mail for my folks? Figured I'd bring it out with me."

"Let me check." She turned toward all the little cubbies on the wall behind her. "Nothing today, sorry."

"That's all right. Thank you for checking." He headed back toward the door.

"Won't Miss Lakeman be surprised to hear you're back."

The words stopped him short.

So Anna wasn't married. That was the best thing he'd heard all week.

five

"Time is fleeting, moments hasten, days are passing, years go by."

~Earl Douglass

Even the long, arduous trek out to his family's ranch didn't diminish the glimmer of hope in Joshua's chest. To hear that Anna was still *Miss Lakeman* had released the shackles he'd wrapped around his heart.

One large hurdle down, about a hundred more to go.

First, much-needed time with his family.

A small figure appeared in the distance, darting back and forth, chasing after something in the dirt. Then the figure stopped, and Joshua smiled.

He'd been spotted.

"Uncle Josh!" His nephew barreled toward him.

Picking up his pace, he ran to meet Caleb. The boy had been his shadow before he left, and Joshua had to swallow down a sudden clogging in his throat from how much he'd missed him.

Long, gangly limbs accompanied Caleb's giant smile, dirt-smudged face, and hair that stood up in a dozen different directions.

Joshua dropped his trunk and braced himself for the boy who launched himself into his uncle's arms.

The unmistakable scent of dirt, manure, and hay clung to Caleb. Joshua couldn't love it any more as he hugged him tight. "You've gotten heavy!" Dropping Caleb to his feet, he gripped the boy's shoulders. "Let me look at you."

His nephew straightened and lifted his chin. "I'm a lot taller, too."

"That you are!"

"I'm glad you're back. Things have been so boring around here."

"Boring? Around here?" Joshua picked up his small trunk and Caleb grabbed his other hand.

An exaggerated groan left the boy's lips. "It's awful. Mama won't let me go exploring by myself and it's the same ol' chores every day."

Oh, how he remembered those days. When all he wanted to do was play in the creek or climb rocks and trees. "Chores have to get done. Otherwise, we wouldn't have food to eat and a way to keep shelter over our heads."

"But I'm tired of being treated like a little kid. I want to be a grown-up like you. Then I can ride the train to the big city by myself."

Covering a chuckle, Joshua cleared his throat. "If you want to be a grown-up, then that means less play time and even *more* chores. And there's no one to do them for you. You should enjoy being a kid while you can."

His nephew kicked a rock with his shoe. "That's what Grandpa said."

"He's pretty smart."

"Yeah, but he's getting old."

"Caleb Dunn!" Joshua guffawed. "Your grandpa is not old."

"He's gotta be. Mama is thirty years old, so he's gotta be a whole lot older than her."

Couldn't argue with the logic of a ten-year-old. "True, but let's not mention that in front of your grandpa, all right?"

Caleb shrugged. "Okay. How long do you get to stay before you hafta go back to Chicago?"

"About a week." He pumped as much enthusiasm into his voice as he could. Caleb hadn't done well saying goodbye last time.

"Will you go exploring with me?"

"Sure thing, buddy. We should have plenty of time to do some good exploring."

"Promise?"

"I promise."

"Joshua!" His sister Martha's voice echoed across the wide expanse of the yard. She ran toward him from the house. "You're here!"

She was followed by his mom, dad, and brother-in-law, Alan. The onslaught of family was a beautiful thing.

He'd been gone too long.

| Friday, June 7

Anna paced her small parlor. Dad had been on pins and needles ever since they'd seen the gulley on the Walkers' property. But then they'd heard of Randall Walker's death and the funeral had only been yesterday.

That put her father in even more of a tizzy. First relieved about approaching Julian rather than Mr. Walker about permission, and then worried that the son might very well want to sell the ranch. Where would that leave them? Time was of the essence.

Anna didn't need her father to convince her of the magnitude of the dig opportunity. But how did they approach it with respect for the dead? And when?

"I think we should go now." Dad's voice brought her around. He was dressed in his best suit.

"To see Julian?" She fidgeted with the hankie in her hands.

"Yes."

As much as she hated the thought of disregarding the etiquette of mourning, it was the only solution. "I agree." The sooner they asked, the better. She raced to grab her shawl, gloves, and bonnet. "Just in case Julian decides to leave town soon."

"I'll get the wagon." Dad's words chased her through the small house.

Once they were seated together on the bench seat, her father lifted the reins and set the horses in motion.

"Do you know what you will say?" At this rate, if she kept biting her lip, there would be nothing left of it by tomorrow. She put a hand to her mouth to stop the action and reached down into her satchel. She never went anywhere without a sketchpad and pencils. Opening the notebook back to the drawing of the bones in the washed-out gulley, she studied pieces of the skeleton. If granted permission, this could be a find greater than they even imagined.

"I will simply appeal to his logic and tell him what an incredible thing this will be for the scientific community."

"Do you think that will work?" She hated to doubt her father, but Julian didn't strike her as one who cared much about science.

Dad tipped his head back and forth. "Hmmm. It might not. But what else can we appeal to?"

"The only thing I've ever seen Julian enjoy was his garden. He and Mary talked about it every day at school. He often brought her flowers."

"I'm not sure how I can connect a paleontological dig with flowers."

"Neither am I." She tapped the book in her lap. "We'll come up with something. Short and sweet is probably best."

They continued on in silence for several moments. The tension increased until Anna could hear her heart thrumming in her ears. She closed her eyes and took several calming breaths. No need to be so nervous. It was just Julian.

As Dad drove up to the Walker ranch house, the wind whipped around them and brought the scent of freshly turned dirt and manure to Anna's nose. "Looks like Julian is cleaning up the place. At least the garden. It was all overgrown the other day." She pointed to the large plot of dark earth.

"It always amazed me what that boy was able to grow here. Definitely has a gift from God and a green thumb." Dad slowed the horses. "I don't think many people ever visit, so perhaps I should call out to make our presence known. I wouldn't want to scare the man."

"All right." Something about this place always made her nervous. Probably because Julian's father yelled at the whole school of kids when they'd come to see Julian's garden one day.

One deep breath in, one long exhale out.

As soon as Dad was down from the wagon, Julian exited the house.

He shoved his hands into his overall pockets and walked toward them.

Dad greeted him with a smile. "Afternoon, Julian."

"Afternoon."

He looked more nervous than she felt. Perhaps because he wasn't used to visitors?

"Son, I'm sorry about the loss of your father, and I'm sure you're probably anxious to get back to your life, but I have a request to make." Her father charged ahead. "When that big ol' storm came through and washed out this gulley"—he pointed across the wide swath of earth the flood had torn through— "it uncovered a scientific discovery of massive proportions. I believe my daughter and I have discovered fossilized dinosaur bones and we would like your permission to dig them out."

The lines in Julian's forehead deepened as he stared across the washout.

Anna's eyes followed his gaze. It had been a rolling prairie area, but now the Walker home and Julian's garden sat on the edge of a bluff above a wide trench. An even higher bluff rose on the opposite side.

A good hundred yards from where they stood was the wall of rock that the waters had exposed. From here, it was impossible to see the outline of the bones. Anna held out her sketch pad. "This is what we saw."

The big man leaned toward her and glanced at it. "I was wondering what you were looking at the other day."

"The digging will displace more of the gulley, but I can promise you that my crew will take the utmost care. These fossils are fragile and need to be handled delicately so that we can preserve them for the future. They will need to be studied and placed in a museum. I can't tell you how important a find like this will be to scientific education across the world." Father raised his eyebrows.

Julian simply stared across the gulley.

Silence stretched and Dad's eyes pleaded with her to help.

Anna glanced around them and saw the garden. A picture of what it once was sprang to her mind. Riotous color everywhere. Maybe a different subject would give him a few minutes to think about it and feel more at ease with them and their request. She took slow steps toward it. "I see you've plowed up your garden."

Julian shifted his face to her and followed. An eager expression in his gaze. "Yes. I'm getting ready to bring it back to life."

"It was always the most beautiful thing around." She continued around the space, and quite shockingly, he stayed beside her. "I've been a bit jealous that you could grow such gorgeous things here in our dry area." She tripped over a rock and bumped into his large frame. She touched his forearm. "I'm so sorry. I wasn't watching where I stepped."

His head snapped up. Wide eyes studied hers. Then the tiniest of smiles tipped the corners of his lips. Something in his gaze . . . warmed. "Takes good soil and lots of water."

"You watered it every day?"

"Yep."

She crouched down and pointed. "This soil is so much richer looking than the rest. Where did you get it?"

"Used a wheelbarrow to haul up river-bottom mud."

Her eyebrows felt like they could touch her hairline. "That's a lot of dirt to haul that far."

"Yep." He shrugged. "Took me weeks. Six to seven loads a day after I finished my chores. But gardening is what I do best."

"You do." Anna was overcome with a memory. "Mary loved it too. She could grow fabulous vegetables with her mother." Clearing her throat, she stood back up. "Me? Well, let's say I have the opposite of a green thumb." She sent him a grin and laughed at her own joke, hoping that he would relax and give them a favorable answer. Mary had a gift for knowing how to get Julian out of his shell.

Anna had never mastered it.

"I'm staying."

His statement caught her off guard. "Staying?" She studied him. "Oh, you mean staying here? On the ranch?"

"Yes."

"That's wonderful news!" She clapped her hands together. Wouldn't Dad be relieved?

"I'm glad you think so."

For a moment she caught sight of the innocent and insecure little boy Julian had been when they were younger. It reminded her of Mary.

He broke the moment and frowned.

Had she done something wrong? She watched him for several moments as he picked through the dirt and pulled out a pebble and then a dried piece of grass. With a glance back to her father, she knew it was up to her to keep trying. "It's good to know you won't be selling"—that sounded far too self-serving—"not that you couldn't if you wanted to." Oh, she'd stuck her foot in her mouth this time. "I'm sorry. That's none of my business. But those fossils are quite precious." She wasn't helping matters.

She tentatively stepped back toward her father, hoping and praying that Julian would follow.

He did.

"So . . ." She bit her lip and then released it. "What do you think of allowing us to dig on your property?"

"You'll stay over on that side?"

"Of course."

He released a shaky breath. "Good. I don't want anything to happen to my garden, you see. I have a large shipment of plants coming in soon."

She held up her hands. "We will not come close to the garden or the house, I promise." Glancing at her dad, she waved him closer.

"Yes, of course." Dad cleared his throat. "We wouldn't dare encroach on any other part of your property."

Julian shrugged. "Then you have my permission."

Anna hugged her father and then grabbed Julian's hand and shook it vigorously. "Oh, thank you, thank you!"

"I'll have the paperwork drawn up immediately." Her father smiled at Julian. "Thank you, son. This means a great deal to me." He walked over to Julian and held out a hand.

"I'll let my foreman know." The big man shook hands with Dad and shrugged. "It's the least I can do to help with your scientific discovery."

After they shook, Anna beamed at the man who'd been her

best friend's project. Perhaps she should take the time to see what Mary saw in him. . . .

A shiver raced up her spine as she gazed back out at the gulley.

Julian Walker had granted them their request. It was the dream of a lifetime.

They were digging for dinosaurs!

six

"Today the earth is a paradise. Almost every disagreeable thing is covered with Eden-like beauty."

~Earl Douglass

The sun was high in the sky as Julian worked a fresh layer of manure into his garden soil. When the train arrived in Green River with all his plants and flowers, he would be ready. The garden would flourish again.

"Why'd you give those people permission to dig here?" Damian's voice disturbed the quiet around him.

"It's what Anna wanted. Her dad's always been nice enough." Julian shrugged.

"If it were up to me, I wouldn't have anyone on my property."

"Well, it's not up to you. You didn't want anything to do with the ranch, remember? Besides, Anna was Mary's best friend." He'd never been bold enough to speak his mind like that with Damian before, but it felt good. Besides, he'd thought

67

about it. The hired hands ran the ranch with precision, and he didn't want anything to do with that work. That had been his father's domain. So he'd let them handle it. His meeting with the foreman had gone well enough. He offered all the men raises to stay on. They agreed.

It would be stupid to not use the wealth that was here. As long as he didn't have to deal with anything but his garden, he'd keep the ranch running. Besides, a steady stream of income from the ranch profits could keep him from having to work for anyone else the rest of his life. Which was a good thing. He wouldn't need to be around other people.

His gaze went to the area where he'd buried his father. The man had done nothing but yell at him, beat him, and tell him how awful he was his whole life. One of the reasons his mother insisted they avoid town. Because that would give fodder for gossip.

As it was, people in Walker Creek called him odd. That wasn't news to him.

Odd. It was more than that. Something was wrong with him. Mother had understood it and done her best to steer him away from the darkness. She was everything good and precious, decent and loving. Had she stayed—or rather had she not been murdered by his father—she could have fixed him.

"Mary again, huh?" Damian's opinion of her was clear in the mocking tone of his voice. "I know you had high hopes that she was like Mother. That she would take her place and find a way to help you. But she did nothing but betray you."

"Hugging Evan wasn't a betrayal."

"Oh, yes, it was. She was comforting him when she should have been comforting *you*."

"Evan's dad had just died."

Damian spat at the ground. "Good riddance. Fathers are horrible."

The bitterness in his brother's voice stabbed Julian in the

chest. More than anything he wanted to ask if Damian had anything to do with Mary's disappearance, but he bit his tongue and stayed silent. The memory of that day washed over him.

Mary had asked to see his garden after school. Something she did often. But after seeing her hug Evan, it had been a balm to his heart to gain her attention again. He adored Mary. Even if she had hurt him.

Then she went missing after her visit with him. The question to his brother lingered on his tongue, but he bit it back, afraid of the answer.

With a shake of his head, Julian pulled himself from the memory and went back to digging and mixing the dirt.

Damian walked toward the trees.

Julian turned his attention back toward the trench. Were his brother's concerns valid? What would it be like to have the Lakemans on his property? He'd informed Scottie, and the man had shrugged as if it didn't matter to him. The cattle had thousands of acres to roam and typically stayed closer to the creek and river. If they came to the washout, the hands would simply have to herd them back.

It wasn't a bad idea to let the Lakemans dig for the fossils, was it? Didn't seem like it would hurt anything and might give him a better reputation in town. Now that his father was gone, people could stop feeling sorry for him.

Anna had been so nice to him. Just like Mary. And Mother.

She touched him twice yesterday. Never yanked back in fear or disgust. Maybe he could try to talk to her more often. . . .

Anna was pretty. And smart, too. If she came every day, he could get to know her. He could grow a beautiful garden in peace and learn how to be a normal person.

No one would ever beat him again. Or tell him it was his fault that everything had gone wrong.

And no one had to know about the bodies in the garden.

The air practically sizzled with excitement.

Anna rushed around and fetched tools, maps, and boxes of unused brushes in various sizes. The number of brushes they went through on digs was astounding. Chisels and hammers were plentiful as well, but Dad always kept extras of all the tools. Just in case.

"My dear?"

Her father's voice, calling from his study.

"Coming." She wiped her brow and scurried back in his direction. "What can I help wi—?" She almost ran right into him where he sat on the floor, surrounded by research and tools.

One quality her father did *not* possess was organization. That was where she came in. Without her, Dad would be lost in his piles and piles of books, sketches, tools, and fossils. "I'm quite certain that I could see this floor no more than half an hour ago."

His laughter rumbled up through the mess. "It doesn't take much for me to tear a room apart, now does it? Probably why my mother called me Peter the Twister growing up."

Anna placed her hands on her hips and surveyed the damage. "Did you need help finding something or simply help to get out from under the weight of all this?"

"Now that you're back here, I've forgotten what I needed." He clucked his tongue.

That was odd. Dad was unorganized, but the man could remember and recite a list of genera at least fifty long. "Are you feeling all right?"

"Sure." One hand held a book, the other a stack of papers. But he wasn't reading either one. "Wish I could remember what I called you back here for. Oh well. I'm sure it will come to me." He set everything down and picked up another stack of books.

"Dad, if you stay on the floor like that, your legs will fall asleep. Remember what happened last time?"

"Quite right." He set the books down and got to his knees. "I know what it was. The investor gave us the go-ahead via telegram—I told you that already, didn't I?"

"Yes, Dad." She pointed toward his desk. "I can see the paper over there as we speak."

"Good, well next, I need to make sure we have the contracts for the men. They'll be here in the morning." He squinted at her. "I hadn't told you *that* good news yet."

"Ah, no you hadn't." Anna held out her hands so he could gain leverage to get to his feet. "I didn't realize they would be arriving so soon. Who is coming?"

"Zachariah, Tom, and Luke. They'll be here tomorrow. In the morning." Dad's words slowed down as he stood.

"Got it. Tomorrow morning." She held onto his hands as her brow pinched. Something wasn't right. First he'd repeated himself. Then his speech wasn't normal. Now his eyes stared blankly at her. "Dad?"

His eyes closed and his hands went limp in hers.

With every bit of strength she had, Anna held onto her father as he collapsed onto the books covering the floor. *"Dad?"*

At least she'd kept him from hitting his head when he went down.

Patting his face, she tried to rouse him. Nothing. Leaning over his face, she could hear him breathing. That brought a smidgen of relief against the worry creeping up her spine. What would she do if something happened to him? Tears stung but she couldn't allow the thoughts to take root. Dad was fine. Maybe overexcited. Or overtaxed.

She ran to the kitchen and fetched a towel and then ran outside to the pump. Once the towel was thoroughly wet, she dashed back inside not caring that a trail of water dripped with her. At Dad's side once again, she wiped his face and neck with the towel, hoping and praying that he would rouse.

If only she had some smelling salts! But they'd never had need of such a thing before.

"Dad! Wake up. I need you to wake up!"

No response.

After fifteen minutes of trying everything she could to wake up her father, she blinked back the tears that threatened to overtake her. What could she do? She couldn't carry him to his bed. She was all alone. Louise wasn't coming until this afternoon. What she needed was the doctor.

But that meant leaving him all alone. The debate raged within. Leave her father to fetch the doctor, or stay and try to take care of him on her own.

The best thing she could do for her father right now was to get the doctor.

She scrambled down the hallway to his bedroom and grabbed a pillow and a blanket. Once she had the pillow tucked under his head and covered him with the blanket, she ran to the barn and didn't even bother with a saddle for Dad's horse. Time was too precious. So she hiked up her skirts and used the fence as a ladder to climb on.

Hot tears squeezed from her eyes as she raced to the doc's house. *Lord, please let him be there. Please.*

Her prayer made the tears surge and for several moments she couldn't see as she blinked them away. Now was not the time to fall apart. Dad needed her. Needed the doctor.

Swallowing against the anguish that churned in her, Anna lifted her chin and swiped at her cheeks with one hand.

It didn't take long to reach Doc's house. She slid off the horse and ran for the building. "Doc Walsh! Are you here?" She burst through the door and glanced around.

Thudding sounded down the stairs.

"What's happened?" The doctor came into view, wiping his hands on a towel.

She put a hand to her heart. Thank God! "It's my father. I need you to come quick. He's collapsed, and I can't wake him."

He put a hand on her shoulder. "Let me get my bag. You head on home, and I'll follow as fast as I can."

She nodded and headed outside. Using the porch to give her height, she brought the horse close and climbed onto his back. "Good boy. Now take us home."

All the way home, tears flowed down her face. *Please, God, I still need him. Please . . . heal him.*

It sounded selfish to her ears, but she continued to beg and plead with the Almighty.

Her home in her view, she stiffened her shoulders and forced herself to stop crying. Now was the time to be strong.

She left her horse at the door where he could munch on some grass and raced back inside. Hoping and praying that her father would be up and around. "Dad?"

But when she rounded the corner to his study, she found him right where she'd left him. Getting down on her knees, she placed a hand over his heart. The faint rhythm of his heartbeat accompanied the lift of his chest.

He was still alive.

"Miss Lakeman?" The doctor's voice called out.

"Back here!" She stayed by Dad's side.

His footsteps echoed in the hall.

"May I?" He pointed to where she sat on the floor.

"Oh, yes, please." She jumped to her feet and backed away, clearing books and papers with her boots. Anna pulled the hankie from her sleeve and twisted it around her fingers.

Doc Walsh put his head to her father's chest. Then lifted his eyelids to look at his eyes. He pulled several contraptions out of his bag and spread them out on the floor. "Would you mind making some strong coffee?"

"Not at all."

The doctor moved so she could exit the room.

As she strode toward the kitchen, she gulped down a steadying breath. Then another. And another. The doctor was here. Surely all would be right soon enough. Dad was still breathing. His heart was still beating.

She poured beans in the coffee grinder and cranked the handle. Dumping the ground contents into the pot on the cookstove, she looked around for the bucket and realized she hadn't brought it in from the pump. As she walked out to the pump by the well, she focused on the task at hand. It was a much-needed distraction.

Out at the pump, she cranked the handle and filled the bucket with water. But tears sprang to her eyes again. Dad had talked about having a pump put into their kitchen. To save her from having to go in and out for water. It had been so sweet of him to think of her.

He'd always been that way.

Ever since her mother passed, he'd tried to fill both roles in Anna's life. A task that was impossible—but he still tried.

With a full bucket, she dried another set of tears with one hand, and carried the water in with the other. Hopefully the news from the doctor would be good.

And soon.

She poured the water over the coffee grounds and placed the pot on to boil. After giving the stove a stoking, she wiped her hands on her apron and gazed around. What else could she do?

Movement sounded down the hall and she sucked in a mouthful of air.

But the doctor didn't appear.

More shuffling and then footsteps.

Doc Walsh entered the kitchen this time. "Anna?" His voice held a bit of resignation.

Her jaw trembled. "Yes? How is my father?"

"I've placed him in his bed. But I'm afraid the news isn't good. Your father has something wrong with his heart. It's beating entirely too fast and wearing him out. That's why he collapsed. His breathing is labored and could stay this way unless we can help calm his heart. He has no strength in his limbs because the pumping of the organ is taking up every ounce of energy in his body."

She swallowed hard. "Isn't there anything we can do for him?"

The doctor she'd known for the majority of her life looked down, his head shaking back and forth. "I'm sorry. I'm going to do everything that I can . . . but your father . . . well . . . he could die."

seven

"Be awake for time is passing
And there's endless work to do
Thou shalt fail but never falter
Every day begins anew."

~Earl Douglass

SUNDAY, JUNE 9

Everything Joshua planned to say flew out of his mind the
moment he spotted Anna on the church steps. Reverend Mills
had a hand on her shoulder as tears shimmered in her dark
eyes. What happened? Was she all right?

Just the sight of her brought all the old feelings to the surface. Problem was, they weren't old. The only thing that had
saved him from losing his mind over her the last three years
was the fact that a good deal of distance separated them.

More than anything, he wanted to rush to her side and
comfort her. But that wasn't his place.

It hadn't been his place for a long time.

Joshua ducked inside the door, taking the moment to recover from seeing her again. How had he let so much time go by? How had he let her go?

As he found his way to a pew, he overheard the whispers: Peter Lakeman had some sort of a heart problem. And might die. Joshua winced. Not Anna's father. She adored him. He was such a gifted and caring man.

Listening in to the conversation behind him, Joshua found out that Mr. Lakeman had collapsed. Anna had gone for the doc, and he had given her the bad news. Her father hadn't woken fully until Saturday evening and couldn't move because he was too light-headed and couldn't catch his breath.

If only he'd gone to see them sooner. What a fool he'd been! He'd put off seeing Anna using the excuse that he needed to spend time with his family. Which wasn't an excuse, it was the truth. But the *truth* was, he'd been nervous to see her. Afraid of her rejection.

Ridiculous really. The person he wanted to see most was the one who frightened him the most.

Now was he too late? How could he even think about imposing on her when her father was bedridden? In a few days, Joshua would be on a train headed east.

But now that he *had* seen her, he couldn't imagine returning to school without at least apologizing.

His sister Martha, her husband, Alan, and his nephew, Caleb, entered the pew.

Martha scooted in next to Joshua. "I heard about Anna's father but that is no excuse for the sad look on your face. As soon as the service is over, we're going to speak with her."

Joshua squinted at her. Typical older sister. She loved to boss him around.

"Don't look at me like that. I'm tired of waiting for you to do the right thing. No arguing."

He opened his mouth to reply, but Reverend Mills greeted everyone while his wife played an introduction to a song.

The reverend led them in singing the hymn and Joshua lifted his voice with the congregation.

"Praise Him, praise Him! Jesus, our blessed redeemer!
Sing, O earth, His wonderful love proclaim!
Hail Him, Hail Him! Highest archangels in glory!
Strength and honor give to His holy name!
Like a shepherd, Jesus will guard His children.
In His arms He carries them all day long.
Praise Him! Praise Him! Tell of His excellent greatness
Praise Him! Praise Him! Ever in joyful song."

Once they all sat down, Joshua's mood was a bit lighter. Martha was correct. He needed to do the right thing.

Reverend Mills cleared his throat. "We have great needs and heartache in our little town. This week, the Lord changed my heart about what Scripture to share. I'd like to read from Psalm 121.

'I will lift mine eyes unto the hills, from whence
    cometh my help.
My help cometh from the LORD, which made heaven
    and earth.
He will not suffer thy foot to be moved: he that
    keepeth thee will not slumber.
Behold, he that keepeth Israel shall neither slumber
    nor sleep.
The LORD is thy keeper: the LORD is thy shade upon
    thy right hand.
The sun shall not smite thee by day, nor the moon by
    night.
The LORD shall preserve thee from all evil: he shall
    preserve thy soul.
The LORD shall preserve thy going out and thy coming
    in from this time forth, and even for evermore.'"

As their pastor expounded upon the passage, Joshua ended up tuning out the man's words. The thought of Anna having to bear this trial alone tore at his heart.

He cringed at the remembrance of their last evening spent together.

It was supposed to be the night he asked for her hand in marriage. With her father's permission, he was going to ask her to wait until he finished medical school. It had been the opportunity of a lifetime to study in Chicago. She'd supported him and shared his excitement.

But then, for some idiotic reason, he'd gotten onto the topic of her going on expeditions with her father. It had been one thing for her to accompany him as his daughter and because he was her only parent. But she'd been talking about doing the sketches for the dig sites. Being in scientific papers and books. Working with all those strange men. It . . .

Concerned him.

When he questioned her about going out on the digs, she took it the wrong way. Thought he said she shouldn't be doing what she loved. Even went so far as to say that he was against what her father was doing.

Every word he spoke made things worse. They'd ended the night in an argument so horrific that she had walked away. Neither of them had said goodbye.

He'd had plenty of time to think about that conversation. Over and over.

He hadn't meant to upset her. He'd worried about her reputation, as every would-be husband should.

No, that wasn't right. What he worried about was much deeper than that.

Martha elbowed him.

Like a little kid caught, he sat up straight and focused on the pastor behind the pulpit. Guess he never grew too old to be prodded by big sister.

". . . Please keep Peter Lakeman in your prayers this week."
Reverend Mills must be done. How had he missed the rest of
the service?

"Along with Mrs. Chisolm and her arthritis and Julian
Walker with the loss of his father."

The congregation stood and sang the doxology together. As
beautiful harmonies lifted to the ceiling and beyond, Joshua
examined his heart.

Anna deserved more than an apology.

As people moved out of their pews and into the aisles, he
kept an eye on Anna as she moved toward the door. Had she
seen him yet? And if she had, would she be upset if he spoke
with her?

The last thing he wanted to do was make things more difficult or uncomfortable for her.

But as his family moved in her direction, his heart felt like
it might burst out of his chest. He had to see her. Talk to her.
Even if for a single moment.

"Miss Lakeman!" Martha waved her hand.

Anna stopped and turned toward them. For a brief second,
her eyes met his. But he couldn't decipher what he'd seen.

Mom and Dad reached her first and gave her hugs. Then
Martha.

Greetings and pleasantries were shared while people milled
about. Just another Sunday in Walker Creek.

Then all of a sudden, he was standing in front of the woman
he'd loved with his whole heart.

"Anna."

"Joshua."

They spoke over one another.

"You go first." He swallowed and twisted his hat in his
hands.

"It's good to see you." Her voice was soft. But she didn't
smile. Not like she had to his family.

A lump now occupied his throat. He swallowed again. It wouldn't go away. "I'm sorry to hear about your father." Her eyes glistened and she looked down. "Thank you."

"How is he doing?"

"He's awake and talking now but is bedridden. He doesn't have use of his legs or arms, he's too weak. And if he does more than sit up, he faints. The doctor is worried about the strain on his heart."

He spotted the slight tremble in her chin. If only he could take away all the pain and anguish of the past three years. "I'm sorry. Is there anything I can do?"

She reached for her sleeve and pulled out a hankie. "I've hired Louise to come live at the house and help. She's with him now. I needed to come to church this morning."

He touched her hand and their gazes collided. "I needed to be here too. I'm sorry, Anna."

"It'll be all right. Dad is strong." She dabbed her hankie at her eyes. "Your family must be thrilled to see you again."

He squeezed her hand and cleared his throat as he inched closer. "I'm sorry about your father, yes, but . . . *I'm* . . . sorry." Would she understand what he was trying to say?

The churchyard wasn't the best place for this but too many years had gone by. What if he didn't get a chance to see her again before he left? He couldn't bear any more time without her forgiveness. Not after seeing her.

For several seconds, he stared.

She blinked.

"Will you forgive me, Anna?" The words were hushed. There were lots of people around. At this point, he didn't care about what any of them heard, except for her.

With a dip of her head, she broke the connection. Then licked her lips. "It was a long time ago. Nothing to forgive." She twisted the hankie in her gloved hands.

So that was it? She'd put it all behind her? He didn't believe it. "Please . . . Anna."

"I can't do this now, Joshua." She blinked in rapid succession. Her words hushed.

He'd hurt her. Again. He shouldn't press her about it. But now that he'd seen her, had touched her . . . he needed more time. "Would your father welcome a visitor? I only have a few days before I need to head back to the university."

Her gaze darted around the crowd as she hesitated. "I'm sure Dad would love to see you."

"This afternoon then?" Patience had obviously left him today. "That would be fine. As long as he isn't sleeping."

"I'll be there."

"Uncle Josh, I'm hungry." Caleb was at his side, tugging on his jacket. The rest of the world had disappeared for the brief moments with Anna.

Anna's light laugh was exactly like he remembered it as she looked down at his nephew. "Uncle Josh better get you home to feed you." Her gaze shot up to meet his again, but her eyes were guarded. "You need to be with your family. I'll let Dad know you're coming to see him." She climbed up into her carriage and drove away.

He allowed Caleb to walk him to the family wagon but couldn't get the look on her face out of his mind. He'd hurt her. What if he couldn't fix it?

Anna brought a tray in for her father. "Louise, you can take a break and get something to eat. I left the pot of stew on the stove. I'll feed Dad."

"Thanks, Miss Lakeman." The younger woman headed toward the door with her needlework.

"I've asked you a hundred times to call me Anna. No need to stand on ceremony here."

"Oh, but I'm not allowed. My parents said that I must use the best of manners while in your employ." She bit her lip. "Thank you again for the work. My family and I appreciate it." The Bowden family was loved and respected in their little community. Feeding a family of fourteen had to be expensive. The three eldest worked to help out. "I appreciate *you*, Louise. You've been a great help to us over the years, and now that Dad is laid up, I can't imagine what I'd do without you. This stew smells delicious, by the way."

A blush crept up into the girl's cheeks. "Thank you. I'll be quick to eat and clean up the kitchen while I'm at it."

"No need to rush, I'll be here."

Only four years separated them and yet Anna felt ancient compared to Louise. Perhaps it was the weight of her father's illness. Or the fact that her friend still had the fresh look of hope on her face.

She'd had that same expression. Before Joshua left. After the shock of seeing him this morning wore off, she'd convinced herself that it didn't matter. She didn't love him anymore.

What a lie.

This wasn't getting her anywhere. She banished the thoughts. "Dad?" With a slight touch to his shoulder, she shook him a bit to wake him.

"Hm?" Several slow blinks and then he focused on her. His mouth tipped up in a slight smile. "Anna." His speech had been slower as he had to breathe often, but Doc Walsh came by early this morning and said that prayerfully they could get his heart to return to a normal rhythm. He was still researching, but the little bit of hope had boosted her spirits.

She would do anything and everything she could to see Dad recover. No matter what it took.

His heart beat so fast that he was in a constant state of exhaustion. So they had to help him eat since moving the slightest made him feel like his heart would tear out of his chest. This was only the second day. Chin up, she could do this. "I brought you some lunch."

He dipped his head in a slight nod, trepidation in his eyes. To survive, people had to eat. But it clearly humiliated her father to have to be fed by someone else.

"Guess who I saw at church this morning?" She made her best effort to keep her voice light and perky.

One of his eyebrows lifted.

She spooned some of the stew into his mouth and waited for him to chew and swallow. Then she wiped his mouth. "Joshua Ziegler. He's home for a few days from school and is coming by to see you this afternoon."

Dad's right hand reached for hers. "You . . . all right?"

Seeing the anguish in her father's eyes almost did her in. But she blinked away the tears and pasted on a smile. "I'm fine. It was good to see him." Time to change the subject. "Zachariah and Luke pitched the tents at the site. Tom is working on all the gear and supplies."

"Good."

As she fed her father lunch, they discussed the next steps to be taken for the dig. It was slow going understanding him, but she waited as he gasped between words. The biggest problem was the use of his limbs. Dad stated they felt like anvils and lifting them made his chest ache with the pressure from his heart. That concerned the doctor. Anna too.

It was hard to watch because her father had always been a strong man.

Doc said to give it time. It might be a long recovery, but that was the goal—recovery. It was much better than the alternative.

Patience had never been Anna's greatest virtue. For Dad though, she'd travel to the moon and back if she had to.

"When . . . is . . . lawyer?"

"This evening. He said he would be by with the paperwork after six."

Another dip of Dad's head. "Good."

Stubborn man. Yesterday, while the doc had still been with them, Dad demanded that Anna set up everything with the lawyer to draw up all the papers for the dig. She'd have to take them to Julian to sign and have every man on the dig sign them as well.

She'd argued that his recovery and health should come first, they could handle the dig later. But that had put him into such a frenzy that Doc Walsh threatened to give him laudanum to calm him down. Finally, Dad cooperated, but made Anna promise that she would continue with the dig without him. The men were there to help and knew what to do. She could be in charge, handle all the sketches, and write the papers on her father's behalf.

There'd been such fear in his eyes. Fear that if he didn't make sure this was done now, he might die and someone else could swoop in.

He might die. . . .

Something she couldn't even bear to think about.

Doc Walsh had taken her to the side and told her to do her best to appease him. Since Louise was willing to be there around the clock, Anna would have the freedom to supervise the dig and Dad could experience it vicariously through her.

At this point, the doctor was sure that the dig was the best thing for her father. Dad needed something to look forward to each day, needed some kind of motivation to rest, recover, and get better.

Well, if making sure that the dig happened helped her dad to heal, she was willing to do whatever it took.

The men certainly wouldn't stand for her to do any of the physical labor, but she was determined to be there every single day and supervise. She would sketch the tiniest of details. And each night, she'd sit with her father, and he could teach her how to write the papers with the correct wording. Even if she had to drag every book from his study into this room, she would do it.

The daunting task before her frightened her and thrilled her at the same time.

Word of Charles Marsh and Edward Cope, two wealthy men bound and determined to win the Great Dinosaur Rush, had spread through paleontological circles. It was information like this that fueled her father's determination.

For one thing, he liked to do the digging himself. He wasn't out for fame or fortune. He simply loved fossils. And the horror stories they'd heard about the lengths to which Cope and Marsh would go to sabotage one another were scandalous.

Well. She'd just have to keep the news of their dig as quiet as possible. To keep the vultures away. Especially with her dad incapacitated.

The more she thought about it, the more the whole thing unnerved her. Was she ready for this? Her father was relying on her. She had to do it. No matter what it took.

When Dad finished his stew, she wiped his face and then held up a glass of water for him to drink. He lifted his right hand a few inches. "Done. Thank . . . you."

Anna cleared away the dishes. "I'll be right back."

But when she made it to the kitchen, she heard a knock on the front door. Her heart jolted into high gear.

Louise answered it before Anna could collect her thoughts. Wasn't it enough to have to think about managing a paleontological dig for her father? Having Joshua here was just too much.

A glance down at her hands showed them trembling. Heavens, she needed to calm down.

Slow footsteps approached.

When she turned around, Joshua stood there, his hat in his hands. "Anna." His timid smile did nothing to calm the butterflies stirring up trouble in her stomach.

His blond hair had darkened a shade or two in the years he'd been away. But his blue eyes were still as captivating as ever. "Joshua." As soon as his name left her lips, she could feel the heat rising up her neck into her face.

Who was she kidding, thinking she was over him?

As sure as her dad loved digging in the dirt, Joshua Ziegler still held her heart.

eight

"I have every day my feelings of deep regret and sorrow
and fears for the future, wounded pride and longing for
what is not."

~Earl Douglass

"I'll bring you to Dad." The awkward welcome was over, now
Anna needed to pull herself together and get over the fact that
Joshua Ziegler was in her home once again.

"Thank you. It will be good to see him." He fidgeted with
his hat.

She turned to Louise. "I'm sorry, I know you have a lot to
do, but would you mind bringing us some coffee?" She needed
something in her hands.

"Of course, Miss Lakeman."

Anna nodded toward Joshua and walked down the hall to
her father's bedroom. "Dad?" She stepped close and touched
his shoulder. "You have a visitor. Joshua is here."

He'd slept a lot the past two days. Hopefully he would wake
up at the mention of Joshua's name. Sure enough, his eyes
opened and he blinked. When he caught sight of Joshua, he
smiled "Josh . . ."

"It's good to see you, sir." Her old beau edged his way closer on the other side of the bed. Leaning over, he gave her father a hug.

The sight of the two of them together again did things to her heart, but she couldn't count on the swell of joy to last. Swallowing back the bitter taste of that last thought, she studied her father. At least this had made him happy.

"I'll go help Louise with the coffee." She took off out of the room as if her dress was on fire. If she didn't get this turmoil inside her under control, she'd never make it through the afternoon, and she needed her wits about her for when the lawyer came.

In the kitchen, she forced a smile. "I'm sorry to throw so much on you, Louise."

"Nonsense. It's what I'm here to do. I finished the coffee and will bring it straightaway."

"I can take it in. I mean, I know you have other things . . . or . . . well, that way you can have a few more moments to yourself. Are you getting settled into your room?" The words weren't necessary, but her nerves were all over the place.

"Yes, thank you." Louise handed her the tray with the coffee and cups, a quizzical look on her face.

The girl probably had a dozen questions to ask but kept them to herself. Anna smiled and turned back toward Dad's room.

With a rapid fill of her lungs to bolster herself, she stepped around the corner and into the room. "Coffee?" She pasted on her best hospitable smile.

She eyed her father with the question first.

He shook his head. "Doc . . . doesn't think . . . it's good for . . . my heart."

Even though his voice was stronger than yesterday, it was odd to hear how many breaths he had to take to speak a simple sentence. She held up a cup to Joshua. "Coffee?"

"Yes, thank you." He took it and sipped.

She did the same with hers.

Silence reigned as Dad looked from Joshua to her and then back again.

Several more seconds passed, then Dad patted the bed with his right hand. "You two . . . need to bury . . . the hatchet."

She almost spewed coffee out of her mouth. "I'm sorry?" Gracious, Joshua had only been there a few minutes.

"I'm . . . tired. Talking is hard." Dad's right hand fluttered at her. "Do it for me."

Certain that her face was crimson, Anna couldn't think straight. Just stared at her father.

He stared back.

She wasn't going to win this. "Should we go into the other room?" She dared a glance at Joshua.

"No." Dad's hand tapped the blanket. "Talk. Now. Then we can . . . catch up."

Nothing like being scolded by her father to make up with the man she wanted to marry in front of said man when they hadn't seen or spoken to each other in three years. And Dad wanted to witness the whole thing.

Not awkward at all.

"I'll spare you both from any excuses on my part." Joshua set his cup down. "It was all my fault. I never should have left the way I did. I'm truly sorry, Anna."

She dropped her jaw to say something, but words wouldn't come.

"Will you forgive me?" His voice was soft as he moved around the bed to her side and took her hand.

His touch sent a jolt up her arm. She stared at their hands for a second. "I told you earlier, there's nothing to forgive."

"That's untrue and you know it." He squeezed her hand tighter. "I'm sorry, Anna. Will you forgive me?"

She couldn't think with him touching her. Because all it did was make her yearn for more. "Um . . . yes. I forgive you."

The lines in his face eased and his shoulders dropped as if he'd released a heavy burden. "Thank you."

"Good. Now that's . . . settled." Dad grinned.

As if it were that easy.

Her gaze collided with Joshua's, and she almost broke under the compassion she saw there. Almost.

He opened his mouth, but she held up a hand. "Let's catch you up with Dad and then we can talk more later."

"I'd like that." Joshua shifted his gaze back to her father and asked about his work.

Grateful for the distraction, Anna worked to stuff all her feelings back into the box she'd hidden them in all those years ago. But her heart was having none of it. Why was love so hard?

The afternoon passed as Joshua got caught up on all of the Lakemans' findings. Anna kept busy bringing different sketches over for the men to look at, and Dad's excitement about the fossils they were hoping to dig made her smile.

When Mr. Gilbert arrived with his legal paperwork, she left him with her father and walked Joshua out to the front. "Thank you for coming today. That meant a great deal to him." It meant more to her than she could express as well, but she worked to keep her expression neutral. Joshua would be leaving again soon and they hadn't resolved anything. Not really.

"May I come see you—and your father—again tomorrow?"

The air between them practically sizzled with the tension. She'd love to go back to that day three years ago and change the course of the conversation that started their argument. But she couldn't. This was where they were now. She'd have to accept that.

"I'd like that. So would Dad."

"It was wonderful to see you." He took her hand and kissed it. The shock of his warm lips on her skin kept her still for several seconds.

By the time she'd regained her senses, he was riding his horse down the lane.

People in town treated him different now that his father was dead. Gone were the pitying glances. Most glanced at him with a wary eye, but at least people spoke to him.

Which was nice. Julian wasn't much of a people person, but several women expressed their condolences for his loss. It made him feel better. Stronger.

Mother always told him she'd be there to help him be good. Maybe someone could take her place now and help him. Someone like Anna.

As he drove his wagon through Walker Creek on his way back from Green River, he dipped his hat to the women and said a brief hello to the men.

Everyone seemed to believe his story that his father died of a sudden fit with his heart. No surprise there.

Julian had built the casket himself and filled it with several heavy rocks and then nailed it shut. What was buried out at the cemetery was as real as his father's love.

Every time he saw the church and the graveyard, he cringed. But his lie to the reverend and everyone else was necessary.

He looked over his shoulder and surveyed all the plants and flowers. Whatever the hothouse in Green River didn't have, they'd sent for from the hothouse in Rock Springs and even from Cheyenne. The prices had been exorbitant, but he didn't care. Amazing what he could buy nowadays.

Several men in Green River had scoffed at a man planting flowers. But it didn't matter. They didn't live here. He could do whatever he wanted. His garden would be beautiful once again.

Six hours later, he dunked his hands in a bucket of water

and worked all the dirt out from under his nails. The sun had been brutal and hot on his arms, but it was worth it. It would probably take him another few days to get everything planted and watered, but that was fine. It kept his hands busy and the clock moving.

Two horses approached from the east.

Julian squinted. Looked like one of the riders could be Anna. The other was a fella he didn't know.

He kept scrubbing at his hands and arms, hoping that the smell of manure wouldn't be too strong for a lady like Anna. When she rode up, her face beamed like the sun. "Good evening, Julian."

"Evening, Miss Lakeman." He tipped his hat at her.

She dismounted her horse while the man rode up and did the same.

"Allow me to introduce Mr. Gilbert to you." She stepped closer to Julian then looked back at the other man. "Mr. Gilbert, this is Julian Walker."

"Pleased to make your acquaintance, Mr. Walker."

Anna clasped her hands in front of her. "Is there a place we could look at all the paperwork? Mr. Gilbert would like to explain everything to you about our paleontological dig."

"Sure." He led them to the house. Thankfully, he'd spent the last few days clearing out everything that was his father's and burning it out behind the barn. Furnishings could be bought or built. The few things he kept were hidden in a box. Things of his mother's.

It had taken all of his anger to scrub down the house. As if he was trying to scrub the sin from his own life. The house was sparse now and he'd started over. Fresh.

Exactly what he needed.

Julian held the door open for his guests. "I guess we could go into the kitchen. There's a table with a couple chairs." Other than his bed, they were the few things he'd purchased.

Once his guests were situated, he leaned up against the sideboard.

Anna smiled at him again. "Julian, I'd like to thank you again for granting us the permission to dig out the fossils on your land."

"You're welcome." He'd do anything for her. Especially when she smiled at him like that.

"Mr. Gilbert, could you explain the papers we need him to sign?"

The older man cleared his throat and laid out several sheets of paper. "As the sole owner of the Walker Ranch, your signature here will give Miss Anna Lakeman and her father, Mr. Peter Lakeman, permission to head up a scientific expedition. This states that you've given them—and their trusted team of workers—permission to not only be on your land, but to dig fossils out of your land for the next three years. The fossils will then belong to Mr. Peter Lakeman and he will cite your property as the location of find in any scientific documentation." He pointed to a line at the bottom. "Are you in agreement?"

"Yes, sir." The idea of workers wasn't his favorite, but if Anna trusted them, so would he.

"Then please sign on the line at the bottom."

Julian did so and looked back up at them.

Mr. Gilbert moved another paper in front of Julian. "This other document states that you are granting only the Lakemans and their work crew access to these fossils and that you will not—in no uncertain terms—allow *anyone* else to dig for them or any other fossils on your property."

Why would he let anyone else on his property? Anna was the one reason he'd allowed this in the first place.

"If you are in agreement, please sign on the line at the bottom."

Julian signed.

Anna released a breath and put a hand to her throat. "Thank

you so much, Julian. This means the world to me and my father."

"You're welcome."

She stood.

"I best be on my way." Mr. Gilbert placed his hat back on his head and went out to his horse.

"When will you start your work?" The more time he spent in Anna's presence, the more he wanted it to continue. He shoved his hands into the pockets of his overalls.

"Tomorrow, if that's all right with you?"

Perfect. "I look forward to it. Will you be out here every day?"

"Yes. Unless my father takes a turn for the worse. And of course, not on Sundays. But I'll be in charge. I promise I'll make sure that we will take good care of your land."

He'd get to see her every day. His heart wanted to bust out of his chest. "Sounds good. I'll see you tomorrow, then."

"See you then." Her dark brown eyes shimmered like they were full of secrets just for him.

She must see the good in him. Like his mother.

He couldn't wait for tomorrow.

~~~~~

WEDNESDAY, JUNE 12

How had the week passed so fast? With a glance to the calendar on the wall, Joshua wanted to kick himself. He was leaving tomorrow.

And he hadn't accomplished anything that he'd hoped. Not the letters. Not the reconciliation. Nothing.

Other than the apology in front of Anna's father, he and Anna hadn't spoken of what had split them apart. How could he let this happen?

He'd gone back to see the Lakemans Monday evening and they had a lot of fun talking about the crazy things they did as children. It had been nice to talk about old times and he fell into the old camaraderie with Anna. Mr. Lakeman had shared more of his excitement about the dig for dinosaur fossils. But then the older man had a coughing fit and Joshua excused himself promising to return on Tuesday.

Which he did, but Anna had been over at Julian Walker's with the lawyer. By the time she returned, she was glowing. Mr. Lakeman shared her excitement. Joshua didn't have the heart to change the subject.

It had all been so cordial and friendly. Now he was about to leave again and he couldn't bear the thought of not knowing where he stood. Or at least letting Anna know that he still cared.

He glanced at the clock. Today they were supposed to work for the first time on the fossils. Perhaps he should ride out there and give her the letters. At least then she'd know his heart. Maybe once she'd had time to read them all and he was back at school, they could send correspondence back and forth.

It was an optimistic thought, but he wanted more than Anna's forgiveness. He wanted her back.

How selfish of him to even think about his wants right now. Especially with her father laid up. And the fact that it was his fault they were in this mess to begin with.

Before he could change his mind, he grabbed the letters and went out to the corral for his horse.

He waved Martha over. "I'm headed out to the Walker Ranch. That's where Anna is."

"Finally gonna give her the letters, huh?" The look she sent him was her typical *I-told-you-so-you-should-have-listened-to-me-sooner* face.

With his foot in the stirrup, he threw his leg over the back of his horse and settled into the saddle. Martha didn't need a response. She knew.

He let his horse meander while he pondered what to say. It

took him almost forty-five minutes to get to where Anna and her team had built a camp. In that time, he'd practiced dozens of ways to tell her how he felt. Not one of them sounded good enough for Anna to not laugh in his face.

She'd have good reason too.

But he couldn't go back now—she'd already spotted him and sent him a slight wave. At least she wasn't ignoring him.

He swung down off his horse and grabbed the packet of letters, shooting a quick prayer to heaven.

She held out a sketch and talked to one of the men as they pointed to the side of the gulley in front of them.

Joshua cleared his throat. "Anna?"

She acknowledged him over her shoulder and then finished speaking to the other man. When she turned toward him, her shoulders lifted. "Joshua. Are you here to see the bones?" Then she pointed to the packet in his hand. Her brows drew together. "What's that?"

He took her elbow and steered her away from the others. "I want to see the bones, because I know they are important to you and your father, but there's something else that's more important to me right now."

"Oh?" Was that a glimmer of hope in her eyes?

Best to just spit it out. "I wrote these for you. Almost every week since I left. But I couldn't get up the nerve to send them after the way we left things. So I kept writing them, week in and week out. Trying to get the words on the page to match what was in my heart. I want you to read them. Maybe . . . maybe there is a chance for—"

Anna's gaze darted behind him and she put a hand on his arm. "Isn't that your dad?"

He turned . . . and frowned. Dad never rode his horse that fast.

His father rode up but didn't get down. "I'm sorry to intrude, but Josh, we need you right away."

"What's happened?" He strode over and mounted his horse.

"It's Caleb. He's missing." Dad looked broken.

Joshua's stomach felt like it dropped to his shoes. Not again. He glanced at Anna. "I'm sorry."

As he and his father raced away from the dig site, he prayed with everything in him that this would have a different ending than what they'd experienced with Mary.

nine

"This dark selfish world needs all the unselfishness it can get, all the love it can command."

~Earl Douglass

Four o'clock in the morning and there was still no sign of little Caleb. Anna rode back to her house to check on Louise and Dad. Her eyes were bleary and dry. Her mind swam with uncertainties. Her stomach twisted.

She should probably change out of her dirt- and mud-covered clothes and drink a good bit of coffee. Might help her to clear her thoughts and think of where to search next.

They couldn't give up.

News had spread fast in their little community. And every man available had come. Many women and older kids too. No one wanted a repeat of what happened to Mary.

When Mary disappeared, they'd searched and searched to no avail. No answers ever came. The searching finally ended after several weeks, but it had only been the beginning of the grieving.

It took years for them to deal with her disappearance. A spark of hope would come at the most unexpected moment and then plunge them all into sorrow anew.

Mary was just . . . gone.

Anna shook away the dark thoughts. This time would be different. It had to be.

At home, Dad was sound asleep. Louise came and updated Anna on his progress yesterday, while Anna had been out searching. His heart was still racing, and he continued to gasp if he tried to speak or move.

But there was good news, too. Dad wiggled his toes last night and Louise shared that he'd gotten so excited, he almost cried. It had been too difficult for him to move his lower body at all since it happened.

Doc had come by with some tea leaves to steep for her father in hopes that they could help his heart calm. So far, nothing had happened, but maybe it took time?

"You go on back to bed, Louise. When the crew stops by in a little bit, would you let them know that we won't be digging? We could use their help in the search." Anna swiped a hand over her windswept hair.

"Of course. I'll make sandwiches for them to take with them as they search."

"Thank you." After a quick change of clothes that were sure to get filthy by day's end, she downed two cups of coffee. The liquid scalded her mouth and throat as it went down. But if that didn't help keep her awake and focused, nothing could. She refilled her canteen with water and put her boots back on.

When she walked outside, the first streaks of dawn started in the distance. It would be another good hour or so before the sun was up.

She rode back into town to check in with the sheriff, who was coordinating the search.

A crowd was gathered in the street with lanterns. Tying her horse on a post, Anna entered the throng.

The sheriff whistled and everyone quieted. "All right, people. We've searched the acreage closest to the Ziegler ranch. It's time to spread out even more. That flash flood a while back opened up all kinds of gullies and crevices. Perfect places for a young boy to go exploring and get lost. Let's put our focus on those for now, especially the ones closest to their ranch, and we will spread out from there. The day will get warm, so he'll need food and water. Everyone make sure you have plenty with you. Fire three consecutive shots in the air if you find something."

The group began to disperse and Anna spotted Martha over by her horse. The woman stared off into the distance.

Anna grabbed Misty's reins and steered her steps in Martha's direction.

The woman stood still as a statue.

No words came, so Anna placed a hand on Martha's shoulder and squeezed.

"My last words to him were a scolding." Caleb's mom sniffed. "He wanted to go exploring and I told him no. He argued with me, and I came down on him pretty hard. Talking about all the dangers out there and he should never go exploring alone." A single tear ran down her cheek.

"This isn't your fault, Martha."

"My mind tells me that, but then this horrible guilt washes over me. Maybe if I'd taken the time to go exploring with him . . . or if I hadn't spoken to him so harshly."

It was one thing to be the friend of the missing person. Another entirely to be a mom, dad, or family member. What must they be going through? It pinched Anna's heart to even try to fathom. "Caleb is a smart kid. He's resourceful and you

101

have brought him up well. There are lots of people looking for him."

"Please tell me we'll find him? Please? Tell me that Caleb won't end up like . . ." Guttural sobs choked off the last word.

Anna gathered her friend in her arms and held her tight. She was sure everyone was thinking the same thing. Fearing it. Praying against it. The town couldn't endure another tragic loss.

"God knows exactly where Caleb is. He'll show us where to find him." The words slipped from her lips before she had time to think them through. So many people said the same words about Mary.

Anna shook the thought away. God Almighty knew where the boy was. She had faith in that. But whether or not He would show them where to find Caleb was beyond her.

As the sun baked the earth beneath him, Joshua crouched down and studied the gulley. There was a small boot print here and another one over there. But how old were they?

His training was in medicine, not tracking. Even so, every available person had dropped what they were doing and were assisting in the search.

Their little town was relatively small, with about fifty families. They all knew each other. All the kids played and went to school together. But the surrounding terrain of Wyoming Territory was rugged and rough with snakes and mountain lions and far too many places for a small boy to get lost or injured.

The negative thoughts weren't helping.

Martha and Alan were looking all over the place for their son. Joshua's dad was out searching too. While his mom— Caleb's grandma—stayed at the family ranch to keep an eye out for the lad in case he wandered home.

Not one of them wanted to mention Mary, but her name hung in the air like the scent of rain after a thunderstorm.

God, we could use Your help.

No other words would come.

He searched the rest of the washout and found no trace of his nephew. The sun was high overhead. How long had he been out here?

He pulled out his pocket watch. One in the afternoon. His train was about to leave. And he wouldn't be on it.

On one of his check-ins with the sheriff this morning, he'd sent wires to Mr. Bricker and Professor Wright telling of the family emergency. At this rate, he wasn't sure when he'd be able to leave. Would he lose his tuition? His spot in the prestigious program?

It didn't matter. Caleb was far more important than his medical degree.

His benefactor would surely be upset to waste a first-class train ticket. But it couldn't be helped. He'd beg forgiveness from Mr. Bricker later.

Leading his horse by the reins, Joshua hiked up the sides of the gulley to higher ground. While the area wasn't mountainous, there were many large, rolling hills, several ravines from the creeks that shot off from the Green River, and lots of craggy, hidden areas.

A ten-year-old boy could be anywhere. Especially this ten-year-old boy, who was an expert at hide and seek.

Certainly, he wouldn't be up to that now? Not for this long. Martha and Alan said that he'd run to the barn after they'd told him not to explore on his own, and Alan had seen him kick the barn door. That was the last time they saw him.

So he entered the barn. But no one saw him exit.

Was there any chance Caleb was still there? They'd searched it high and low earlier. Or at least, in their panicked state, they all believed they had.

With no other good ideas, Joshua climbed back on his horse and headed home. He'd give the barn a good search and if he didn't find the boy, he'd head into town and check in with the sheriff again. And the telegraph office. Just in case there was word.

By four in the afternoon, Joshua was back in town after his search at home. Their barn was a bit worse for wear, but he could clean it up later. He'd gone from top to bottom three times, tearing into every inch of space. But no Caleb.

He tied his horse out front of the telegraph office and walked in.

"Joshua! I've got two telegrams for you. They came in a few minutes ago." Mr. Mavery handed the papers over the counter. "I'm sorry about Caleb. My sons are out helping with the search. Sure as shootin', he's bound to show up soon enough."

"Thank you, sir." He tapped the papers against his palm and headed out the door. Even though Mavery already knew what the wires said, Joshua wanted a bit of privacy. Just in case the news wasn't favorable.

Out on the street, he grabbed the reins for his horse and mounted. Then he opened the first paper.

Mr. Joshua Ziegler,
*   Leave is granted for the remainder of summer term. If you do not return a week before fall term begins, you will lose your place in the program. Prayers for your family.*

Professor Wright

A bit of the tension in his neck alleviated with the note. Not losing his spot in the medical program was a huge gift. A miracle, to be honest. He was sure to be behind by the time he returned, but he could make it up. Work extra hard.

Here was hoping that the next telegram would be as favorable.

He tore into the second paper.

Joshua,

Praying for nephew to be found. Spoke with university. Your funding is guaranteed if you return before fall term begins. New return tickets will be purchased for you. Advise on date.

Matthew Bricker

The news was much better than he expected.

Heading back to the sheriff's search checkpoint, Joshua eased breath into his tight lungs. He hadn't realized how much anxiety he'd built up in his body over the requests he'd sent to Chicago.

He rode up and listened as the sheriff was directing different groups to search specific areas. Since Caleb went missing yesterday, the people of Walker Creek had covered a lot of ground.

As search parties dispersed, Joshua waited for the sheriff to finish giving instructions and turn his attention toward him.

Sheriff Turner strode over. "How are you holdin' up?"

"About as good as can be expected, sir. I'd like to see where I should search next."

The older man opened up his map of the area and pointed to a section over by the Lakemans' home. "Haven't heard any news out of here. Miss Lakeman searched around her home last night, but it wouldn't hurt to look again."

"Thanks. When is the next check-in?"

"Six o'clock."

Joshua dipped his chin at the sheriff and rode toward the Lakemans'. It was an area he knew well, though he normally traveled to it from his own home.

This route would take him right past a corner of the Walker ranch.

As Joshua rode by, he slowed when he caught sight of Julian out in his garden. What was the man doing planting flowers when the rest of the community was hunting for Caleb?

A burning sensation started in his gut. How *dare* that man ignore the fact that a little boy was missing!

Kicking his horse into a gallop, he went straight to the Lakemans' home. He jumped off his horse and went to the door. Anger wasn't something he allowed often, but right now? He was furious.

Louise answered his harsh knock. "Mr. Ziegler, have y'all found Caleb yet?"

He shook his head. "No. Not yet. Is Mr. Lakeman awake?"

"He was a few minutes ago. Would you like to see him?"

"Yes, please." He needed to calm down. This was getting him nowhere. But he had to talk to someone. And Mr. Lakeman had been like a second father to him. He respected the man and his opinion.

Louise led him down the hall to the familiar room and Joshua held his hat in his hands as he approached the bed.

"We haven't found Caleb yet, but I needed someone to talk to."

"There's a . . . storm brewing . . . on that face of yours." Mr. Lakeman's right hand lifted a few inches. "Sit. Talk."

"Sir, I'm sure you can understand the emotions that are surging through me after we lost my little sister. It's hard to think of us never setting eyes on Caleb again." He swallowed and cleared his throat, doing his best to keep the tears at bay. "But as I was riding out to the next place the sheriff asked me to search, I passed the Walker homestead. Julian was out in his garden. Planting *flowers*." He almost spat the last word. "Why isn't he out helping with the search?"

"Maybe he . . . doesn't know?" He tapped the bed. "I wouldn't know . . . without Anna."

The response took a little bit of the wind out of his sails. But it didn't take away the gnawing inside him that something wasn't right. "This is all too familiar, sir. I hate to say it, but I want—no, I *need*—someone to blame. And I'm sorry, but Julian Walker fits the bill. He had a weird crush on Mary all those years ago. Granted, she was nice to him when hardly anyone else was, but that was simply who Mary was." His thoughts were gaining steam now and he barreled on ahead. "Julian was the last one seen with Mary after school the day she disappeared. Is there any chance he could be responsible for Caleb's disappearance too? I mean, I know that sounds awful, but everyone in this town knows his father was a crazy lunatic who beat Julian and his mother. No wonder the woman left—"

"Joshua Ziegler!" Anna's sharp tone stopped him cold. "How dare you gossip about poor Julian Walker that way!" She stomped over with her hands on her hips and glared up at him. "The poor man obviously suffered at the hands of his own father and the wagging tongues of the town. I can't believe you would stoop to such a level."

Of course she'd defend the man. Instead of *him*. "You know for a fact that he was a little obsessed with Mary! Could you by chance be blinded by the fact that the man was kind enough to allow you to dig on his property?" He narrowed his eyes and stepped closer to her.

She inched closer and stuck her finger in his face. "You are horrid. The fact that you would even say such awful things shows me that you have no heart, Joshua. No, we're not blinded by his kindness. The poor man has been shunned by people in this town long enough because of his father. I think it's time for you to leave."

"Anna." Mr. Lakeman's tone was sad. "His nephew . . . is missing."

Her face softened for a moment but then that defiant little chin of hers lifted. "That's no excuse. The Joshua I knew and loved would never gossip or slander someone else." Her lips pinched into a tight line after the words were out. "Besides, Julian didn't even know that Caleb was missing. The sheriff told me you were coming out here to search, so I followed you. I wasn't far behind, but when I saw Julian outside in his garden, I went to ask him if he'd seen the boy. The poor man had no idea there was a search. He dropped everything and went to get all the ranch hands to help out." The heat in her stare reminded him of their last fight.

He'd been wrong then, too.

Shame flooded his gut and washed away the anger. "You're right."

His statement defused a bit of her ire.

"I'm sorry." He turned to her father. "I'm sorry for what I said. Like Anna stated, my words were nothing but gossip and slander. I hope you both will forgive me." He plopped his hat back on his head and headed out the door before anyone could say anything else.

He'd said enough.

And probably lost Anna forever.

ten

"To despair and willingly give up I cannot, on account of my folks. I must be a man. I sometimes think death is preferable to what I will suffer but it is not for me to choose. I must make the best of it and live for others, not myself."

~Earl Douglass

THURSDAY, JUNE 20

A week had passed, and the search parties had returned empty-handed. No sign of little Caleb. Anna's heart broke for the Ziegler family. Again.

Staring out her bedroom window at the dawn, she had a decision to make. The team of men that Dad hired needed to be working on the dig. That's what they were getting paid to do. But she'd asked them to help search instead. Today, she needed to get them back to the site. A decision that made her want to cry.

The worst was now feared but no one wanted to say that Caleb was . . . gone. Not out loud. Members of the community kept searching when they had time. Kept giving the family tidbits of hope. Not a single person in their town wanted this family to go through what they'd endured with Mary.

Memories of her childhood friend forced their way into Anna's mind. Mary's laughter. Her smile. Her joy for life. She was the epitome of everything sweet and good. The day she disappeared, she was excited to go see Julian's garden after school.

Usually Anna went with her friend, but Dad needed her at home.

She'd always regretted not being with her friend that day. But if she'd gone . . . what if something had happened to her too? The thought always made her feel selfish and petty.

Mary was a wanderer. She'd get distracted and lost in her imagination all the time. The best everyone could tell, she'd wandered off. No one wanted to speak about what could have happened to her. The West was a hard and unforgiving place. Danger lurked around every corner. Wild animals. Snakes. Treacherous rivers and canyons.

Anna put a hand to her forehead. No good would come of these thoughts. Dad had prayed with her last night about the decision. All the other families had gone back to work on their ranches and in their gardens, or back to work in town after the first few days. Cattle needed tending. Chores needed to be done.

In extra snatches of time, the community of Walker Creek still searched with the Ziegler and Dunn families and the sheriff. Many had volunteered to take care of things out at the Ziegler ranch too. There had been plenty of people to help.

But life also had to move on.

The thought made her stomach ache. Martha and Alan probably wished that the world could halt until Caleb was found. Christian and Elizabeth Ziegler too. Not only did they understand what it felt like to be the parent of a child missing, but they were having to experience it as grandparents now too.

Then there was Joshua.

The bags under his eyes each time she'd seen him broke her heart. Had he slept at all the past week? The whole town knew that he'd put off his return to school so he could help his family. Everyone understood what a sacrifice that was.

When he'd received word three years ago that he'd been accepted into the prestigious medical program and his tuition was being paid for by a wealthy benefactor, the town had celebrated and rejoiced with him. Anna had been by his side as his biggest supporter.

Until the day before he left.

Why had they argued like that?

Turning away from the window, she looked at the stack of letters on her small desk. All her time and energy had been spent on the search and she'd glanced at them each night before falling into bed. Now, they called to her.

Standing up, she walked over to the desk and pulled the packet to her chest. She took it back to her bed and sat down on the quilt. Her fingers trembled as she untied the twine.

Sifting through the stack, she discovered that he'd written the date on the back of each envelope. The bottom of the pile had been the first ones he'd written.

Perhaps she should start there.

Pulling her knees up to her chest, she leaned against the headboard and opened the earliest letter.

August 22, 1876

My dearest Anna,
   Sleep has eluded me the last few days since I left Walker Creek. I'm still in shock over our harsh words to one an-

other and can't seem to make heads or tails of them in my mind.

I'm hoping over time that I will be able to convince you that I am truly sorry.

I love you,
Joshua

A single tear slipped down her cheek. Such a simple note and yet it cracked open the wound of losing him. She still loved him. But she had no idea what to do. Where to go from here. She opened the next envelope.

August 30, 1876

Dear Anna,

Classes have started and I am overwhelmed beyond what even I could imagine. I wake up several times a night thinking of you. Hating myself for allowing our argument to take place. Several of my fellow medical students say I'm lovesick and should go home. The competition is fierce. I'm sitting here wondering if you even think of me or if you've decided that you do not care for me anymore.

I'm exhausted and this probably doesn't make sense. But I have to communicate with you somehow. I will pour my heart out onto the page and pray that my words are enough.

I'm sorry, Anna.
I love you.
You have my address. I'm hoping to hear from you and that all is right between us.

Forever yours,
Joshua

She set the letters down as she exhaled a shaky breath. It wouldn't do her any good to fall apart right now. There wasn't time for it. With Dad laid up, she had to supervise this dig.

But this . . . she glanced at the letters again. This would take more emotional stamina than she had right now. To think that he'd written her all these years and she never knew. Why didn't he mail them?

For months, she'd held onto her anger toward him while secretly hoping for a letter. Even though she told herself she'd burn it, it wasn't true. Any word from Joshua would have been welcomed.

She'd been so immature back then. Foolish. Allowing her temper to take over and to think the worst of the man she claimed to love.

As she tied the stack back together, she clamped her jaw against the rush of tears that threatened. She placed the letters back on her desk and went to grab her sun hat. There was work to do.

But something else gnawed at her mind.

The stark truth of her own stubbornness and pride.

Joshua had pleaded with her for forgiveness. Now it was her turn.

New blooms covered many of the small plants.

It made Julian smile. Something good needed to come out of the last weeks. He'd poured his heart into the garden. Watering it. Tending it. Weeding it.

"It's not going to help the townspeople think of you any different. You'll still be mean ol' Walker's son." His brother spit out the piece of straw he'd been gnawing on.

"I don't expect you to understand." Julian examined the next row of new plants.

"I know. I just don't want to see you hurt."

Damian had always protected him, and he appreciated it. He did. It didn't stop Julian from wishing for something different though. Helping with the search for the missing boy had shown him several things. People still thought he was odd. They were wary around him. The Walker ranch might be the biggest and most prosperous ranch around, but the Walker *name* wasn't respected. All thanks to his father.

That's why the workers out at the Walker ranch were paid more than any of the other ranches. That's what it took to keep them there. But maybe now that his father was gone for good, things could change.

Not that he minded paying the workers. No. He'd pay them more if he had to. Just to get them to stay. But if people could see him differently . . . that would help him to be a better person.

"Don't you think it would be good if people respected me?"

Damian gripped his shoulder. "Sure, it would. I just don't think it's going to be easy. It's not like the Walkers are known as good people."

Julian longed to be a good person. "Offering to help out with the search was the right thing to do. I wanted to do it."

"Yeah, but that's not enough for these folks."

If only Mother was still here. She could help him be good. Save him from the darkness.

Movement out of the corner of his eye drew his attention to the tents over on the other side of the gulley. The men had returned. Would Anna?

She was so kind to him.

Mother's voice floated through his mind, stopping him in his tracks. "You're a good person deep down, Julian. Don't let the dark take over. Be good."

Be good.

There was still hope for him. Anna Lakeman was good. She could help him. He knew it in the depths of his heart.

He would do anything for her.

Anything.

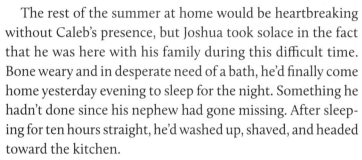

The rest of the summer at home would be heartbreaking without Caleb's presence, but Joshua took solace in the fact that he was here with his family during this difficult time. Bone weary and in desperate need of a bath, he'd finally come home yesterday evening to sleep for the night. Something he hadn't done since his nephew had gone missing. After sleeping for ten hours straight, he'd washed up, shaved, and headed toward the kitchen.

The house held an eerie quiet this morning. His sister and brother-in-law were in the parlor with Mom and Dad. Little comfort could be given right now.

There was a pot of coffee on the back of the stove, so he filled himself a cup and stared out the kitchen window unwilling to think there was no hope. But the more his mind went over the situation, the more his physician training kicked facts and statistics into the center of his attention.

God, You are God of the impossible, but I can't see past the grief in front of me. Hope doesn't even seem fathomable. Forgive me for my lack of faith. A miracle would be most welcome to my family, Lord.

The silence was broken by gut-wrenching wails.

Martha. His sister had always been stronger than the rest of them. He wasn't sure if it was being the firstborn, or if she was simply made of sterner stuff. Hearing her break now was enough to send a tremor through Joshua's bones.

Father, give me Your strength to help my family through this. He squeezed his eyes against the tears that burned in the corners and took another sip of coffee. Would the nightmare ever end?

"Why? Why Caleb?" His sister's voice echoed throughout the house. She'd shed a few tears when Caleb first went missing, but this was the first time he'd heard her sob like this. Joshua's heart threatened to crack in two at the sound of it.

"Mornin', son." Dad's gravelly voice made him turn from the window.

"Morning." One look at his father's face told him the man hadn't slept.

Swollen and red-rimmed, Dad's eyes conveyed the weight of the sorrow of this family. He walked over and wrapped his arms around Joshua. He held on for several seconds. "I love you, son."

"I love you too, Dad."

His father patted his shoulder. "I hate that these are the circumstances, but I'm glad you're home. At least for a little while." His jaw clenched. "I need to get out to take care of the cattle." Dad swiped at his face.

"Do you need help?" Anything to get out of the house and away from the sorrow.

"No. I need some time alone, if that's all right. But there's a note on the table that came for you earlier. From Peter Lakeman."

Watching his father walk out the door was brutal. The man had always been strong and spry. Today the weight of ten thousand pounds seemed to rest on the man's shoulders as he trudged his way to the barn.

Joshua forced his gaze back to the table. He swept up the note and opened it.

Mr. Lakeman expressed his sincerest apologies for what Joshua's family was going through, but asked if since he was home, he was in need of a job. Since Mr. Lakeman was laid up, their team was down a man, and they needed to accomplish as much as they could at the dig site while the weather cooperated.

While he longed to see Anna and spend time with her, the thought of leaving his family tore at him.

"Joshua?" Mom lowered herself into a chair at the kitchen table. "Did you sleep?"

"I did." He went to the stove to refill his cup. "Would you like some coffee?"

"No, thank you, dear." Her monogrammed handkerchief was gripped tight in her hand. "What did Mr. Lakeman have to say? Is he recovering?"

"I think he is. It will take some time for Doc to figure it all out and for Mr. Lakeman's body to recover." Joshua refolded the note and tucked it into his pocket. "He asked if I would consider helping out on the job they are working on since he's not able."

"Is that the dig you were talking about? Sounds like a good way to earn some money while you're home." Her gaze drifted out the window.

"You and Dad wouldn't mind? I mean, I'd love to be able to help the family more . . . but with C—"

"Son. Nothing else can be done. I don't know why the good Lord is allowing us to go through another trial like this, but I'm going to rest in Him. Go help Peter—he's a good man. And who knows, maybe you and Anna can patch things up?" Mom reached across the table and patted his hand, then stood up and left him alone with his thoughts.

Anna. They hadn't really spoken since he gave her the letters and found out Caleb was missing.

It didn't take another second to make his decision. Yes. He would accept Mr. Lakeman's offer.

He went out to the barn for his horse and then headed over to their home.

The whole ride there, he had to keep his heart in check. How many times had he taken this path, eager to see the woman he loved? He couldn't wait to see her again—and with this job, he'd potentially see her every day—but he didn't want to risk getting his hopes up. Not after how he'd hurt her.

He loved her. But had to give her space. Quite possibly forever.

He rode up and tied his horse at the hitching post. Offering a brief knock at the door, he removed his hat.

The door swung open and Louise greeted him. "Hi, Mr. Ziegler."

"I've come to see Mr. Lakeman. Is he awake?"

"Doc Walsh is supposed to be here soon, so I need to wake him anyway. Come on in, I'm sure he'd love to see you." She led the way. At the threshold of the older man's room, she tapped softly on the doorjamb. "Mr. Lakeman?"

"Come in." The older man's words were stronger than they had been last week.

"Go ahead." Louise turned back down the hall. "I'll be in the kitchen if you need me."

Joshua approached the bed and smiled at the man he'd hoped would one day be his father-in-law. "You're looking quite chipper today."

"Feeling . . . mighty fine. All things . . . considered." Mr. Lakeman's gray hair was neatly combed and his eyes were full of life.

"I received your note." Joshua reached for the note in his pocket.

"Good. Does that mean . . . you accept?"

He stepped closer. "Yes, sir. I appreciate you thinking of me."

"I think of . . . you as a son. And . . . I trust you." The man blinked several times. "Sure hate to hear . . . about Caleb."

Joshua looked down at his boots. "Me too. I could use your help getting my mind off the sorrow."

With a slight wave of his hand, Mr. Lakeman motioned Joshua closer. "Sit. If you're . . . going to help out . . . at the dig, I need . . . to teach you. A lot." He lifted his other hand and accidentally knocked over his water glass. "Sorry. My co-ordination . . . is off."

Joshua spotted a towel on the table beside the bed and picked it up to wipe up the mess. "All right, sir. I'm sure there's a lot I need to learn. Where do we start?"

"Fetch some tools from my study." He attempted to shift in the bed but wasn't successful.

"Would you like to sit up some more? Would that help?"

"Please."

Joshua helped him lean forward and then moved the pillows behind him so he could prop him up a little higher. "Here. Let's try this." After a little work, Mr. Lakeman was sitting higher, leaned up against the headboard.

"Good."

"I'll go get those tools. I probably need some paper and a pencil too so I can take notes. I'll have to study them tonight so I remember what to do tomorrow."

"There's some . . . in the desk."

The afternoon passed with Joshua bringing Anna's father one tool at a time and the man explaining how to use it. Everything had to be precise. Great care had to be taken not to damage the fossils when using chisels and hammers to free them from the rocky layers. The little brushes in various sizes were used to painstakingly work the debris away from the bones.

"One of the hardest . . . things will be . . . gaining your balance."

Joshua wrote as fast as he could. As Mr. Lakeman explained the way they used scaffolding to climb up the walls and gain access to the fossils, Joshua wondered how hard it would be to lean his weight against the rock and yet still have leverage for the hammer and chisel.

The more he learned, the more excited he became. No wonder Anna and her father loved this work so much. Regular animal fossils were exciting enough, but to think that he would get to learn of dinosaurs. It was beyond his imagination to think of creatures like that roaming the earth. He couldn't wait to see the skeleton in the wall and study Anna's drawings.

"Promise me . . . you'll come visit me in the evenings . . . before you go home?" The man's voice was hoarse by now. His head laid back on the pillow.

Joshua held up the water glass for him with the towel underneath like he'd seen Anna and Louise do.

"Thank you."

"I will come after work each day. I promise. I'm sure I'll have lots to share and many questions."

"Anna can answer . . . most. She's pretty . . . much a paleontologist herself."

Footsteps sounded down the hall. "Dad?"

Anna's voice. Vibrant and full of life. She was obviously excited about something.

"You won't believe—" She clamped her mouth shut as soon as she entered and caught sight of him there with her father.

Joshua stood feeling a bit like an intruder. "Your dad has been teaching me about his work."

"I've hired Joshua . . . to help out at the dig."

Her eyes widened as she stared from her father then to him and then back again. "Oh?"

"We're a . . . man short." Mr. Lakeman was matter of fact.

She nodded.

A horrid thought came to Joshua's mind. "Does this make you uncomfortable? To have me working with you?"

She blinked several times. "No. Not at all." The smile she

gave them wasn't convincing. "It will be good to have another set of hands."

Even though the words were honest, they nicked at his already bruised heart. She didn't want him around because she cared for him. No. He was just another worker.

Well, if that was all he was good for right now, he'd take it. Love meant serving one another. Over time, he would prove to Anna Lakeman that he loved her.

eleven

"And so they searched and labored
To find a way from night
And sin and pain and sorrow
To Truth's and Freedom's height."

~Earl Douglass,
from his poem *Nature's Noblemen*

It had been seven days since they stopped searching for Caleb.

Six out of those seven—Sunday, they rested—Anna's team had worked out at the dig site.

Five of those Joshua had helped.

Anna wasn't sure how she felt about that yet. She'd been ignoring the fact that he was there every day. At least, that's what she'd told herself each time her thoughts drifted to him. Which was often.

She looked down at the paper in her lap and then back up to the bones in the wall in front of her. The layer of white rock that held them was quite beautiful.

Joshua had voiced the same thought yesterday. His admiration of their work and marvel at the fossils was invigorating. So why did she continue to keep him at arm's length?

He hadn't pushed his way in. In fact, he steered clear of her most of the time. With a grunt, she shifted her thoughts. Her sketches kept her busy and her pencils dull. Every single fossil would need to be well documented. Multiple times. Before the digging started. During the process. And then once it was removed. So far, they'd retrieved one small bone out of the rocky wall, but she'd filled pages and pages working to make sure her representations were perfect. Complete. Without mistake. It was crucial for the scientific journals and papers she and her father hoped to publish.

She'd sketched the whole wall. Ten times. Now, she was working on it in sections. In finer detail. Up close. She worked at one end of the dig site while the men worked at the other end so she wouldn't be disturbed.

Not that she hadn't worked side by side with her father. But that was different. They understood each other. Knew each other's quirks and working habits.

Oh, she had worked just fine with the other men too, so she should give up with the excuses. Time to be honest. She preferred to keep her distance from Joshua. Plain and simple.

Wiping the sweat from under her wide hat with the back of her wrist, she caught sight of the dirt and grime that had accumulated on her hands and under her nails. That was why ladies weren't supposed to do things like this.

She'd heard the whispers and murmurs as she'd traveled with her father and schmoozed with the investors. One of the wealthy women had even stated that she would faint dead away if she were found unclean like that.

The thought made her chuckle. Good thing she wasn't rich and part of high society. Of course, if she wanted to be respected in this field, she had to follow society's rules. Wouldn't it be nice if one day she could have a name for herself as a paleontologist and not just as the daughter of one? To capture people's attention with a specimen *she'd* uncovered and not just sketched.

She winced. That sounded so ungrateful. It was a privilege to work alongside her father. He'd made sure that she was credited for her work every step along the way. Now that he was laid up, her sole focus should be doing this job well and making him proud.

Wiping at her sweaty forehead again, she shook her head. The heat was intense. Even with the shade of the canopies, it was sweltering today.

Anna took a sip of water from her canteen and chanced a peek at the men.

Joshua had been a huge help. The team had welcomed him and appreciated that Dad hired him.

Every evening, Joshua left the dig to fill Dad in on the day. Rather than be a part of those conversations and deal with her emotions, she'd stayed out at the site re-drawing the same bones she'd already documented. Zach and Luke stayed as well since the long summer days gave them plenty of light to work by. But Anna kept an eye on the watch pinned to her shirtwaist.

Each night, she'd tried to time her arrival home so that she wouldn't have to cross paths with her former beau.

Each night, she'd been too exhausted to think.

Each night, she'd stared at the stack of letters on her desk.

As she gazed at the wall of bones, weariness invaded. Something had to change. It wasn't wise for her to be draining her energy simply to keep her distance from Joshua.

Besides, she'd gotten used to him being around again. Not that they'd said more than a few sentences each day to one another. He probably wanted to give her space. But, he'd been such a large part of her life since before she could even remember, she didn't realize the hole that had been left. A hole that no one else had filled. Or even *could* fill for that matter.

Dad had been disappointed that she hadn't spent more time with him in the evenings, but avoiding Joshua meant avoiding her father.

Her focus completely gone, Anna covered the sketches and stuffed all of them into her satchel. Maybe she should go home early today and try to do something nice for her father. Spend some time with him.

"Good afternoon, Anna."

Julian's voice behind her made her jump. She put a hand to her pounding chest. "Julian. Good afternoon."

"I didn't mean to frighten you."

"Not at all. I was deep in thought."

He held out a beautiful sunflower. "I thought you might like this. It's the first one."

She took the gift and smiled. "Thank you. But how did you get them to grow so fast?" Peering past him to his garden, which sat on the bluff above the gulley on the opposite side, she noticed many colors breaking through the greenery. "Your whole garden is flourishing. I'm amazed."

"I didn't plant everything from seed or bulb. I ordered an entire wagonload from hothouses in Green River, Rock Springs, and some came from Cheyenne." His smile stretched across his face. The big man was like an eager child, seeking approval.

"Well, it's magnificent what you've done. It must have cost a great deal to ship all of that here."

He shrugged. "Money doesn't matter as much as the beauty of the garden."

"You've definitely brought a smile to my face with this. Thank you, Julian."

"You're quite welcome." He tucked his hands into his pockets. "Looks like you have a great deal of work to accomplish this summer."

She allowed her shoulders to droop as she released a long sigh. "We'll see how much we can get done before the snow flies and the weather prevents us from working, but it's a slow, tedious process."

"I can see that." He tipped his hat. "Don't worry about the time. You can take as long as you need." He shrugged again. "It doesn't bother me any."

"Thank you."

"Miss Lakeman!"

She glanced at Zach, who had called to her. "I better go see what they need."

"Goodbye, Anna."

"It was good to see you, Julian. And thank you again for the flower." For a moment, she watched him walk back across the wide washout, then glanced back up to the garden before heading toward Zach and the others. How she'd love to grow things like that. But she couldn't seem to keep anything alive. A fact that Dad teased her about on a regular basis.

Dad, on the other hand, often talked about growing all kinds of things when he was young. He knew most plants and flowers by name. When she was younger, he'd often talk about the plethora of flowers at the Walkers' garden, and how he was always amazed at what they'd been able to grow in the dry heat of Wyoming.

Granted, this area was close enough to the river to have much more vegetation and greenery than a few miles east. That's probably why Walker built his ranch here to begin with.

Hmm . . . what if she could do something to surprise her father? Rolling the notion around, she strode over to the guys. "Hey, Zach, what did you need?"

"I wanted you to double-check something. I think I might have found another piece of the skeleton when I chiseled through this layer." He squatted and pointed.

Crouching down next to him, she craned her neck to get

as close as she could. Peering through the opening in the first layer of rock, she could see the dark lines that they always hoped to see.

More fossils.

"Incredible. I think you're right. We might be looking at another layer. At this point, I don't know if it's the same dinosaur or a different one. But why don't you see how much you can chisel out today? I'll sketch it real quick and take it to my dad to look at."

He nodded and went back to work.

Anna walked back to grab her satchel. She could do a quick sketch and would then have the perfect excuse to head home early. Once Joshua arrived for his evening chat, she could make herself scarce and maybe implement her idea.

Thirty minutes later, she rode Misty home and prayed that Louise had made sure all the windows were open to let the breeze come through. This heat was fierce. A cool bath would help, but she wanted to talk to Dad first.

"Dad?" She rounded the corner to his room and stopped.

He was sitting up. Staring out the window. He didn't even acknowledge her.

"Dad? Are you all right?"

"I'm fine." But his voice held a hint of defeat.

She stepped into the room and pulled the chair up beside the bed. "Doc Walsh wanted Louise to start working with you on your exercises for your legs today. You didn't give her any trouble, did you?"

He turned his head toward her. "No. But I . . . couldn't do much."

Ah. So that was it. "It's the first day. You have to start before you can finish." She repeated the phrase that he had used with her dozens of times in her lifetime.

After a shaky breath, he dipped his head. "You're right. I don't want . . . to admit it, but you're . . . right." He glanced back out the window. "This is a greater burden . . . than I ever thought I'd have to bear."

Her idea came back. From his place in the bed, there was an amazing view out his bedroom window. It would be the perfect place, if she could do it without killing everything. "Perhaps this will cheer you up. Let me show you something Zach discovered today." She pulled a paper out of her bag. "It's a rough sketch, but I think there's more bones there that we are unable to see in the first layer."

A smile almost reached his eyes. "This is remarkable."

"You know what that means, don't you?"

He stared at her, question in his eyes.

"We could spend years digging out at the site and possibly find more than one intact skeleton. Perhaps several."

The light in Dad's eyes was back.

"All the more reason for you to work hard on those exercises, rest, and do everything Doc says. Every little bit of progress counts, Dad. We need you out there."

Days out at the dig site were hot and long. But Joshua enjoyed the manual labor more than he'd imagined he would.

Perhaps it was because Anna loved this work and he wanted to feel connected to her. Especially since she'd been avoiding him like he had the plague.

Tonight, he was determined to do something about it. He'd allowed years to pass without any communication with her and now that he saw her on a daily basis, he couldn't bear to let this rift between them continue.

Of course, she could always tell him to take a hike and leave her alone. A possibility he had to consider. But he didn't think she would.

Not with their history.

Their history.

If he included all the years *prior* to the day of their hideous fight, it was quite good. Funny how one day—one explosive argument—could change the course of everything.

Well, he'd had days to plan and think about this. He wasn't wasting any more time.

As soon as they were done at the site, he took off on his horse and rode straight to the Lakeman home.

If Anna wasn't there, he would wait until she returned home. A lady had to sleep at some point.

When he arrived, he made short order of tying up his horse and getting him a bucket of water. By the time he reached the door, Louise stood there with a smile on her face.

"Come on in. Mr. Lakeman is waiting for you."

"Thanks." He removed his hat and headed down the familiar hallway.

To his surprise, Anna sat there with her father. She hadn't run away from him again.

The softest smile flitted over her lips. "Hi."

"Hi." He cleared his throat and turned his attention to her father. "Evening, Mr. Lakeman."

"How many times . . . must I request . . . that you call me Peter?"

Every night, the man said the same thing. "Sorry, sir. I forgot." In his defense, it was hard to think of him as a colleague . . . because he would always be Anna's father first and foremost. When he'd messed things up with Anna, he'd lost the privilege—at least in his own mind—to call the man by his first name.

"Anna showed me . . . the sketch of the new layer."

"It's fascinating. It will take the team a long time to get through the first layer, but how marvelous to think there's more underneath." He stole a glance at Anna. What was she thinking?

They chatted about the day and all they'd found. Mr.

Lakeman—Peter—began to droop. "I'm afraid the exercises . . . today drained me . . . of all my energy." The man's eyes slipped shut for a long moment. Then they opened halfway. "Any news . . . on Caleb?"

"No." He hated the answer. Wished he could do something about it.

"I figured you . . . would have said something, but there's still . . . a piece of me that hopes."

"Me too, sir." He shifted toward the door. "I better get on home. Get some rest, Peter. I'll come back tomorrow."

The older man nodded and closed his eyes.

Joshua's resolve nudged him, and he whispered to Anna. "I need a moment of your time." He didn't wait for a response as he walked out the door and toward the kitchen. Would she follow? Her soft footfalls behind him gave him a bit of hope.

"Josh?" She hadn't called him that since he left. There was a hitch in her voice.

"I was hoping we could talk." He turned and gazed into her dark eyes. Rich like coffee with a splash of cream. He blinked away the thoughts and studied her face. "Is something wrong?"

"I need to ask you a favor." She tugged at the cuffs of her sleeves.

"All right."

"Would you help me with a project for Dad?" Stepping toward him, she kept her voice soft and low. "He seems to be discouraged and I'd like to lift his spirits, keep him on the road to recovery."

"What can I do to help?"

"When I was a little girl, he used to love to talk to me about plants and flowers. But I didn't inherit my mother's green thumb. Maybe it's because I've spent my life sketching and drawing dead things. Not just dead. Beyond dead—fossilized." Her half laugh was a good sign that she was getting comfortable with him again. "But I have an idea."

He smiled with her. "All right. I'm all ears."

"Would you go with me to ask Julian if he would teach me how to garden? Maybe he could give me some advice about what to plant and how to take care of it. Then I would need your help to bring it about. I'd like to put a garden outside Dad's window, give him something beautiful to look at."

Spending more time with her was, of course, exactly what he wanted to do. "I'd love to help. I still have things to do at the homestead to help out, but I think it can be arranged. There's plenty of daylight nowadays."

"Thank you." For the first time since he'd been home, she looked at him without any walls up. No guarded expression. No apprehension in her eyes.

"But this means that you'll have to stop avoiding me." He held her gaze. Could she tell he was teasing?

She shook her head at him but smiled. "Let's go outside."

"All right." He followed her out the door.

"Shall we walk?" Pushing errant strands of hair off her face, she didn't wait for an answer and headed toward the creek.

It had been their favorite place to sit and chat.

Rather than push, he waited for her to open up. They strolled side by side for several minutes.

"I'm sorry for my behavior since you came home." She held a bit of her skirts in one hand while the other hung free. At least she wasn't fidgeting. That would be a sure sign of her discomfort.

"I'm sorry for how we left things."

She stopped and turned toward him. "I know. I'm sorry, too." Her eyes closed in a long blink. "I read a couple of your letters." Then she started walking again.

He had no choice but to follow. The silence was deafening. He counted to twenty. "And?"

"I loved you, Josh. With all my heart. I was crushed—beyond crushed—when you left. It would have been difficult enough to face you leaving even knowing that we had a future to look forward to, but with how things happened . . . I cried in my room for days. Refused to eat. It was the worst time of my life."

He deserved that. But he hated hearing it. "I'm so sorry."

She held up a hand. "I forgive you. I do. But I need to apologize. I'm sorry. And I hope that you forgive me."

"Oh, Anna." He moved toward her, wanting more than anything to take her in his arms. But he held himself back. They were so close, their toes could almost touch.

She reached her hand toward his shirt and laid it on his chest. "Can we start over?" Tipping her chin up so she could look at him, she sent him a soft smile.

"I'd love to."

"Good." She stepped back and broke the connection. "Maybe one day we can talk about why you didn't want me to go on paleontological digs with my father."

"Anna, that's not what I—"

"It's one thing for you to not have faith in me, Joshua Ziegler, but don't you dare disrespect my father's life work."

twelve

"And they went, fearless, forward,
For when they but looked back
They saw in the ways of error
Only a blood-stained track."

~Earl Douglass,
from his poem *Nature's Noblemen*

THURSDAY, JUNE 27

Two riders approached in the early morning hour. Julian watched out the window, and a tingling sensation prickled its way up his spine. Visitors had never been welcomed on the Walker Ranch. And as much as he wanted to be different from his father, he wasn't too keen on them himself.

The foreman on the ranch—Scottie—was a decent enough fellow. He treated Julian with respect and did whatever he was instructed. But the rest of the hands steered clear of the house and Julian.

Not that he could blame them. Nor did he mind.

They kept the ranch running and making money. That was all that mattered.

"I hate that he left us with this reputation. Just because he was the worst human being since the beginning of time didn't mean that he had to make the town hate us too."

Julian was certain his brother's words were true. "Maybe they don't hate us. The one good thing our father did was build this ranch. Not that it was *good* necessarily, but it has done a lot for the community. And it makes money now. Perhaps good can be done with it."

"Good. You go right ahead and try that."

Julian waited for his brother to leave and glanced back at the riders. Why were they coming here?

He filled his lungs and counted to ten. Watched. But as he held his breath, he recognized Anna and Joshua.

Two people he knew wouldn't try to hurt him.

He went out to meet them and stood by his garden. The seeds he'd planted were beginning to sprout among the other flourishing plants. This fall, he'd plant all the bulbs he ordered. Come spring, the tulips, daffodils, iris, and lilies would paint the area in vivid color.

"Good morning, Julian." Anna slid off her horse with ease. "I hope it's not too early to visit?"

"No. I was up." He needed to do something with his hands, so he shoved them into his pockets.

"Morning." Joshua greeted him.

Anna stepped forward, her dark brown eyes seeming to peer through to his soul. "I have a request to make, and I'm hoping you'll be willing to help me."

"Okay." What else could she want since he'd already granted them permission to dig on his property?

Anna peered over her shoulder at Joshua and then back at him. She fidgeted with her horse's reins. "You see, my father is laid up for a while. His recovery will likely take a great deal of time, and I was trying to come up with a way to cheer him up. Encourage him, you know?"

He didn't. He couldn't imagine ever doing anything for his father.

When he didn't say anything, she continued. "He used to always talk about how beautiful your garden was and would remark about all the unique flowers and plants you were able to grow. I've never been able to grow anything"—she winced— "so I was hoping you could teach me? That is, if you have time?"

What did she mean? "You want me to teach you . . . how to garden?"

Her head bobbed up and down. "Yes. I'd like to start a lovely garden outside Dad's window, so he can watch it grow."

A tingling sensation started in his middle. Anna loved something that he did. Wanted to learn more about it. His favorite thing in the whole world. But he'd never taught anyone anything ever in his life. "It's a lot of work and you spend a lot of time there." He pointed out to the site where they'd been working.

"I know." With a thumb over her shoulder, she pointed at Joshua. "He's offered to help me, and Louise told me she could help with the watering and weeding."

The hopeful look on her face was something he couldn't deny. "Okay. I'll do it."

Her shoulders lifted and her face beamed, her smile was so full. "Thank you."

"You're welcome." He toed the dirt with his boot. "Just let me know when you are ready to start. I'll order some plants and seeds for you if you'd like."

"Oh, would you? I wouldn't have the foggiest idea where to start." She went to the side of her horse and Joshua assisted her up. "I can't wait. I have a feeling this will help Dad with his healing."

Joshua mounted as well. "Thanks, Julian."

Anna turned her horse toward her home. "I'll come see you

this afternoon to get started, if that's all right? I'm sure there's a lot we need to do to prepare the ground. Didn't you say you brought in a bunch of better dirt?"

His mind spun with all the details of what needed to be done. A nod was all he could muster. He'd have to put his thoughts together after they were gone. Perhaps make a trip into town and wire in another order. He'd been wanting a few more things for his own garden too.

His two visitors rode back the way they'd come and Julian scratched his head.

More time with Anna would be nice. Talking about plants and flowers and getting things to grow out of the dirt was his specialty.

Wouldn't Mother be happy for him?

***

Anna walked into her father's room that evening and enjoyed hearing his hearty chuckle. Her eyes darted from him to Joshua.

"Our new paleontologist-in-training here . . . was just entertaining me with stories from the site." The twinkle in her father's eyes was good to see and his speech was smooth and strong. Not all staggering breaths. Perhaps the herbal teas Doc recommended were helping.

"I didn't know I was much of an entertainer, but then my blunders have been quite impressive." Joshua's amusement lit up his face.

She took a chair. "Don't let me interrupt, it sounded like you were getting to the good part." They shared a smile since she knew what he was about to say. He'd matured the last three years and grown into the man she always knew he'd be. Kind, intelligent, generous, strong, hardworking.

"All that work. And then your daughter informed me that I'd been chiseling around a smudge." Joshua's eyes twinkled with merriment. "Apparently, she'd drawn on the rock with her pencil to show Zach something." Shaking his head, his shoulders shook with laughter.

It was good for all of them after a long day. Especially Dad. "I think this proves that I should stick with medicine." He held up his hands and caught her eye.

They shared another brief smile.

The long days out in the sun were exhausting, but the team was making progress. About four o'clock today, she'd packed up her sketching supplies and headed over to Julian's garden. With a notepad and pencil in hand, she'd walked with him around the garden and listened to him explain what he called the basics. Which was still more information than she could remember. Gracious, he'd named so many plants that she was tongue-tied when she tried to repeat one of them.

And understanding the soil? That was beyond her. But she was determined to do this for Dad.

When she'd left, she shoved the notepad into her satchel. She'd much rather be working with the bones. For one thing, they didn't need her to keep them alive. Just the thought of growing something made her shiver.

However, she was not a quitter. Perhaps if she conquered gardening, she could move onto something even more adventurous. Like cooking.

It was unheard of for a woman of her age to be unable to cook. Or garden.

But after her mother died, Dad kept them fed. He was quite a good cook. They'd traipsed all over the country together as he dug for fossils. As soon as she could handle a pencil and paper, she'd started to draw what she saw in front of her. Her scribbles in the beginning weren't perfect, but he saw the potential and had placed her in art classes one summer when he was working in Chicago.

She'd excelled, and the teachers raved about her amazing talent.

They'd been a duo ever since. Dad digging and preserving the fossils, while she sketched everything.

It was why she desperately needed to do something for him. She needed her father around. For a long time. She couldn't imagine life without him. Nor did she want to.

But it was more than that. She still needed him to teach her. She loved the field of paleontology. The quest for knowledge. The constant pursuit of understanding in science. There was so much they didn't know. Couldn't explain.

Like dinosaurs.

Probably why Dad had always dreamed of having his one big dinosaur find.

It didn't help that the Great Dinosaur Rush had made men do crazy things, all in the name of science. But not her father. No. He was a good and decent, hardworking and honest man.

"Anna?" Joshua's voice broke through her thoughts.

She blinked at him. "I'm sorry. What did you say?"

"I asked if you wanted to take a walk with me, but I know it's late. You must be tired."

Tired of pushing her thoughts of and feelings for Joshua aside, yes. She needed to stop pining for days gone by and move forward with her life. "I'd love to take a walk." Without hesitation, she stood, then turned to Dad. "Do you need anything?"

"No, my dear. But thank you."

Anna kissed him on the forehead. "I'll see you in the morning then."

"Good night." Dad yawned. "Thank you for coming by, Joshua. The laughter was indeed good medicine. My heart feels like it's almost beating normally."

Anna walked toward the sitting room where Louise worked

on some embroidery. "I'm going to take a walk with Mr. Ziegler. Dad is resting."

"Very well, Miss Lakeman."

Joshua headed out the door and Anna second-guessed herself. "I'm not asking too much of you, am I?" It had been a while since she'd thought about poor Louise and what she might need.

"Heavens, no, Miss Lakeman. It's a wonderful job and I'm grateful to you for allowing me to help you and your father. We have such lovely chats. I learn something new from him every day."

"You don't mind all the nursing duties?"

"Not at all. I enjoy spending time with older people. They have such great stories to share and a lifetime of wisdom to pass on. I helped take care of my grandmother before she went on to glory." Her eyes widened. "Not that your father is even close, I didn't mean it like that. I just meant that—"

"It's all right. I understand. No need to worry. I simply wanted to make sure that you are well taken care of and that you know how appreciated you are."

The younger woman smiled. "I appreciate that. And my parents are grateful as well." One of her eyebrows arched up. "I don't think you should keep Mr. Ziegler waiting on my account."

"Oh." Anna glanced to the door. "You're right. I'll see you in the morning."

"Yes, miss. I'll have breakfast ready for you and your father and pack a lunch for the dig site." Louise waved her hand at her. "Go on now. Shoo."

Armed with the younger girl's encouragement, Anna headed out the door and found Joshua waiting by the hitching post.

"I was wondering if you'd changed your mind." His deep voice calmed her nerves.

Honestly? What had been her problem? Why was she doing everything to avoid him? "Louise and I were chatting."

They took slow steps down the path.

A nice breeze blew across her yard this evening, which helped diminish some of the heat of the day.

They walked in silence for several minutes. Taking their time, meandering their way down to the creek.

"You haven't told me about medical school. How do you like it?" That should be a safe enough subject.

"It's incredible. Truly, it is." He let out a grunt. "But it's also much harder than I imagined. Every day the work is intense. There's so much to memorize and understand. It keeps me busy."

"I'm glad you're enjoying it even though it's difficult. You never were one to back away from a challenging subject in school." Memories of Joshua tackling the higher maths for extra credit while the rest of them were content to simply do what was required brought a smile to her face.

His steps halted and he tugged at her arm to stop with him. "I wanted to share all of it with you from the very beginning. I wrote to you about everything in those letters. It's been incredibly difficult to do this without my best friend." He trailed a finger down her cheek. "I'm sorry, Anna."

"Stop apologizing, Josh." Wrapping her arms around her middle, she didn't know how to feel. It had been easier to pretend nothing mattered.

"It was my own foolish pride that kept me from mailing them. I kept thinking one day I would, and then as the weeks passed and I didn't hear from you . . . I guess I thought that meant you didn't want to hear from me. But I continued to pour out my heart to you because *you* were the one I wanted to spend my life with. Who I wanted to share everything with."

"Oh . . . Josh." Why did love have to hurt?

"What I'm saying is that I know we agreed to start over, but *if* you choose to read them, you'll notice that you still hold my heart. I don't want to start over. I want to move on. With you." He let out a breath, shoved his hands into his pockets, and started walking again.

Her heart seemed caught in her throat. More than anything, she'd wanted to spend time with him tonight. Each morning she woke up and was determined to knock down the wall that was between them. And each day, she'd find some reason to convince herself to hold back.

He'd written her all those letters. And what had she done? She'd wallowed in the aftermath of their fight and then held a grudge that he didn't even bother to communicate with her. But did *she* try? No. She hadn't.

Watching his back as he continued on down the path, she hated herself for what she'd done. She was as guilty as he was.

Lifting her skirts, she ran to catch up to him. "Josh . . ."

He turned. The anguish in his eyes pierced her. Had she put that there? "I'm sorry." Between breaths, she brushed the front of her skirt. Needing something to occupy her hands because she wanted to touch him but didn't have that right anymore. "Let's move on. Together."

His eyes crinkled at the corners. "I'm willing to try if you are."

Without another thought, she walked up to him and wrapped her arms around his waist. This was where she wanted to be. The strain of keeping her heart locked up for all this time slowly melted away with the rhythm of his heart under her ear.

"Anna . . ."

The hoarse whisper from the trees made her jump. She gripped Joshua's arm. "Who said that? Who's there?"

thirteen

"Youth is short and age is dreary; cheer these early days with a song or thou wilt grow sad and weary if the journey should be long."

~Earl Douglass

FRIDAY, JUNE 28

The crow of the rooster came too early. Anna moaned as she sat up on the edge of her bed. They'd searched the trees for twenty minutes and never found a sign of anyone else, but Joshua assured her she wasn't the only one who heard her name called.

It had taken another half hour for her to convince him that she was safe and he could return home. She'd scurried in the door and locked it as soon as they said goodnight but that still didn't make her feel comfortable enough to go to sleep. Her dad had been asleep when she came in and she couldn't bear the thought of waking him with her paranoia. Once she was in her room with the lantern burning bright, she'd kept herself distracted by reading more of Joshua's letters.

She'd started over with the first two and put the rest in chronological order. After the first few haunting missives, where she could almost feel the grief over how they'd ended things, he started sharing everything about school. His hopes and dreams. Which still included her. If she could forgive him.

She'd finally relaxed and snuggled up under the covers. More than once, she'd laughed aloud while reading, and multiple times she'd teared up as he'd shared the depth of his heart.

To think that she'd missed out on all of this because of her temper.

They still needed to discuss the argument. And whether or not he still felt that way toward her father's work and hers. But they were walking a fine line right now. Trying to put the past behind them and move forward.

That hard conversation could wait. For now.

Anna dressed and prepared for the day. Another long one at the site most likely. So much needed to be done. She missed her dad's presence. His knowledge. His skill. Without him, even with more men, it would take double the time. Because no one was quite like her father.

But they were doing their best.

She threw water on her face. Oh, to be in two places at once. But she couldn't stay here and care for Dad if she was needed out at the dig.

And she *was* needed. The guys looked to her for her expertise and knowledge. Their respect boosted her confidence a little bit each day.

Louise had been a godsend. Anna would forever be grateful for the young woman's help, but it didn't keep the guilt from gnawing at her.

Of course, Dad would never want her to feel guilty. He *wanted* her out there. To stretch her paleontological prowess. Now that he was doing small exercises every day, there was a bit more progress with his right leg. Doc Walsh said that as soon as he had enough strength on the right side, they could begin working on the side hit worse by the apoplexy.

Time. That's what it would take. *Everything* took time. Time for Dad to heal. Time for the dig. Time for her to grow a lovely garden.

If that last one was even possible. Which she doubted, but she would give it a try.

She walked into the kitchen and her stomach growled at the wonderful aroma of bacon and coffee. "Good morning, Louise."

"Morning." She turned, her blond hair still hanging in a braid down her back.

"I think I'll take my breakfast in with Dad today. I can spare a few minutes before I head out."

"Sounds good. I'll go ahead and get some bread going so it can have plenty of time to rise."

Anna walked over and kissed Louise on the cheek. "I am so thankful for you, my friend. You are amazing. Some young man is going to snatch you up soon and I won't know what to do around here without your help." She picked up the stack of mail she'd left on the table last night, dropped it on the tray, and then took it all to Dad's room.

"Good morning!" Carrying in the tray, she beamed a smile at her father. She set the tray down in the chair. "Here. Let me help you sit up and then we can have breakfast together before I get back to work."

"Sounds good." He *was* getting stronger because he was able to help her a little in the process.

Once she had him settled, she picked up the tray and set it on the bed. "I went by the post office yesterday and picked up our mail. It's been a week since I went in last, so there's a decent pile. One of the letters is from Mr. Oppenheim. Wasn't he the investor who wanted to build his own museum?"

The smile slid off Dad's face. "Yes. That's him."

"Why don't we eat first while it's still hot, and then I'll help you open the letters?"

Dad shook his head. "Open the one from Mr. Oppenheim first. Then we can eat."

She did as he asked and slit open the envelope, unfolded the single sheet of paper, and handed it to her father's right hand. He could hold it up high enough to read, which was good. Gave him a bit of independence when so much had been taken from him.

While he perused the missive, she took a sip of her coffee. She couldn't feed Dad and herself at the same time, so maybe she should go ahead and eat a few bites. Her stomach was ravenous.

Anna ate several slices of bacon and sipped her coffee.

Then Dad let the paper fall.

"Is everything all right?"

Her father's eyes connected with hers. "I asked Mr. Oppenheim to invest in our dig."

That wasn't unusual. So why did he look upset? She waited for him to continue.

"He agreed to invest as soon as we had permission from Julian. I had wired Mr. Oppenheim that day. But I never did get the correct contracts to him, because of my collapse."

Legal stuff wasn't her favorite. "What does that mean?"

"It means that he sent his money in good faith, but the parameters weren't laid out." Dad sighed. "Now he wants to change those parameters. He wants his name on the dig and the scientific papers as well."

⁓

Teaching Anna to garden was a dream come true. She appreciated him. Enjoyed spending time with him. Praised his garden.

Not only all that, but she also was kind to him and listened to everything he had to say. She took lots of notes and asked even more questions.

Talking to people had always been a chore, but talking to Anna about gardening? It overwhelmed him with good feelings.

Today she said that he was smart. No one ever told him that before. No one. Not even his mother. Not even Damian. Over and over again, she'd complimented him on his skills, the beautiful flowers, and said that he was an excellent teacher. It was like he could walk without even touching the ground. Now he couldn't wait for her to come back. Julian had been watching them dig across the gulley with a set of field glasses. Anna was so busy. It seemed every time he looked, she had moved from one perch to another so she could make another drawing.

The work she did was interesting. But the other men at the dig didn't speak to Julian when he came by. Just nodded and kept chiseling away at the rock.

Joshua talked to him, but they'd known one another since they were little.

"I thought good ol' Joshua Ziegler left for medical school years ago." Damian's thoughts brought Julian back to the shovel in his hand.

He'd probably spent too much time staring across the gulley. "Yeah. He's back. But only for the summer."

"Hadn't they talked about getting married?"

"I don't know what happened other than they broke it off a long time ago. But they haven't talked about it since he's been back. In fact, Anna hasn't mentioned him. She's asked me to teach her gardening, you know. No one else can teach her what I can."

Julian lifted the field glasses up again. Anna was making her way across the washout toward him. "You better go. She's coming."

His heart thudded in his chest as he went to wash up and comb his hair. By the time he walked outside, she was almost up the bluff.

With one hand on her chest and another lifting her skirts, she approached, eyes wide. "I should take the path I normally take from my home next time. Whew! That's quite the climb." She put a hand to her stomach and sent him a smile. Her cheeks were red from the heat and her walk up the incline. "I forgot to ask you this morning when I need to have the dirt ready at my house. I mean, for planting."

"In four to five days we should have everything we need to plant."

"Oh good, I still have some time to prepare. I need to stay later at the dig site this evening because my dad asked for some specific drawings and the guys are trying to make a good bit of progress while the weather is hot and dry. Dad's having a tough time not being a part of it, so I want to make sure he can *see* as much of it as he possibly can."

"That's awfully nice of you to do that for your father." He tried not to choke on the last word.

She pulled a fan out of her waistband and began fanning her face. "We've been working together for so long, it's not right to *not* include him in everything." She walked along the edge of his garden. "How did you learn all of this anyway?"

"My mother. She was very talented in the garden."

"I'm sorry I don't remember her well. She must have been a wonderful person."

Julian looked away. "She was. You remind me of her."

"Julian, that is such a lovely compliment. Thank you." Her fan made little wisps of her hair fly this way and that. It was mesmerizing.

"You're welcome. She would have loved helping you with a garden to cheer your father."

She tucked the fan back and clapped her hands together.

"I'm so excited. I can't wait for everything to arrive, but I guess that means I better get busy preparing the ground."

"I'll help you make it beautiful. I promise."

"Thank you, Julian." She stepped over to him and gave him a quick sideways hug. "Don't forget to let me know how much I need to pay you for all the plants and flowers or whatever you ordered." The words were thrown over her shoulder as she walked away.

He watched her and couldn't move for several moments. She'd hugged him.

He couldn't even remember the last time someone had done that.

Anna must really care for him.

By ten in the morning, Joshua had already sweat through his shirt. Now it was half past three and it seemed every inch of him was covered in perspiration, which made the dirt and rock particles stick to any skin that was exposed. But they were getting awfully close to retrieving a large bone out of the rock face. He couldn't wait to hold it in his hands.

The tedious work of chiseling the rock away from the fossils was more than just holding the hammer and chisel. It was the odd way they had to stand since the rock wall was at a slant that must be close to forty-five degrees. To get to the top part, they had to climb up the scaffolding and lay on their sides, then reach, chisel, and pray they didn't slide back down.

It was an easy way to get cramped arms and legs, but it wasn't a process that could be rushed. Having a greater understanding of what Mr. Lakeman had done all these years was eye-opening. In his mind, they'd just dug things out of the dirt. Not out of massive slabs of rock. Big difference.

Now he understood. There was no such thing as *easy* in

paleontology. The work was tedious, meticulous, and time consuming.

Anna had been sketching a tight grouping of several bones so that her father could help them see how they fit together. Rarely were skeletons of animals discovered in the exact placement. She'd told Joshua that her father had to study the bones for days, sometimes even months, to know exactly how they fit together. Which made sense when he thought about how the fossils got there. That the majority of them had to be from the Flood. A catastrophic event to be sure. Thousands of years ago.

He snuck a glance at her. The dry wind had pulled a good deal of her hair out from its pins. Tendrils of it moved around her face as she was bent over her sketch, her pencil moving in swift strokes.

Her head popped up and when she saw him, she smiled. Had she sensed his gaze?

She set her sketch down and walked toward him. "You look like you could use a good dunk in the creek."

He grunted. "That, Miss Lakeman, is an understatement. I'm looking forward to doing just that."

"Well, not to deprive you of that, but I was wondering if you would help me tonight? I need to start digging for the garden and it will be shaded on that side of the house by the time we get there."

What was a few more hours of dirt in the heat? "Of course, I'll help. I told you I would."

"Will your family be all right with you being gone? I know it's hard ever since . . ." She bit her lip and let the sentence hang.

The cramp of grief that hit every time he thought of Caleb made him close his eyes. "It'll be fine. We're all dealing with it the best we can."

"I'm sorry." Her gaze softened. "I never know if I should say anything or keep my mouth closed."

"The work is helping me to keep my mind off it. Which is helpful right now."

"All right then. Well, since Julian's been so kind to order plants for me, I better have the ground ready to plant. He said he would have one of his hands bring over a wagonload of manure."

"Oh good. That should make things smell even better." He couldn't help but laugh. "What are you doing with an entire wagonload of it?"

"*We're* going to mix it into the dirt."

"Exactly what I was hoping to do this evening. You read my mind."

Her laugh echoed off the rock wall.

The other guys studied them for a moment and then went back to work.

"I need to finish these sketches for my dad, but thanks for helping. I appreciate it."

"You're welcome. Just tell me when you're ready to head that way."

A few hours later, they stood alongside her home outside her father's window, shovels in hand.

True to Julian's word, a wagonload of manure sat waiting for them. Plus a wagonload of rich river-bottom soil. Flies buzzed around and Joshua had to tie his bandanna over his nose and mouth to keep the stench partially out of his senses.

"Sorry. I know that's strong." Anna held her nose and sounded a bit like a duck. She pulled out her handkerchief and tied it like Joshua's. "Why do I feel like we're about to rob a bank now?"

They laughed for a few seconds and then attacked the grass, weeds, and dirt with a hoe and shovel.

She came closer to him for a moment. "We've got to get

all the grass and weeds out and get down to the soil." She shrugged and went back to slicing her hoe into the ground.

This was a good bit of work. "How much do you want to clear?"

"How about thirty feet by thirty feet? That's big enough, don't you think?"

"Sure. Sounds good to me. I'm here to do what you tell me."

They worked for a half hour before a whistle came from the window. Louise smiled at them as she waved a hand in front of her nose. "Shoo-ee, it stinks."

"Sorry about that." Anna approached the window.

"Your dad wants to know what you two are up to and I didn't want to be the one to spoil the surprise." She stepped back from the window and covered her nose.

Anna waved Joshua over to stand with her by the window. He stood next to her and smiled down at the top of her head.

"Well? Who wants to tell me what's going on?" Her dad tilted his head, his brow furrowed.

"I'm planting you a garden. Joshua is helping me. I know how much you love flowers, and I thought it would be nice to look at while you recover."

Mr. Lakeman's eyes widened. Then he burst into laughter. "Joshua, I hope you know what you're getting into, because my Anna here has never been able to grow anything. Ever."

Anna's hands went to her hips. "Now see here. I asked Julian to teach me. You've never complained about *his* gardening capabilities." Her tone made it sound like she was offended, but the smile on her face gave her away. Joshua loved seeing the teasing glint back in her eyes. It had been years since he'd seen it.

It reminded him of so many good times growing up.

"And so you wrangled Joshua into helping you?" Mr. Lakeman's face was lit up in a grin.

Joshua held up his hands. "I believe she can do it, sir."

Anna swatted him. "Of course I can do it."

"That's exactly what I said! The manure must be getting to your brain."

"All right, you two. Well, I'll ask Louise to close that window because I'd like to eat my dinner without gagging on the stench."

Joshua turned and picked up his shovel. "This is a great thing you're doing for him. Not just the garden, but the dig, the sketches. Everything. You're a wonderful woman, Anna." He dug into the ground and turned over another large clod of grass and weeds.

"Thank you." The words were soft, but he'd heard them.

It didn't take long before his back was aching, but they'd gotten a lot accomplished. Louise brought them glasses of water and Joshua chugged his down in seconds.

A rider in the distance was coming at them awfully fast. "You expecting anyone, Anna?"

"No."

Then he caught sight of his brother-in-law, Alan. His heart perked up. Maybe they found Caleb! Wouldn't that be a miracle.

Alan's expression wasn't one of delight. "Joshua, it's your mother. She's been thrown from her horse."

fourteen

"I am getting wonderfully interested in my bones."

~Earl Douglass

It was almost lunchtime, but if Joshua knew anything about Anna, she'd be at the dig with her team. So he rode out to the Walker Ranch and the gulley that had become his second home. Last night had been touch and go. Getting Mom back to the house was awful because she'd been in so much pain. But once Martha got her cleaned up and in bed, Doc was able to see that Mom had broken her femur. Not that a broken leg was a good thing, but it could have been so much worse. Joshua had expected more than one broken bone. Multiple rib fractures were common for women when they were thrown from their mount. He'd seen far too many of these cases in the hospital back at school.

His mind had gone to all the worst-case scenarios, which hadn't been helpful. And he'd questioned Doc Walsh a bit too much, but this was his mother they were talking about. He'd gained a new understanding of what his own patients might

153

feel one day when a family member was ill or hurt. Once he'd calmed down, he took notes about ways to ensure his patients' families were well informed.

When the good doctor was ready to set his mother's leg, he'd requested Joshua's help. Something Joshua did many times in school, but it was different watching the pain move in waves across his mother's face.

The bone would take a long time to heal, but his mother was strong. Keeping her in bed and off the leg would be an adventure for Martha and his dad. Mom had never been a good patient.

As Joshua approached the dig site, he spotted Anna studying the wall of bones from about twenty feet back. What was she looking for?

She must have heard his horse approaching because she turned. "Oh my goodness, how's your mom?"

"She's okay. Broken femur. It's going to take a long time to heal, but she should be all right. No other broken bones, which is miraculous." He swung his leg over the back of his horse and dismounted.

She leaned in, her brows drawn together, and touched his arm. "I wasn't expecting you to come work. And seriously, if you are needed at home, I understand."

For a second, as their gazes collided, he was transported back to the Joshua and Anna they'd been . . . before. But then she pulled back and stared at the ground.

Taking a moment to school his thoughts, he turned and patted his horse's neck. "No, Martha is taking good care of Mom, and I promised your dad I would help while I was home. So here I am."

"Well, thank you for coming. We could definitely use your help." She shifted her gaze back to the wall.

He stood next to her and tried to see what she was seeing. "You looking for something in particular?"

154

Tipping her head back and forth, she squinted. "Just trying to envision what my father saw in the drawing." She held up the sketch she'd made of the wall and then looked back at the actual thing.

"What'd he see?"

"He thinks this is the fossilized remains of an Allosaurus. Which would be exciting. Especially if most of the skeleton is here."

"A what?" Over the years, he'd heard her and her father spout dinosaur names, but he had no idea what any of them were.

"Allosaurus. A large carnivorous biped."

"And that means what, exactly?"

"Well, for one, its size would be about twenty-five to thirty feet long. It would have large, sharp teeth to eat meat, and it ran on its hind legs." She kept staring at the wall, pointing at sections as she spoke. "The first thing I saw when the flash flood exposed this was the curved spine here. Now I can clearly see the tail over there." She pointed to a higher section of the wall. "Then over here"—she shifted to another section—"Dad thinks that is part of the neck, but we won't know until we start getting it out of the rock." Stepping forward, she went straight up to the wall. "Look, right here. Dad must be correct. I'm pretty certain this is one of the talons."

"Yikes. I wouldn't want to run into this guy when he was hungry."

She chuckled. "You wouldn't want to run into him *any* time. Their arms were short, but they ended in three-clawed fingers. Sharp claws, I might add."

He stared at the wall and tried to picture it but couldn't. All he knew was that some of the bones visible were much larger than any other animal bones he'd seen before. "I'm amazed at what you and your father do. How you can see what's there. It's definitely a gift."

When she turned her gaze toward him, the look in her eyes

took his breath away. She laid a hand on his arm. "Much like the gift you have for healing people."

He held her gaze. Every bit of love he'd ever known for her flooded his heart and soul. It was like he was looking into Anna's eyes from *before* he'd left things in shambles. "I still believe in you, Joshua. I always have and always will. You were meant to be a doctor."

So she'd read more of his letters. The ones where he doubted himself. Doubted why anyone would ever believe in him. Without Anna those first few months, he'd been lost and so alone.

He didn't want the moment to end. "Thank you. It hasn't been easy. But I'm grateful for the generous opportunity at school."

She dropped her hand and began walking toward her satchel on the table where she'd set up several of her sketches under rocks. "Have you ever met your benefactor?"

"No, but Mr. Bricker has corresponded with me regularly. He has been a great encouragement. He said he will be at my graduation."

"Any idea why he chose you?"

"I have no idea."

"One day I hope to be able to thank him. I'm so glad someone gave you this chance. You deserve it." She picked up another sketch and a pencil. Every now and then she would add a little mark here or there on the paper.

Watching her sketch was like watching the waves on Lake Michigan. Soothing, yet ever changing. Beautifully exciting and calming all at the same time.

She caught him staring. "Josh?"

"Sorry." He tugged his hat a bit lower. "I'll get to work with the rest of the guys."

"Will you help me out at the garden tonight? We're almost done and Dad loves seeing you."

"Sure." Didn't she know that he would do anything for her? The afternoon passed in the pinging of his hammer and chisel making progress millimeter by millimeter around a fossil. He'd brush away the rock fragments and then do the same thing. Over and over again. His left leg had a cramp in it from holding his position. He stood up and stretched. Every muscle in his neck and shoulders screamed at straightening his spine. He needed to pay better attention and move every quarter hour or so. Good grief, he should know better.

He went over and grabbed his canteen under the shade of the canopy. After draining almost half of it, he wiped his mouth on his sleev—

What was this?

Julian Walker was headed in Anna's direction. A bouquet of flowers in his hand.

Searching around him, Joshua hunted for something—anything—that would give him an excuse to go ask Anna a question.

A tool he hadn't used before sat in one of the crates. Huh. He grabbed it.

After Julian was at Anna's side, Joshua casually strolled in their direction and listened in.

"I thought you might like these." The big man handed the bouquet to Anna.

Her face softened into a smile. "That is so thoughtful of you, Julian. Thank you."

Julian yanked his hat off his head. "They are some of the same kinds of plants I ordered for you. They should be here tomorrow." Holding his hat in his hands, he curled the brim.

"Gracious, that was fast. Perhaps we could start planting them on Monday, since tomorrow is Sunday?"

"Sure. I'll pick them up in Green River tomorrow. I need to meet the train or they'll get damaged and scorched in the sun."

She offered the bouquet back to him. "These are lovely, but won't *they* wilt in the sun without any water?"

Walker blinked several times as he studied Anna.

Joshua watched. Something about the expression on the other man's face reminded him . . .

Of Julian with Mary.

Julian had looked at Mary the same way every time he brought her a flower from his garden.

Julian Walker was smitten.

With Anna.

A stirring in Joshua's gut wasn't pleasant. No one else should look at Anna that way. As soon as his mind registered it, he cringed. Jealousy. Green and ugly.

Julian slapped his hat back on his head and took the flowers. "I'll take them back to the house and put them in water. Then you can come get them later. Or I can bring them to you. Whatever you like." With an awkward shrug, he turned on his heel and strode away.

"Thank you for the flowers," Anna called after him.

Joshua stepped up to her side. "What was *that* about?"

Her gaze snapped to his, a frown covering her face. "Why the angry tone?" She placed her hands on her hips.

"You didn't answer my question."

"Probably because I didn't like how you asked it."

He worked to tamp down his frustration. "I think you need to be careful."

"Careful? Around Julian? That man wouldn't hurt a fly. He grows *flowers*. I mean, really."

"It's clear that he is enamored with you. Just now, it reminded me too much of the way he looked at Mary. And look what happened to her." The words slipped out and he wished he could yank them back.

She put a hand over her mouth.

The look on her face pierced him. "Wait. That's not—"

"You think Julian"—her hand fell back to her side—"had something to do with Mary going missing?"

Why couldn't she see it? "He was the last one to see her." His words were digging him in deeper, but at this point, he was too far in to backpedal.

She clucked her tongue at him. "You think he did something to Caleb too, don't you? Because his father was a mean man and a horrible father and Julian is a bit odd"—she flung a hand in his direction—"go ahead and blame him for everything bad that happens around here."

He did. But the look she sent him made him clamp his mouth shut.

"I should have known." She stomped away.

Not so fast! He couldn't allow her to leave in anger. Not again. "Known what?" He stomped after her.

"You're jealous." The words were thrown over her shoulder.

There was that. He couldn't deny it. He followed her fifty yards out from the site.

When she turned on him, the tears streaking her red cheeks deflated all the ire from his chest. What had he done?

He held up his hands. "Anna . . . look. I'm sorry." He took off his hat and ran a hand through his sweaty hair. "Between the heat, and all the stress at home, I guess I lost my mind for a bit."

She sniffed and narrowed her eyes. Then crossed her arms over her chest.

He met her anger. "I saw Julian give you those flowers and you're right. I got jealous."

"That doesn't give you a right to think so poorly of Julian. Can't you see how much he's helped us? Shouldn't we give him a chance? Isn't that the Christian thing to do?"

He bit his tongue before what he wanted to say came out. He gave a slow nod. "You're right. I'm sorry." He still didn't like the situation, but he'd have to deal with his issues later.

Her stiff posture relaxed, and she closed the distance

between them. "Look. I know you're hurting. Losing Mary affected all of us. With little Caleb gone, I'm sure that has simply pulled the scab off that wound and made it bleed all over again. Then your mother got hurt last night. You didn't get to go back to school as planned. I know things have been difficult. But I believe Julian needs the benefit of the doubt right now. Deep down, there's a beautiful heart there. Nobody has ever taken the time to see it before except for—"

"Mary." He wiped a hand down his face. Another reason to be protective of Anna. Whether she could see it or not. "I'm sorry for losing my temper."

"Me too."

They stared at each other and then at the ground.

He broke the silence. "Truce?"

She stared at him for several seconds. "Fine. Truce." She shook her head. "You do bring out the worst in me, Joshua Ziegler."

It was hard to keep from glancing at Joshua. They'd worked in silence for the past half hour, and the longer it stretched, the more Anna wanted to spill everything out of her heart. But something held her back. Was it her own stubborn pride?

In all the years that she'd known him, she'd never encountered discomfort like this with him. What was wrong with her?

"I think I'm going to head home now." Joshua leaned on his shovel.

Anna lifted her gaze once more to him. She pasted on a cordial grin because that's what normal people did even though she felt nothing of the sort. "It's been a long day. I appreciate you helping."

"Please tell your father I'm sorry I can't stay. I didn't get a lot of sleep last night." The smile he sent her was weak.

"I will. He'll look forward to chatting with you another time."

Ever since their argument this afternoon, things had been tenuous at best. Granted, he'd still come and helped her with the garden, but the sweet camaraderie they shared earlier in the day was gone. And it was her fault. Why was she her own worst enemy?

Life had been simpler when they were younger. They told each other everything. Never held anything back. Now it was like there was a thousand-foot wall up between them. Oh, it had a nice little window that she'd fashioned in all her caution. Every now and then it opened to show her how close they still were, how they cared for one another. But then she'd find herself slamming the shutter closed on that glimpse into what could have been—what might *still* have a chance of coming to life.

He leaned the shovel up against the side of the house. "Do you need me to help you put all this away?"

"No thanks. I'll need it on Monday to plant, so I'll roll the wheelbarrow into the shed real quick. You go on home. Give your family my love. Tell your mom I'm praying for her."

"Will do." He trudged over to his horse. "See you at church tomorrow?"

"I'm staying home so Louise can go. The poor girl has sacrificed enough for us already, I can give her that." Time for her to sacrifice her fear as well. She bit her lip. "But . . . if you have time, could you come by tomorrow afternoon and visit with Dad?" Somehow she needed to mend all that was broken between them. Even if he was judgmental and in the wrong. Again.

She flinched. There . . . *she* did it again. Went straight back to blaming him.

He studied her for a moment and then rubbed his jaw. "Are you sure you want me around?"

So he'd seen her face. Of course. The man had once known her better than her own father. Grief, she was exasperating, even to herself. "I'm sorry. My thoughts . . . that is . . ." She groaned and waved her hands back and forth. "Let me start again. Yes. I do want you around. I would love for you to come visit *us* tomorrow." And she meant it. She would get on her knees tonight and beg God to help her get over whatever ridiculousness she'd allowed in her heart and mind. This constant battle was making her dizzy and sick of her own thoughts.

"I would enjoy that."

"Good. Me too."

He slapped his hat on his head, gave her a quick dip of his chin, and then rode away.

Anna watched his back. If she was honest, she loved him just as much today as she had before he left. Perhaps even more. Leaning up against the house, she relaxed and let her shoulders drop.

God, You're gonna have to guide me through this because I obviously can't do this on my own. Somehow I've got to climb out of this manure pile of my own making and truly forgive Joshua. I want to forgive him. But then I get riled up so easily that I ruin every tenuous step we make toward healing.

She closed her eyes and leaned her head back. What kind of a child of the King was she? In the past three years, she'd pushed the Lord to arms' length as well. Losing Josh had made her stuff her bruised heart inside a box. Then she carried it around like it was fragile and not to be used or touched or opened up for anyone . . . ever.

The parable of the ten talents rushed to her mind. She was just like the servant given the one talent.

She'd buried her heart—and herself—in the dirt. Unwilling to allow it to grow. Unwilling to let it be touched. Hiding away.

Forgive me, Father. Tears filled her eyes and slid down her cheeks.

Her heart gushed out in great sobs until she finally opened her eyes again and stared up at the clear sky above. When she'd had no other words, her Savior understood her tears. The reconciliation seemed even more beautiful.

He knew her.

He understood her.

He'd been waiting with open arms, and she'd run into them.

On shaky legs, she stepped away from the house and wiped at her cheeks. Maybe after she took care of her things and cleaned up, she could share her heart with Dad. He'd been waiting for her to open up. The man was a saint with the patience of a thousand men.

Once she took care of the tools, she went inside and drew a cool bath. When she climbed into the tub, the chill of the water washing over her woke up every one of her senses. Which was a good thing. She wanted to spend some quality time with her father this evening. And talk about the dig.

Maybe even about Joshua.

She'd never discussed her courtship with him with her father before. There'd been no need. Dad was with them most of the time and saw everything that transpired. Everything except their horrible blowup.

She hadn't shared much with Dad about that other than the fact that they disagreed.

He'd given her space and allowed her to cry. And he'd kept her busy by taking her to dig after dig. Probably figuring that was the best thing for her.

Over time, she'd healed. Or at least pushed her feelings aside.

But her parents had been married a long time. She knew how much they'd loved each other. Perhaps Dad had some insight that could help her through this crazy puzzle that was love.

After they'd eaten and she'd caught him up with everything at the site, she tucked some hair behind her ear and ventured into the tough topic. "Dad? Could I perhaps . . . talk to you about . . . love?"

His soft chuckle put her at ease. "I would hope that you would feel comfortable talking to me about anything after all we've been through."

It was good to hear his speech almost back to normal and he was building strength every day. "It's about Joshua."

"I could have guessed that." He released an exaggerated sigh.

She sent him a teasing glare.

"Well, go on then. Don't leave me in suspense. I've been waiting three long years for you to come out of that shell you've built around yourself."

She grimaced. "I know. Why didn't you just tell me what to do?"

"Daughter . . . you've never been one who enjoyed being pushed into anything. In fact, pushing normally makes you dig in your heels and put up every defense you have."

His words hit closer to home than she would have liked. Which made her want to argue. She opened her mouth—and then snapped it closed. "Point taken."

"Your mother was the same way, God rest her soul. Time was the best thing I could give you. So I did. And kept you busy in the process." He chuckled and then folded his hands together.

"You're a smart man." She took a sip of water and then opened up. She told him about the letters, her argument with Joshua that afternoon, and even told him all about their argument years ago. Once it was off her chest, she felt a lot better. "Well? What do you think?" She reached for his hand.

He patted the top of hers and then squeezed. "You're in love. That's what I think. Joshua has been in love with you since he was five years old. I think you two are simply going to have to work through these things."

"You don't believe that he was wrong in what he said before he left?" Why wasn't her dad taking her side—

Good heavens, she was going right back to her old habits. Her father laughed again.

"I don't think this is a laughing matter, Dad." She leaned back in her chair and crossed her arms.

"I'm not sure why you got your knickers into such a knot over his questions. I'm sure there's a fine explanation for what he asked, and you just didn't give him the chance to explain."

"He questioned everything we do. Everything *you* do." Her temper was roaring back to life.

Dad shook his head. "No. Sounds to me like he was being protective of the woman he loved and was trying to understand something, but without all the information. Have you two discussed this since he's been back?"

"Well . . . no." She deflated a bit. She needed to calm down, and this wasn't helping.

"Maybe that's where you should start, rather than getting all riled up at me for speaking truth." He stared at her. His eyes conveyed his love, wisdom, and grace toward his only daughter.

Oh, why she was so good at jumping to conclusions? That was exactly how she'd gotten upset at Joshua. What a hypocrite. "Fine. I'll talk to him." *Lord, You're going to have to do a mighty work in me because I'm failing at this over and over.*

"Good." He patted the bed. "Was there any mail?"

Thank heaven for a change of subject. She stood. "I left it on the table. Let me go get it. I know there was a wire from Mr. Oppenheim."

She went to the kitchen to fetch it and took several deep, calming breaths. If she wanted to conquer this problem of hers, she needed to face it head-on and eradicate it once and for all.

She picked up the wire. Hopefully it wasn't anything too important. She couldn't believe she'd forgotten to bring it to her father.

Opening the envelope as she walked back to Dad's room, she pulled out the paper and then handed it to him. "Here you go. I'm so sorry. I should have brought this to you first thing."

Dad read the wire and she watched for his reaction.

His brow furrowed. "It appears we will be having a visit from Mr. Oppenheim, his daughter, and his son."

"What for?"

"I'm not certain. But I need you to get ahold of Mr. Gilbert. We need to make sure we have all the paperwork in order and know our rights since Mr. Oppenheim wants to have his name on the dig."

"Are you concerned?"

Dad grimaced. "More than a little, I'm afraid. What if he wants to take away his funding if he doesn't get what he wants? Or . . . worse . . . what if he threatens to tell Cope or Marsh or any of the other scoundrels who would drool over a find like this? We can't fight against people like that . . . we could lose it all."

fifteen

"I must think twice before I speak once."

~Earl Douglass

SUNDAY, JUNE 30

Walking down to the creek with Joshua was just like old times. Except there was a lot more silence.

Anna had left her dad and Joshua to chat for a while this afternoon while she gathered her thoughts. She'd gone into her room and read a few more of his letters, needing to connect with the man she loved. But her father was correct, they simply needed to talk about it.

Once Louise came back from church and a visit with her family, Anna had asked Joshua to go for a walk with her. Now that they were out here, she needed the nerve to discuss what she should.

"Are you going to tell me what's on your mind, or are you going to twist that dandelion to shreds?" He'd reached the edge of the creek and turned toward her.

Fine. Might as well get it over with. "I talked to my dad about us last night."

"And?"

"Well, he thought it was silly that we hadn't discussed our big fight."

"The one yesterday, or the one before I left?" The teasing glint in his eyes took some of the edge off her nerves.

"You know which one I'm talking about, Joshua Ziegler."

"Oh, *that* one." He nodded and took a seat in the grass. "Go ahead. You can ask me anything." He bent his knees and rested his elbows on top. Casual and calm.

Okay. This wouldn't be so bad. If she could spit it out. "Do you think that paleontology is so horrible?"

He jerked back. "What gave you that idea?"

"Because you questioned whether I should go on digs with my father. Then questioned what people would say about it!"

He didn't look at her, but his shoulders sagged as he let out a long sigh. Turning toward her, he clenched his jaw. Then dipped his chin. "I didn't understand a lot back then, Anna. Hadn't quite wrapped my mind around the thought of you going out and working with a bunch of men. It was one thing when you were a kid and followed your dad around. It was cute. Your sketches were amazing. But when I thought of you going out on those expeditions as my future wife . . . well, part of me didn't handle it well."

She opened her mouth but he held up a hand and she bit her lip. It was only fair to allow him to finish before she jumped in with her opinions.

"I didn't handle it well because I didn't understand. Yes, I was worried about what people thought. I'd read plenty in the medical journals about what people thought about women working in areas that some believed they shouldn't. Oh, the good folks in Walker Creek knew you and your father well. Paleontology had always been a part of your lives. It was normal.

But the more I studied, the more I realized that the last couple decades have brought about a huge rift between the scientific and church communities. They used to go hand in hand." She and Dad had many discussions about this in the last few years. She nodded.

"But now it's almost like the two have shunned one another. Especially after Darwin's book came out. As soon as you left the safe haven of our little community, people were going to judge you. The church shuns science because of the new prevalence of evolution. And scientists shun the church because they think we're ignorant."

"I know. We've encountered a lot of that. Especially since science has been trying to understand dinosaurs and *when* they lived on the earth. I don't get why they think the two have to be separate. To me, they go hand in hand. Dad's never once had trouble with it, and you know Dad's passion has been on finding his own dinosaur." She picked up a blade of grass and peeled away one skinny piece at a time. "He's in your corner, by the way. He said you were being protective."

Joshua grinned at her and wiggled his eyebrows. "He knows me well. And yes, that's part of it. I didn't want you to be ridiculed or shunned because of your work. The other part was my own ignorance. I didn't understand yet how my faith and science could be woven together. Not until I went to medical school. I faced a lot of opposition but also found a greater understanding." He scooted closer and took her hand. "It's important for you to keep doing what you're doing."

Her heart soared. "Really?"

"Yes." With a squeeze to her hand, he scooted closer still. "Not only for the science—finding dinosaur fossils is amazing, by the way—but for women everywhere. There are women right now fighting for the right to go to school and study in the sciences. You're incredibly talented at sketching, but I know you, Anna. Deep down, you would love to be a paleontologist yourself. I've seen the light in your eyes as you're supervising the work that we are doing. You love every facet of this, don't you?"

She let his words sink in and held onto his hand. "I do." What powerful relief flooded her heart with saying the words out loud. "I'm not as good at writing up the scientific data as my father is, but he's teaching me."

"You'd love to have your name on this dig as more than the artist . . . wouldn't you?"

She flicked a bug away from her face. "Yes. Very much."

"So . . . why don't you dig with us? Let's make it happen."

With a shake of her head, she dropped his hand. "I don't know. What if someone discounts the work we've done because a woman was helping? There's so much riding on this for my father. . . . I would never jeopardize the find."

His eyes softened. "Okay. I won't push. But you could think about it. Even talk to your dad about it."

Studying him for several moments, she tipped her head to the side. "So you don't object to me going on digs anymore?"

"No. I admit I was afraid of you getting hurt, but that was because I didn't understand. Like I said, I needed to be educated. Ignorance almost always leads to fear. I'm sorry for that. But it was because I loved you so much."

Heat filled her cheeks. "I rushed to judgment, Josh. And I'm sorry. I got offended that you didn't support me and I thought you were questioning not only my validity, but my father's as well. His reputation. His life's work."

They stared into each other's eyes. As the seconds ticked by, she could almost feel the invisible walls crumbling around her. Yes, let them fall. Tears pricked her eyes. Her shoulders relaxed as the weight was finally gone.

Joshua leaned closer to her. "So instead of a truce, instead of starting over, instead of all the things we've said the past couple weeks, how about we pick up where we left off?" He stood and offered his hands.

When she placed hers in them, he lifted her to her feet and pulled her close. He kissed her forehead. And then her temple.

Chills raced up and down her spine as he inched closer. She'd never been kissed before. Had dreamed of this moment with him since she was sixteen.

He placed his hands on the sides of her face and lowered his lips to hers. It was soft, sweet, and full of promise.

Her heart pounded in her chest.

He deepened the kiss and tugged her closer.

Every inch of her felt alive and cherished. Heat rushed to her middle.

Then his lips released hers and he leaned his forehead against hers. With a moan, he stepped back. "I love you, Anna."

"I . . ." She caught her breath. "I love you, too."

The rumble of a wagon in the distance brought Joshua down from the cloud he was on and back to his senses.

He stepped another pace away from Anna, his heart threatening to pound out of his chest. But he couldn't peel his gaze away. Her lips were pink and matched her cheeks.

Joshua had felt attraction and desire for Anna before, but the passion that jolted through him right now was blinding.

She loved him!

Deep down, he'd hoped that she did. But until she said it, he hadn't been sure. He'd thought they might have too much to overcome.

He wouldn't mind finding the good ol' reverend right now and whisking Anna off to marry him.

The rumbling grew louder.

No. He couldn't ask that of her right now. He still had school to finish. She had a bedridden father.

They had a dinosaur dig to work on.

She put a hand to her lips and cleared her throat. "I guess I better go see who that is."

The moment broken, he followed her back up to her house. The wagon approached and Joshua recognized the driver. Walker.

Tamping down his frustration at the interruption, he worked on his attitude. Anna wanted to give Julian grace. On top of that, the big man *had* granted the Lakemans permission to dig on his land and was helping Anna with the garden.

Besides, she'd declared her love for Joshua, so what was he upset about?

She sent Joshua an intimate look and then turned and waved at the wagon. "I thought you were bringing everything tomorrow?"

Perhaps she didn't appreciate the interruption either. The thought made him grin.

Walker pulled the horses to a stop. "I was going to, but I had a feeling Joshua might be here and figured he'd want to see what I found." He lifted a thin blanket off the mound at his feet.

The mound moved, and a dirt-covered face blinked at him.

"Caleb!" Joshua surged toward the wagon, his heart pounding. "Caleb? Where have you been? Are you all right?" What was he doing in Walker's wagon?

The boy whimpered and lowered his head.

Filth covered him from head to toe and he was skin and bones.

Joshua looked up to Walker, fire in his belly. What had he done?

"I found him hopping off the train in Green River. Recognized him right away from all the search posters. So I offered him a ride back home." Walker shrugged. Looked uncomfortable. "I gave him some water, bread, and ham I brought with me. After he ate it, he fell asleep on the floor."

Joshua lifted his nephew out of the wagon. Doubts filled his mind about the man in front of him, but he could deal with that later. *Thank You, God.* His gaze went back to Walker. "Thanks for bringing him back." He cradled the boy against his chest. Kissed the top of his head.

The big man sat back down on the wagon seat. "I'll take all these flowers back to my place and water them real good. Then tomorrow we can talk about planting everything." Walker nodded at Anna and then put his horses back in motion.

"Thank you, Julian!" she called out after him.

Joshua held Caleb close until the wagon was a good distance away. He set his nephew down and crouched in front of him. "Did that man do anything to you?"

"Joshua!" Anna's reprimand echoed.

He clenched his jaw. "I need to know the truth."

Caleb shook his head.

"Are you sure?"

The boy nodded.

Joshua wasn't sure he believed it. "Where have you been?"

Tears pooled in Caleb's eyes. "I ran away."

"What?" He jolted back as if he'd been slapped. "Why?"

"I got mad at Mama so I snuck into Gilbert's wagon when he was headin' to Green River, then jumped on the train. I made it as far as Cheyenne and realized maybe my idea wasn't as smart as I thought."

"Oh, kid. Where have you been staying?"

"Nowhere." He sniffed and wiped at his nose with his sleeve. "Which ain't fun, that's for sure. Especially when there's no food." The tears started in earnest now. "I stole food, Uncle Josh. And I had to sleep in people's barns or up in a tree so critters wouldn't get to me. It was *awful.*" Caleb dove back into his arms.

Anna leaned down. "I'll go get him something to eat and drink. He probably needs more nourishment before you take him home."

She walked away and Joshua tugged on Caleb's shoulders and pulled him back so he could look him in the eyes. "You tell us who you stole from, and we'll pay them back. The only thing that matters is that you're all right." He glanced over his shoulder to make sure Anna was inside. "Are you certain that man didn't have anything to do with this?"

"Who? Mr. Walker?" Caleb scrubbed at his face with his hands. "Nuh-uh. But I sure am glad he found me at the train station. At first I thought I was in big trouble 'cause he looked real serious, but bein' in trouble is better than starving. I don't care what punishment Mama and Daddy give me. I just wanna go home."

Joshua nodded and then hugged the boy again. He smelled almost as strong as the big pile of manure they'd worked into the ground for Anna's garden, but nothing that a good hot bath and a bar of soap couldn't cure.

Anna returned with a sandwich and a glass of milk.

Caleb devoured it in a matter of minutes. "Thanks, Miss Lakeman."

"You're welcome. Now I'm sure your family will be thrilled to see you." She tousled his hair.

Caleb handed her the glass and plate. He nodded and turned back to Joshua. "Will they be mad?"

"They'll be so relieved to see you alive, son, there's no need to worry about that." He lifted the boy up onto his horse.

Anna tugged at his elbow. "May I speak with you for a moment?"

"Sure." He followed her a few feet away.

"Did Julian have anything to do with this?" Her chin jutted forward.

He deserved the challenge. "No. Caleb said he found him at the train station."

"Good."

No *I told you so*, or any other angry retort.

She studied him for a moment. "I meant what I said."

The look in her eyes took him back to the creek. "I did too."

"Good." She blushed.

"Good," he echoed. "I better get Caleb home. I might be late tomorrow."

"That's understandable. Take care of your family. I'm thankful he's all right."

She broke the connection and headed toward her house.

Now he had an entirely new problem to deal with.

How could he leave his heart behind when he returned to school?

sixteen

"It is terrible to lose a mother . . . there is none left to love me with a mother's love now."

~Earl Douglass

MONDAY, JULY 1

Julian couldn't stop thinking about the way Joshua Ziegler had glared at him when he brought Caleb back from the train station.

"Ziegler was awfully suspicious of you."

Why couldn't Damian stop needling him? "I told him what happened. Just wish he believed me."

"He was angry too. I don't appreciate that."

Julian didn't appreciate it either. He'd done a good thing. He'd even fed Caleb and brought him home, knowing how much it hurt Anna that the little boy was missing. "People will respect me when they hear what I did." At least, he hoped that was true.

"Don't get your hopes up. That's what gets you hurt every time. That's why you need to nip this in the bud."

176

He yanked on the rope. "I am!" He flung the words as he finished tying the rope to the base of a tree trunk.

"Good. This is a good idea. Just don't go soft on me. I see the way you look at Anna."

Anna.

He hadn't realized how much she hurt after Mary was gone. He didn't want Anna to hurt any more.

But now Joshua was spending too much time with her. He was going to ruin everything.

Julian's mind drifted to thoughts of Mother. Teaching him out in the garden. Their special place. The only place his father wouldn't beat him.

"If you water them, feed the soil, and remove the weeds, the flowers will bloom all summer."

He'd loved seeing the flowers continue to bloom. It had been the one bright thing in his life. Especially after she was gone.

"You have to fight the darkness, Julian. Fight it with everything in you. You're a good boy."

Right now, the darkness was winning. But only because he allowed it. After he fixed things, he would concentrate on the light again. On Anna. And their flowers.

She could help him fight the darkness.

He'd finally be fixed.

The joy around the breakfast table demolished the cloud of sorrow that had hovered over Joshua's family for weeks.

Caleb was clean and rested. Martha and Alan had their son back.

Mom and Dad were ecstatic to not have to endure another loss.

After the reunion last night and Caleb's confession, tears of happiness had flowed. They'd all slept better than they had in weeks.

Mom had even insisted on everyone coming into her room for prayer and she'd eaten better than she had since her fall.

Alan had one arm around Martha and one on the back of his son's chair. "Thanks for staying after Caleb went missing, Joshua."

"You're welcome. I wouldn't want to be anywhere else." With his family. With Anna. Healing was happening in every area of his life this summer.

His brother-in-law dipped his chin. "Well, we know what a sacrifice it was for you to miss a term."

Caleb's eyes welled up. "You missed school 'cause of me?"

Joshua sent him a smile. "Don't you worry about that, little man. I'll still be able to finish in a little more than a year."

"And we're so proud of you, son." Dad patted him on the back. "The first in our family to go to college."

"*And*," Mom chimed in, "the first doctor in the family. Don't forget that part!"

He held up a hand. "All right, all right. That's enough. I have to actually finish before we celebrate." To get the attention off him, he took another bite of food.

Caleb got up from his chair and walked over to him. "Uncle Josh?"

"Hm?" He answered around a bite of eggs.

"Will you take me to pay the people back? Ya know, like you said last night?"

He caught his sister's eye. "Is that all right with you?"

She looked to her husband and Alan spoke. "We think it will be a great lesson for Caleb. I'm needed here at the ranch, so we appreciate you taking him. We've got money set aside and have already talked to him about how he will work to pay off his debts."

Joshua's gaze went back to his nephew. "I'll be glad to take you."

"When can we do that?"

"Let me talk to Miss Lakeman about my duties at the dig and I can give you a better estimate on which days."

He seemed to think about that for a minute. "I understand. You've got responsi . . . responsi . . . Daddy, what was that word again?"

"Responsibilities." Alan winked at him. "Good job remembering our little talk last night."

Joshua grinned. "Well, as much as I would like to stay all day and enjoy this fun, I should probably head out to work."

He patted Caleb on the head, shook Alan's hand, kissed his sister on the cheek, and then went over to his mother. He kissed her on top of the head. "No wrangling cattle today, deal?"

Her laughter was so good to hear. "Give Anna our love, please?"

"I will." He couldn't tell them what was on his heart and mind yet.

"Is she doing all right? What with all she's carrying on her shoulders?" Mom always was a softy for people struggling.

He gave her shoulder a squeeze. "I think she's doing pretty well, all things considered. I know her face lit up when she saw Caleb last night. I could tell part of the burden on the shoulders had been lifted."

"But she's got a bedridden father and a monumental task in front of her—what with the dig—should I send her a note?"

"I think she'd love that, Mom." He patted his dad on the back and sent a wave. "I better get." Walking out of the room, it was great to hear the family's happy sounds. Back together and whole again.

Something they'd lacked after Mary went missing.

Thank You, God. He'd whispered that prayer so many times over the last twelve hours. But God understood how grateful he was for the safe return of his nephew.

After he saddled his horse, he grabbed the two canteens

he'd filled earlier and headed to the dig. Looking to the sky, he shook his head. They were headed for another scorcher, that was for certain. Not a cloud in the sky and he was already sweating—and it was barely mid-morning.

The trail to the dig was worn thanks to his many treks back and forth. Funny thing was, he had come to enjoy the work. And not because it was with Anna—although that definitely added spice to his life—but because the science truly was fascinating.

Over the last three years, he'd learned about the leaps and bounds they were making in scientific discovery. It was changing the face of medicine. Which was a good thing. Healing people always needed a boost when new ailments seemed to crop up overnight.

If only faith and science could be reconciled. Why couldn't the two come together?

It didn't make sense. They went hand in hand. Perhaps that was something he could talk to Mr. Lakeman about. Unlike many others in his field, he didn't seem to have a problem with the two coming together in his life.

The last bit of shade was ahead. Right before the washout. Joshua better enjoy it while it lasted because that sun beating down on the white rock face made it feel like he was an egg frying right there.

His horse knew the way, and Joshua gave him the signal to move into a canter. He wanted to see Anna.

Anna. Whew. That kiss last night had kept him awake for a good while. Because he wanted more. And he wanted everything to be good and right between them so he could go back to university, finish up, come home, and marry her. As soon as possible.

Guess he better work on his patience.

The edge of the gulley was close, so he'd have to let his horse navigate the steep incline down into the area washed out by the floo—

Joshua was flying through the air . . .

And then tumbling down the washout.

Two large bones of the spine. Anna laid them out on the table and began sketching them. They were remarkable. It had taken a good deal of time to get them out, but now that she could see them, hold them in her hand, she was amazed that they seemed to be—for the most part—intact.

Which was always a wonder considering that most of these bones were fossilized during a great catastrophe. That's why, on so many of their digs, they found partial skeletons. Sometimes just a skull.

But now. Well, now they were accomplishing her father's dream.

Two hours later, she had two sketches done. Not all the detail was there yet, but even so, just wait until her father saw these! It was almost enough to have him jumping out of bed. If only he could—

Stop. Be thankful for the progress Dad *has* made.

She pulled her mind from worry to the garden. The project scared her more than she wanted to admit. Maybe, with Julian's help, this time would be different. Maybe the garden would grow and flourish.

Checking her watch for the umpteenth time, she scanned the horizon for Joshua. How odd that he still wasn't here. When he'd said he would be late, she hadn't expected him not to show up at all. That wasn't like him.

But then again, Caleb was home. Their family had a lot of celebrating to do. And dealing with the old wounds of Mary's loss, which Caleb's disappearance had stirred up.

What would it be like if Mary were still here today?

Maybe Anna could have learned to garden earlier. Maybe

even learned to cook. At ten years old, Mary had already been a wonder in the kitchen. She made apple pie for every church picnic and it was so good. Mrs. Ziegler even said it was better than hers, which was why she allowed Mary to make it each time.

Such good memories . . . but hard, too. She'd never had another friend like Mary.

Joshua had soon taken his sister's place in Anna's life. At school. At church. Running around climbing rocks and exploring. Joshua had become her best friend.

"What's got you smiling?" Zach stood in front of her, his hands on his hips.

"Good memories." She hopped down from the crate she was sitting on and walked toward him. "Have you found something interesting?"

"Yep. Your dad is gonna love this." He pointed to the bones of the spine they'd been working on. "Look in the hole from where we removed the other two parts of the spine."

She peered in and gasped. "There's more! *Yes!*" Bouncing up and down, she clapped her hands. "Gentlemen, I think we might be sitting on a quarry of bones. Wouldn't it be amazing if we found one of the most intact skeletons of a dinosaur ever?"

Luke huffed. "As long as Cope or Marsh don't hear about it, we'll be fine."

"Don't rain on my parade." She frowned at him.

Both men had too much money. They could fling around whatever they wanted and hire whoever they wanted to accomplish *what* they wanted.

No one but her team could know about this dig. It would ruin everything.

Oh, wait. Mr. Oppenheim was coming. She groaned. Why, oh *why*, did Dad let him know what they'd found? Sure, they probably needed the money because it was expensive to do this kind of work, but would Oppenheim keep his mouth shut?

There was a confidentiality clause in the agreement. There always was. But rich people did whatever they pleased.

She gave the guys more instructions for the rest of the afternoon because she wouldn't be able to stay out for too much longer. There were plants that needed to get in the ground while it was still daylight and she'd asked Julian to bring everything this evening.

Dad would be so thrilled! Especially if she could keep everything alive until it bloomed. Wouldn't that be a wonder?

She added a little more detail to the sketches before she wrapped each of the bones in burlap and laid them in the straw in the crate where they kept the fossils. They didn't have that many out of the rock yet. There were hundreds more to go.

She glanced around at her table. Looked underneath it. Where was her other sketchpad? Hadn't she brought two out here today?

Good heavens, she must be losing her mind. That's what being in love did to a person.

What would she do without Joshua when he left for his next term? His extra set of hands had been a lifesaver. But then again, Dad could be a good deal better by then. Probably not strong enough to wield a hammer and chisel, but maybe he could sit out here in a month or two?

That was optimistic thinking. But she needed that right now.

A lot.

Where *was* Joshua? And why hadn't he let her know that he wasn't coming at all? It was so odd.

She wanted to see him again. Their time together yesterday had been . . . *really* nice. Better than nice, it had been the most incredible day of her life. In fact, she hoped that they could repeat it again soon.

Heat filled her face at the thought of kissing him again.

Checking her watch, she tried to put it out of her mind for

the time being. "Guys, I'm headed home to check on Dad. If Joshua shows up, would you ask him to come by my house tonight?"

"Sure thing." Zach, the designated leader of the group, waved at her. "We'll stay while we still have light. Thanks for bringing all those sandwiches today."

"Thank Louise. She's the one who made them for us."

"Well, pass on our thanks to her. We've got food and water and plenty to keep us busy."

"Thanks, guys." She headed to her horse. "I'll let her know." This team of men had been wonderful over the years. They were almost like brothers to her. Dad trusted them, and it was great to see their loyalty and their excitement for the dig.

Things could change a lot over the coming years if Marsh continued to push and rile up everyone around him. A paleontological dig could become a place of argument and unsafe working conditions. She wouldn't wish that for anyone, but she could see the writing on the wall.

Something had to change, or her beloved science would forever be tainted.

As she rode home, the wind in her hair and on her face helped her to cool down from the heat of the day. She better not get used to it, though, because she was about to dig in the dirt for hours.

Manure-filled, stinky dirt.

But it would be worth it.

If she said it a hundred times would she believe it?

Eh, probably not.

At home, she raced inside, determined to eat and chat with her dad before Julian arrived with his wagon.

Dad and Louise were excited to share that he had been able to move his legs without overtaxing his heart today, which had given him a boost of confidence.

As long as he kept up with the daily medicine for his heart

and his exercises, surely he would get stronger each day. At least, that's what the doctor said to them each time he visited.

Her father had a million questions about the dig, especially after he examined the sketches she'd brought.

Before long, she heard the rumble of a wagon approaching. "I better change into clothes fit for digging in the manure." She sent Dad a horrified look as she pinched her nose.

Dad's laughter encouraged her. He struggled from day to day with the melancholy that came in spurts and bouts.

But she couldn't blame him. He couldn't move much on his own, he had to have someone feed him and change him, he couldn't be out at the dig site—of the most exciting find of his career—and he was having to live vicariously through his daughter bringing him sketches.

Didn't sound like a whole lot of fun.

Not for anyone.

She wouldn't handle it well, she could say that.

After changing into her worst dress, which she'd worn when they'd mixed the manure into the dirt, she went outside to the garden plot and waved at her dad through the window. "Just wait. This is going to be amazing."

"Miraculous, is more like it."

"I heard that!"

Julian pulled up in his wagon and she peered over the side at all the tiny little green plants. "Thanks for doing this."

He shrugged as he hopped down. "I enjoy it. Growing things makes me happy."

"Well, let's see if it can make *me* happy. And if I can keep anything alive."

The look he sent her wasn't humorous. In fact, the man appeared downright horrified.

"My apologies, Julian. It was in jest. I'll do my very best, I promise."

He studied her for several seconds. "All right."

For the next hour, they unloaded the wagon and he explained every plant. Which was completely overwhelming. How would she keep them straight?

He tried to convince her that once they bloomed she would know. But she shook her head at that.

"Why don't we mark each row with a stake, and you can make yourself a drawing of what is in each row?"

"Great idea." She ran inside to grab some paper and a pencil. When she came out, she practically ran over Joshua.

Blood coated his forehead and dotted his shirt.

She put a hand over her mouth. "What happened?"

He put a hand on her shoulder, and she tried to lead him to the bench outside their door.

But he collapsed at her feet.

"Josh!"

seventeen

"How can fossils in such great numbers be deposited in the earth and be preserved except by catastrophe?"

~Earl Douglass

A whooshing sounded in his ears. Joshua worked to get his eyes to open.

"Josh? Are you all right?"

Anna's voice sounded far away.

His next attempt helped him to lift the curtain off his eyes. With a groan, he pushed himself up to a sitting position. "As well as can be expected." His head pounded as he got to his feet. Maybe that wasn't such a good idea. "I'm sorry I didn't make it to the dig today. I was on the way when my horse tripped and we went tumbling down the washout." He gripped her outstretched arm.

"What did he trip on?" She steered him toward a chair and pushed him to sit, then examined his head.

He shrugged. He'd seen the rope as he'd tumbled over the back of his horse. It had been intentional, of that he was certain. But as much as he wanted to tell her his suspicions, he didn't dare until he had more proof. She was already on edge enough about his qualms with Walker. "Must have been a trap for some animal, maybe?"

"That's awful. How's Indigo?"

Of course she'd ask about his horse. When Josh's dad gave him the Appaloosa, she'd helped name him saying his black spots appeared to shine indigo in the light. "He's okay. Much better than I am, I'll say that. I was the one who went flying."

"You poor thing. I'm so sorry. Are you certain nothing's broken?" She went and grabbed a clean cloth.

"Yeah. At least from what I can ascertain." As he shifted, he winced.

"I'll be right back. I need some water for that cut on your head."

Sitting in the chair made every bump and bruise come to life. As long as he'd kept moving, they hadn't bothered him too much. But now? Ouch.

Anna rushed back in with a bucket of water and the clean cloth. "All right, let me get some of this cleaned off. There's a lot of dried blood on your head." She dunked the cloth in the water and went to work on his face and head.

"Head wounds tend to bleed a lot, so I wouldn't worry." Except for the fact that he'd been passed out on the ground for a while, but he wouldn't tell her that. She was so close, it did funny things to his insides. "You look nice."

A soft laugh brushed over his face. "You lie. I'm wearing the absolute worst and oldest thing I own, and I smell like manure from working in the garden. Try again, Joshua Ziegler."

He tugged on her waist and pulled her into his lap. "I don't care what you're wearing. You still look nice." Tapping her nose with his finger, he released her.

But she stayed for an extra moment. "Thank you."

"Miss Lakeman?" Louise's voice carried from down the hall.

Anna bolted to her feet, a deep pink filling her cheeks.

"Oh, there you are." The young woman who'd been nursing Mr. Lakeman appeared. "Mr. Walker is out there planting and asked a question, but I didn't know what to tell him."

"Tell him I'll be there in a moment." Anna kept her face averted. Probably to hide her blush.

"Julian is here?" He wanted to growl but refrained.

"Yes, he's helping me get the garden planted, remember? I was coming to get some paper and pencil so I could draw a diagram of what is planted where when I ran into you." She wiped the cloth over his head again, rinsed it out, then made another swipe.

"I can help you finish planting, if you'd like." He certainly didn't want Anna alone with Walker.

"It's sweet of you to offer, but you just collapsed outside my door."

"I'm okay. Besides, I want to help." Maybe if he sounded sweet enough, she'd comply.

She placed her hands on her hips. "How about this? You can come sit and supervise. I'll ask Louise to fix you something to eat and then after you've rested a bit and eaten, I *might* allow you to help." She dabbed at another wound. "But only because it's taking forever to plant everything, and my back is already aching something fierce."

"I'm fine. Doctor in training, remember?" He sent her what he hoped was a convincing smile but she didn't budge. "Okay fine. I'll supervise."

She kept her stance. "Promise me that you'll see Doc Walsh as soon as possible, and I won't nag you about it anymore. Or ask you how you are doing."

"Deal." Lifting his eyebrows, he smiled at her. "So are you done? Can we go work on the garden now?"

"Most of the blood is off your head and face, but you could still use a good bath to get rid of the rest. I'll take this water out for the garden and speak to Louise."

As he got to his feet, every ache screamed for attention. He had to work at it not to groan in front of her. Tomorrow was sure to be brutal.

He grabbed a chair and headed outside. Walker eyed him but didn't smile. He went right back to planting the next seedling in the row.

Anna was back with a tray and handed it to Joshua, then surveyed the little garden plot. "Gracious, Julian. You've accomplished a good deal. Where'd you find the stakes?"

He shrugged. "I had some in the wagon. The different colored string will tell you what's planted there. So draw it up and I'll explain the colors."

Anna made a quick sketch while Joshua ate a sandwich. He watched them work for several minutes, then couldn't stand it any longer.

He got down on his knees next to a wooden crate filled with little green sprouts. "Tell me where you'd like these, Julian."

Anna quirked an eyebrow at him but shook her head and smiled. Walker shuffled over, gave him specific directions, and Joshua went to work. Not that he wouldn't pay for it tomorrow, but what was a little more pain to ensure Anna was protected?

As the three of them made headway in each row, Joshua listened to Walker explain the plants to Anna. The different colors and blooms that she would eventually have if she kept it watered every day. As he talked about growing things, the man did seem to come alive. Perhaps Joshua was wrong. And his suspicions unfounded.

Walker seemed perfectly normal. Maybe he simply didn't care to be around many people.

Except for Mary. He'd followed her around like a lost puppy dog, and now . . .

Anna.

And yet, he was gracious and kind. Soft spoken. Didn't seem like he would ever want to hurt anyone.

Joshua dug in the dirt and examined his heart. Why was he on edge around Walker? What made him think Julian couldn't be trusted? Was it simple jealousy?

God, if I'm off here, please help me to see that. Guide my heart and my mind.

"I ordered plants in different stages of growth so you would have blooms longer. I can teach you later how to encourage the plants to continue blooming. That's what I do."

Walker's voice made him look up.

"Thank you, Julian. I have no idea what that means, but I appreciate your help. This will be beautiful to look at over the summer."

Anna's voice was light and happy. Did he really want to put a damper on that? No. He needed to keep his mouth shut and pray God would show him the way.

A carriage came down the lane toward them.

She stood and brushed the black dirt from her hands. "Oh good. It's Doc Walsh. He must be coming to check on Dad." She turned to Julian. "I think we'll have to be done for tonight. Would you mind coming back tomorrow so that we can finish?"

"Sure." He didn't say anything else, just packed up his tools and unloaded the rest of the plants and seedlings.

As he drove his wagon away, Doc pulled up.

"Good evening, Miss Lakeman, Mr. Ziegler." He secured the reins of his carriage, picked up a black bag, and hopped down. "As you can guess, I'm here to check on your dad."

"Go on in." Anna smiled and held out her hands. "Joshua and I will get cleaned up and meet you in there."

Doc quirked an eyebrow at him. "Looks like I might have another patient."

He'd been hoping the man wouldn't notice. But he'd made a promise to Anna. "Yeah, if you have time, Doc . . ."

"Not a problem." He headed into the house.

Joshua went to the pump and started cranking the handle. It was going to take more than a little water to get rid of all the dirt and grime. And the manure stench.

"I'm proud of you." Anna beamed at him right before she splashed water on her face.

With a roll of his eyes, he grinned back. "You better be. That wasn't easy."

The rest of the evening passed in easy conversation with Mr. Lakeman and Doctor Walsh. The good doctor looked over Joshua's bumps, bruises, and abrasions, and bandaged a few of the deeper ones. Then he leaned forward on his knees. "All right, young man. I've been waiting three long years to ask this question."

Oh boy. What was this about?

"I know you're getting close to finishing up your medical training. Any chance I can convince you to come back here and join forces with me?"

He hadn't expected that. Doc Walsh was a relatively young man. And their town wasn't all that big. "I'd love to come back home, but I didn't think we needed another doctor in the area."

"I'll be honest with you. Doctor Williams left Green River and a few weeks later, Doctor Lansam went on to glory. That leaves Doctor Miller and he wants to retire. He's almost seventy and doesn't think he'll be able to do it much longer. I had a discussion with him last week and he's willing to stay on until you're done. Then you and I would cover the entire area. Probably need to find another doctor to join us as well. As you know, there aren't a lot of people willing to come out to the Wyoming Territory right now. It's unknown. There's Indians. And there's not much out here other than the train going through."

Joshua looked around the room. Anna's face was expectant. Mr. Lakeman's was encouraging. A dream come true. "I gladly accept your offer, Doc."

The next half hour was spent in a flurry of questions and excitement. But now that he knew where he'd end up after school, he had one singular focus.

Speaking with Mr. Lakeman. As soon as he knew the man still approved, he would speak with Anna alone.

The doctor told Joshua to keep his wounds clean and to try not to take any more tumbles. He also gave instructions to Anna and Louise for Mr. Lakeman's exercises and care. Keeping Peter from stress was a big part of the healing for his heart now that it had calmed down out of the severe rapid heartbeat.

After the doctor left for home, Anna's father turned to him, a twinkle in his eye. "I'm excited for you, son. It's the perfect opportunity."

In that moment, emotions surged, and for a second, he thought he might even tear up. "I may never make a lot of money as a country doctor, but this is what I've always wanted to do. God called me into this. God paved the way." He thought of all the times he'd been tempted to stay in the big city—that's what his professor and adviser wanted for him after all—but he couldn't imagine that kind of life. What he wanted was right here.

"I'm so happy for you, Joshua." It looked like Anna had more to say, but then she closed her mouth. "Let me go refill Dad's water." She left the room.

That was okay, he would ask her to walk him out later and he could ask her what was on her mind.

Mr. Lakeman lifted his right hand. "I can see you've got something on your mind. I'm listening."

No time for hesitation. Anna would be back any moment. "Are you still agreeable to me asking for your daughter's hand in marriage?"

"Yes! You should know that, son."

Joshua leaned forward and gripped the man's outstretched hand. "Thank you."

"Thank *you*. But you've got to promise me something."

"What?" Joshua prayed it wasn't anything out of his realm of expertise. Mr. Lakeman had always been a dreamer.

"You have to take all of her. Not just her hand."

They laughed together and Joshua shook his head. "You had me going, sir."

"I know. But you looked entirely too stiff. First, Caleb's return, then the doc's offer, and now this!"

"What's all this?" Anna walked through the door and her gaze shifted between them.

"Speaking of Caleb"—he placed his elbows on his knees and leaned forward—"I promised that I would take him to repay some debts that he incurred when he ran away. I'm planning on taking him Saturday and Sunday, so I'll miss working on the dig on Saturday, if that's okay?"

She walked over and sat on the edge of her dad's bed. "I'm glad you're doing that. It will be a rich memory for him. Don't worry about the dig. We'll be fine. A day or two shouldn't delay us much."

Mr. Lakeman nodded. "You should go. And bring him back here so he can tell me all his stories. I need some entertainment. Tell him anytime he wants to come by and chat, I'd love to see him."

Joshua laughed. "Sure thing, sir." He glanced at Anna and then back to her father. "Would you mind if I take your daughter out for a quick walk? I know it's late. I promise I won't take up too much of her time."

He held the older man's gaze, hoping and praying that he would understand the underlying question.

"Go on, you two." The lopsided smile on his face grew. He knew.

Once they were out in the hallway, Joshua reached back for Anna's hand and took it in his.

They walked out of the house and down the lane a bit before he got up the courage to go ahead and speak.

He stopped walking and turned toward her. Her hair had come out of its confines and he reached forward to touch it. It was soft and smooth under his fingers. Her dark brown eyes searched his.

"Anna Lakeman . . ." He almost couldn't breathe.

"Yes?" She bit her lip.

With a squeeze to the hand he held, he summoned all his courage and lifted his other hand to her cheek. "I have loved you since I first chased you in the schoolyard all those years ago. You've been my best friend and if the past three years have taught me anything, it's that I don't want to live without you. I know it's a lot to ask you to wait until I'm done next year, but I want to marry you, Anna. I want to spend the rest of my life showing you how much I adore you. I want to raise a family together, grow old together, argue and debate, discuss and learn, dig for fossils with you, and anything else that means we spend the rest of our lives together. I love you."

Her eyes sparkled in the twilight.

"Will you give me the honor of being your husband? Will you marry me?" Holding his breath, he waited.

The seconds that passed felt like an eternity.

But then her eyes changed. Almost shuttered.

What was happening? He released his breath.

She squeezed his hands and then released them. "Could I have some time to think and pray about it?"

What? What was there to think about?

Still, it'd be callous of him to say no. But her answer—or lack of one—hurt. "Sure." His voice cracked and he swallowed against the sudden desert that had taken up residence. "I'll be praying too. I love you." He couldn't bear any more. Leaning forward, he kissed her on the forehead and went home.

Shattered.

eighteen

"This dark selfish world needs all the unselfishness it can get, all the love it can command."

~Earl Douglass

TUESDAY, JULY 2

Anna rubbed at her gritty eyes. Not a wink of sleep last night. And she deserved it.

Her annoyance with herself for not answering Joshua right away kept her up last night and would probably make her a downright grump this morning.

What kind of a woman does that to a man she loves? *Had* loved with her whole heart for years? It was ridiculous. And she'd paid for it.

What was wrong with her? Yes, she wanted to marry him. Yes, she wanted to spend the rest of her life with him. Yes, she loved him.

But at the last second, she'd gotten nervous. Remembered what it felt like to not hear from him for three years. To constantly chastise herself for her temper and her words.

After hours of tossing and turning—and scolding herself—she'd gotten up and read the rest of his letters. All of them. Now she got up out of her bed and went back to her desk. One letter lay open on the top. The one that had gripped her more than any of the others. Anna picked it up and read again:

My dearest Anna,
You will always be my dearest because you are the only woman that I will ever love with this depth. I love my mother and my sister, but it's a mere fraction of what I feel for you, which is hard to even fathom because they are my family. My blood.
I don't know if we will ever see each other again. I hope and pray that we do. I hope and pray that one day you will forgive me. I hope and pray that I am given the opportunity to hand-deliver these letters to you so that you can know my heart has always been yours.
Medicine is such a hard course of study. There are so many procedures we must know how to perform. So many medicines that we must memorize and understand how much to dose. It seems like every day there's a new condition or ailment, and we have to learn all about the symptoms, treatments, and prognoses.
I've always wanted to help people. To heal them. But I feel inadequate.
In truth, the one thing that keeps me going is you. I can hear your voice in my head. The day I received word that Mr. Bricker was funding my schooling, you said, "Joshua Ziegler, you are going to be the very best doctor who has ever walked this world. You are gifted by God. You are compassionate and caring. And you have great discernment. Don't you dare

doubt yourself. Ever. Or I will have to hop on a train to Chicago and give you a stern talking-to."

I can still see you there. With your hair blowing in the wind, your hands on your hips, and fire in your beautiful eyes. You have always challenged me to be better. Encouraged me in my faith. Urged me to continue and not quit.

What will I do without you if our parting words were the end?

Another round of exams starts tomorrow, so I must get to bed.

I am ever thinking of you, dreaming of you, and loving you.

Forever yours,
Joshua

Her heart overflowed with everything she felt for this man. Years and years of memories raced through her mind. Closing her eyes, she clutched the papers to her chest and smiled. With a sigh, she opened her eyes again, folded the letter, and placed it back in its envelope.

She would see him at the dig site today and ask him to walk with her this evening.

Then she would give him her answer.

The day had been even longer than Joshua imagined it could be. And not *just* because Anna hadn't answered his proposal.

It didn't help that every inch of his body hurt from the fall. The intense labor at the dig site brought out every ache and pain. He knew it would happen but had hoped an affirmative answer from Anna would make it all go away.

So much for that.

She'd smiled and laughed with him throughout the day, which had helped some. She'd even invited him for a walk later that evening, all of which hinted that she would give her answer.

But the discomfort, the pain . . . the *uncertainty* just made the day drag even more.

He'd gone back to see the location where his horse had tripped and found a rope tied low over the trail and bark torn off the bottom of a tree. In a ring.

Why had someone done this?

Had he been the intended target?

Walker seemed focused on Anna. He *had* to be the one behind it. Trying to get rid of Joshua. Who else?

Who else had bad blood—?

He winced. They were all sinners. Anna's words had convicted him. Society might love to throw around the term *bad blood,* but as a believer in Almighty God, Joshua knew that wasn't possible. Sin was responsible. Not someone's blood.

Of course, history did show though that plenty of people who were raised in horrid environments ended up doing some nasty things themselves. And Walker definitely had a horrible example.

But Julian was quiet. Grew flowers.

Things didn't add up.

Wait. What about the brother?

Joshua shook away the thoughts. Julian made it clear his brother had left. No one ever saw the brother. At least, not for a long while.

He checked his watch. Should be a decent time to head over and see Anna. The wait had been eating at him, but once he was on his way, his gut churned.

What if she said no?

As he rode up to the Lakeman home, he heard laughter coming out of Mr. Lakeman's window. It was good to hear the man getting back to his old self. If anyone could make it through, Peter Lakeman could.

Joshua tied up his horse and strode up to the door.

Just as he lifted his hand to knock, the door opened in a great swoosh of air.

"Joshua!" Anna's face was positively giddy. She grabbed his hand and dragged him to her father's room. "Look!"

Mr. Lakeman lifted his right leg about an inch off the bed. Then his left. And then he bent his knees and tugged his legs toward him. It wasn't a ninety-degree angle yet, but it was close.

Joshua clapped. "That, sir, is amazing. Great job."

"Thank you, son." He rested his head back against the head-board. "I can't tell you how good that feels, even though it's not a tremendous amount of progress."

"It's a *remarkable* amount of progress, sir. Don't sell yourself short." He stepped forward and held his hand out to shake the older man's hand.

Mr. Lakeman's grip was stronger than it had been, another great sign. Joshua squeezed the man's hand and nodded. "God is good."

"Amen to that." Mr. Lakeman let out a long breath. "Now I'm exhausted, and I hear you two have a walk to take." He closed his eyes and then peeked through one. "Go on. Get outta here."

Joshua reached for Anna's hand and they wandered out of the house and down their favorite path toward the creek. His heart pounded. Would this be the last time?

The evening's breeze helped to cool things down. The blue sky wasn't disturbed by a single cloud. A perfect evening.

"I know you're waiting for my answer." She sent him a teasing grin.

"Oh, not at all. I haven't thought about it one bit." He squeezed her hand as they walked.

Her light laughter filled the air. "Liar. It's all I've been able to think about."

"Glad to know I'm not the only one."

"I want to give you my answer and then I need to ask you something."

"All right." Deep breath.

"My answer is yes. I would love to marry you, Joshua Ziegler."

He couldn't resist it—he picked her up by the waist and spun around. When he set her back down, he gave her a quick kiss on the lips. Then he stepped back. "I'm sorry, I know you said you wanted to ask me something."

The gleam in her eyes told him she didn't mind. She put her fingers to her lips. "Your kisses are dangerous to my heart." She patted her chest.

"Mine too. Now go ahead. I'm all ears."

"How do you feel about me continuing my work with my father? I mean, not just this next year while you finish schooling. But after that? What are your expectations?"

They walked several more steps and he thought hard about her question.

"From where I stand, our home base will be here. I will work with Doc Walsh and you will work with your father. This is what you are called to do, Anna. I understand that now. Whether you want to continue with the sketching, or if you want to dig, or if you want to write the scientific papers . . . I will support you."

"Really?" Her eyes shimmered with tears.

"Yes, really." He pulled her into his arms. "I love you, Anna. I love everything about you. And I love the work that you do. I would never ask you to stop."

She hugged him tight.

"Well . . . I take that back."

With a frown, she pulled back. "What do you mean?"

"I might ask you to stop if . . . well . . . at least for a little while . . . if you were in the family way." He wiggled his eyebrows at her.

She swatted at him as her cheeks turned fiery pink. "Joshua Ziegler!"

But as much as she tried to wriggle out of his grasp, he held on. "You know, you keep on blushing like that and I might never let you go."

She sputtered and pushed at his chest. "You, sir, are incorrigible."

"And you, miss, love it."

WEDNESDAY, JULY 3

Helping Anna in her garden was almost as good as working in his own. Granted, hers was much smaller and didn't have as much care put into it as his own, but it would be beautiful. It would give Mr. Lakeman something to look at while he recovered.

At least, that's what Anna wanted. If it made her happy, then Julian was happy.

He'd waited years and years for the blackness to go away. Had begged for God or whoever was up there in the sky to make him normal.

Damian's snide words pushed to the forefront of his mind. *"But God hasn't done anything to help you. Besides, Anna doesn't love you. She can't. Not as long as Ziegler is around. You just need to let me take care of it."*

It wasn't wise to have these thoughts now. When Julian finished the row he'd been planting, he stood up and looked down at their work. "Anna?"

"Yes?" She was lovely with her sunbonnet on, kneeling in the dirt, planting the last few seedlings.

"We're almost done." He risked a smile. He didn't do it often because his father had always smacked it off his face.

Leaning back, she surveyed the garden. "You're right! I only see five more." She stood up and went to the window. "Dad, you're going to love it! We're almost done planting."

"Ask Julian to come to the window." Mr. Lakeman's voice drifted out toward him.

A sense of panic sprang up inside him. Why did her father want him closer? His limbs shook and he gulped.

Anna took his arm. Her hand was warm and comforting. "Come on, Dad wants to talk to you."

He couldn't say a word. Couldn't stop the fear from growing. Fathers were horrible men. They did horrible things.

He allowed Anna to walk him to the window.

The man in the bed had tears in his eyes. "Son, thank you for helping my daughter with this surprise for me. I've admired your work in your garden for years. Once you were gone, it broke my heart to see it wither up and die. You are talented. I wanted you to know how much I appreciate all this."

Julian stood there. He had no idea what to say. The man was . . . nice. Thankful. And had complimented him.

Mr. Lakeman waved his right hand at him. "Anna showed me the diagram with all the plants, I would love it if you would come back sometime and visit with me. We can talk flowers. I've always wanted to be an *anthophilous* myself."

He blinked several times. The man understood what it was like to love living among flowers. "I would love to talk flowers with you."

"Good, good." He leaned back. "I look forward to visiting with you."

"I look forward to it, too." As hard as it was to believe, it was the truth. Julian waved his hand and walked away from the window. He turned to Anna. "Is your father always that nice?"

The look she gave him was quizzical, then she laughed. "Yes. He's a wonderful man."

Huh. Wonderful man.

Julian cleaned up his tools while Anna finished planting.

What would it be like to be called a wonderful man?

nineteen

"Bitterness and despair rolled away and left me happy again."

~Earl Douglass

Anna fanned her face as the heat of the day was upon them. But she wouldn't trade this for the world. The Independence Day celebration in Walker Creek this year was better than ever before.

Little Caleb was safely home. Dad was improving each day. Their community was thriving and had come together for a big picnic.

And she'd said *yes.*

Her cheeks lifted in a smile. She was going to marry Joshua Ziegler!

The news had spread like wildfire, and she couldn't be happier.

"If I could have your attention, please." The good reverend held his arms up in the air and then clapped. The sound echoed across the crowd, and the happy chatter diminished as everyone turned to face him.

"The choir has prepared a few songs for us. We invite you to join in on the final song."

After the choir finished "My Country 'Tis of Thee," the reverend waved for all of them to stand and join in on "The Star-Spangled Banner."

Tears sprang to Anna's eyes as the words sank into her heart. Ever since the end of the Civil War, the healing of the nation had been slow going. Out here in Wyoming Territory, they hadn't dealt with as much division as they'd read about in the papers back East. But here, right now, she felt they could heal from the horrific war that had turned brother against brother—if Americans would simply come together in love and community. Like Walker Creek.

Oh, she'd seen the brutality and lasting effects of the war that had left large portions of the country in shambles as she'd traveled with Dad. Memories she wished she could erase. But her community prayed together this morning that God would bring them back together in unity and that beauty would rise from the ashes. Fueled by her own passion to see that happen, she was determined to do her part. However large or small that might be.

Joshua nudged her elbow as the song ended and handed her his handkerchief.

Swiping at the tears, she beamed up at him. This man. This wonderful, wonderful man. If she hadn't admitted how much she loved him before, she would've been shouting it from the rooftops this morning when he'd brought a wagon over to pick up her father so that he could participate. Dad had been so overjoyed that he'd cried. And so many people rallied around him, telling him they were praying for his full recovery and soon.

It was healing for him to get out and be among folks again.

To feel a bit normal again. To talk about the dig and share his excitement.

People were curious about the dinosaur and asked if they could come out and see what they were doing.

She couldn't contain her smiles and enthusiasm as she talked about it. It wasn't just Dad's excitement anymore. It was hers. They spent a good portion of the celebration talking about what was entailed in a paleontological dig, but asked for people to please keep their distance until the team had excavated the fossils since it was a fragile work site.

It had been a perfect day.

"Ready to head home? I think your dad is fading in the heat." Josh whispered close to her ear.

With a nod, she glanced at her father. It had been wonderful to see his face light up and fill with color. But he was drooping. At least the celebration hadn't caused his heart to beat too fast again. "That's a good idea. I'm quite tired myself."

He loaded her dad into the wagon bed with the blankets and pillows around him and then helped her up onto the wagon seat.

"This was the best Fourth of July in history." The smile on his face didn't look like it could ever dim.

"I agree."

They chatted about the weather and their daily tasks as they rode. Dad's soft snoring accompanied the sound of the wheels rumbling along the lane.

Once Dad was back in bed and under Louise's watchful eye, she and Joshua headed out for an evening walk.

Hand in hand, they strolled to the creek. Anna took a long inhale. "I love the scent of the water."

He chuckled. "Guess I hadn't thought about how water smelled."

Turning toward him, she squeezed his hand. "Think about

it. Take a good long breath. It's alive with movement and growth. I'm so used to working in the dusty and dirty and extremely dry conditions that the smell of water and wet earth makes me happy. Probably why I love the rain so much."

He shrugged. "It makes sense. Next time it rains in Chicago, I'll be thinking about that rather than complaining."

Unable to resist her feelings any longer, she stood up on tiptoe and threw her arms around his neck. With all the love that she'd shoved deep down for the past three years, she kissed him again. And not just a peck.

He placed his hands on her waist and leaned into the kiss. For the first time, Anna felt complete. Whole. Like this was exactly where she was supposed to be. Forever.

He ended the kiss and then kissed the tip of her nose and then her forehead. With a soft moan, he pulled back. "That could be dangerous."

She frowned. "What do you mean?"

"I love you, Anna. More than you could ever imagine. And that kiss . . . well, that brought the fire of passion inside me to a roar."

Feeling the heat rush to her face, she dipped her chin.

"I'm sorry. I don't mean to embarrass you, but I have to be honest. I want to marry you and spend the rest of my life with you. You are the only one for me." He trailed a finger down her cheek.

"I feel the same about you. I love you." As they stared into each other's eyes, it would have been easy to allow the magnetism of their love to take over.

But Josh stepped back. "I don't want to do anything to disrespect you, so I think we should head back."

With her heart beating wildly, she couldn't argue. "You're right. It'll be a long day tomorrow."

Taking her hand again, he led them up the trail back to her

house. "I will probably smile the whole ride home. And all day tomorrow. And the next . . ."

She giggled and bit her lip. "Me too. Whatever will people say?"

When Josh arrived at the dig site, he shared an intimate glance with Anna. Zach, Tom, and Luke snickered as they headed with the tools over to the wall of bones. He would get ribbed about it, that was for sure. Probably all day. But he didn't mind one bit.

He would marry the woman he loved. He would finish medical school now with a new inspiration. A new challenge and encouragement to give it all he had. Because Anna was waiting for him after graduation. And a lifetime of memories were waiting to be made.

With a long breath, Josh took in the scene around him. Anna was correct. The scent of a dig site was nothing like that near the creek. Perhaps he should pay a bit more attention.

Of course, his nose was accustomed to the sanitary smells of a hospital. Thanks to the work of Pasteur and Lister, antiseptic surgery was now a must. But the disagreeable odor of carbolic acid had become the scent of his trade, too. Not that he liked it. Perhaps his sense of smell was dulled because of it. Coming back to work here would help him appreciate the little things in life again.

Funny how fast the big city and all its dressings had pressed him into submission.

With a smile, he took another big whiff of dirt, earth, and metal. Only a year left. Then he could return.

The offer from Doctor Walsh had been more than generous. Joshua even had an idea of a friend back at university who might be adventurous and willing enough to venture out to their rugged territory and spend a few years working with them.

Of course, his friend would have to be willing to leave the city and all its amenities. That might take some convincing.

He shimmied his way up the slanted wall, wishing he had some scaffolding around him, but the degree grade of this section wasn't as steep. Working with his hammer and a tiny chisel, Joshua took tedious care to excavate another bone that they assumed was part of the spine. The more Joshua gazed at the bone, the more beautiful it became. He could picture the beast thanks to her drawings. All the time and energy Anna had put into this dig made him proud.

Oh, there were lots of other fossils. Bones out of place. With at least two layers. Perhaps many animals other than just their Allosaurus. But the more they worked, the more excited the team became to bring this great beast out of its resting place.

The pinging of his hammer and chisel was a steady rhythm, with a few seconds' breather in between as he used the brush to clean the debris from the specimen. Then the pinging would begin again.

Each man had their own way they worked. But every day it became a rhythmic symphony. Even the pitches of each hammer and chisel added to the resonant percussion.

A sound he'd come to love. It was beautiful.

Zach's whoop echoed through the gulley. "Lookee here!"

"Whatcha got?" Luke scrambled down the wall from where he'd been working and peered over Zach's shoulder.

Josh stopped with the hammer and watched. He tipped his hat back and swiped the sweat off his forehead.

Tom stood at the base with his hands on his hips. "Well?"

Zach's eyes were wide as he pointed for Luke examine it. "Anna! Come quick! I think we've found the skull!"

She was off her perch and darting across the gulley in an instant. Joshua slid down the wall too.

As the guys assisted Anna up to Zach's side and helped hold her in place, she held a stoic face. But after examining it, her gaze shifted to Josh. The pure delight in her eyes gave him the answer. She then looked at each of the others. "I'm quite certain Zach is correct in his assessment."

She sounded so proper. In charge. The true leader of their little expedition.

The guys hollered and threw their hats in the air, and then once they were all back on safe footing, Anna headed straight for him and wrapped him in a big hug.

Zach whistled while Tom and Luke clapped. Josh gave them all a wink.

When Anna released him, she turned to each one of them. "This is a big day for us. Not only does it appear that we have an intact spine, but we now have the skull." Tears shimmered in her eyes and she held out her hands. "I know this is a bit unconventional, but I would appreciate us taking a moment to thank God for this."

Joshua removed his hat and moved to her side taking her outstretched hand.

"Would you pray?"

The request only made him smile. How amazing that God had brought them back together and now this. "I'd be honored."

The others bowed their heads as they removed their hats and placed them over their chests.

"Heavenly Father, we thank You—"

A rumble in the distance interrupted his words and drew his attention to the south end of the washout.

A wagon was headed their direction with several people.

One of them was obviously a woman. Her frilly parasol gave that away.

Joshua looked to Anna.

"I wonder who that could be?" Then her shoulders drooped. "Oh no."

"What?"

"I completely forgot that Father's investor said he was coming out for a visit." She rubbed her forehead. "If that's them, I don't know what to say."

Joshua rested a hand on her shoulder. "You'll do fine. You know this dig upside down and backward. You're in charge, remember? Just give them the facts. You know rich people, they don't have any idea what manual labor is all about. They want to hear that their money is being used to make them famous or add to their wealth."

She grimaced. "That's awfully cynical. But I guess it's true." Straightening her shoulders, she lifted her chin. "You're right. I can do this."

"We'll get back to work." He glanced at the others. "But I'll be right here if you need anything. Anything at all. The others have your back as well."

"That's right, Anna." Zach placed his hat back on his head.

"Me too." Tom nodded.

"Thank you." With a straightening of her shoulders, she strode back over to her table where she kept the day's lists, sketches, and fossils they'd recovered from the rock.

Joshua watched her for several seconds. She smoothed her hair and studied her papers. What he wouldn't give to give her the boost of confidence that she needed to be able to deal with whatever came.

He went back to work. The other guys lifted their gaze to the coming wagon here and there, but they all kept at it.

When the wagon reached them, Joshua kept his head down. He wasn't going to encroach on Anna's leadership. If she needed him, he'd be at the ready.

Anna welcomed the visitors.

"Why, Joshua Ziegler."

That voice.

Ugh. He closed his eyes for a moment to gather his thoughts and control his expression before he slid down from his spot again. Why, oh why, did the frilly parasol have to belong to that Rosemary Oppenheim. Her father was the investor? "Miss Oppenheim." He tipped his hat to her.

With a dip of her chin, she batted her lashes. "When my father said he was coming out to see his newest investment, and I heard where it was, I knew I had to tag along. Wyoming Territory is such a rugged place. I had to see it for myself."

"That's nice." No it wasn't. It was horrid. But he couldn't ruin this for Anna.

"Wouldn't you know, I was so surprised to see you here. What a coincidence." Her tone was smooth and musical. Albeit fake.

Coincidence? Not hardly.

"Well, it's nice to see you, miss." He shimmied his way back up to his spot.

She didn't take the hint. "This work is so fascinating. You simply must tell me all about it. As soon as my father said that he was investing in dinosaur hunters, I had to see this. You know, I've always had an eye for the sciences."

"Uh-huh." Maybe if he kept hammering, she would go away. He pulled a larger chisel out of his belt and started pounding on rock that wasn't anywhere near a fossil so he could smash it as hard as he could.

"What are you working on right now?"

He hammered again, hoping she would think he didn't hear her.

"Mr. Ziegler?"

"Yeah?" This whole time he'd been praying for God to help Anna with the new visitors. Now his prayers turned to *his* patience and sanity.

"Isn't that part of the spine? My father said this is an exceptional find. An Allosaurus, if I'm not mistaken?"

He paused his hammering. "Yes, it's part of the spine. Forgive me, but it's best to direct all your questions to Miss Lakeman. She's in charge and is much more knowledgeable than I. Truly, I must get back to work. We don't want to waste any daylight. It's a long and tedious process."

She let out a tiny huff. "She's busy talking with my father. Besides, I would much rather talk with you since we've been friends for so long."

Friends. He deflated a bit. Yes, Rosemary Oppenheim had been a good friend to him. Not until recently did he realize she'd grown interested in him.

After all their conversations, surely she knew how he felt about Anna.

Of course, Miss Oppenheim couldn't possibly know what had happened since he'd been home. He'd have to make sure that she understood. Ensure he didn't hurt her along the way.

"You've been a good friend to me, Miss Oppenheim. I do appreciate that."

"Well then, don't you think it's highly providential that we are once again thrown together." She giggled and then fanned her face. "And out here in the middle of no man's land."

"I wouldn't call it providential. This is harsh territory. Hardly a place for a lady like you." He turned his gaze to the chisel and went back to work.

"Not a place for a lady, huh?" Miss Oppenheim purred. "I wonder what Miss Lakeman would say to that?"

<hr/>

The past hour had been far more excruciating than it should have been. Mr. Oswald Oppenheim seemed kind enough. His son, Albert, stood next to him, appearing as if this whole thing was beneath him. Unworthy of his time.

The endless litany of questions in the heat of the day had frayed every last one of her nerves. Especially after having to listen to every giggle the wealthy man's daughter aimed at Josh.

Every now and then she snuck a glance in their direction. Maybe one of the other men had caught the beautiful socialite's attention. . . . But no. She hovered below Josh.

Anna's Josh.

How did they know one another?

"Why don't you show us the site, Miss Lakeman?" The older gentleman pointed his shiny black walking stick at the wall of bones.

"Yes, of course. I'd love to." Paste on a smile. Be nice. Dad needed this. So did she.

As she walked over to give them a tour, she decided the best thing would be to ignore the man's daughter for now and focus on the bones. The details of what they'd found so far. What they hoped to accomplish during the dry summer season. She could do this. Be professional and knowledgeable. Yes, she could.

"Aren't you going to introduce us?" Miss Oppenheim's voice had such a lovely tone.

It made Anna feel . . . frumpy. Inadequate. She cleared her throat. "My apologies, miss. This is Tom, Zach, and Luke." She pointed to the long-time members of her team. "These three men have worked alongside my father and me for many years. We couldn't ask for a better crew."

Each man nodded and then went right back to work.

"And it appears you know Mr. Ziegler." Now why did she go and get so formal all of a sudden? Was she jealous? No. No. She was going to marry Josh. He loved her.

"Yes, we've known one another for several years." That lilting voice could probably make any man come whenever she called. But it was the way that she tipped up her head to look at Josh that made Anna take note. Best to get rid of the visitors as soon as possible.

She glanced at her watch pinned to her shirtwaist. "Well, gentlemen, miss, thank you for coming out today, but if you don't mind, I—we—must get back to work."

She strode back toward her table.

Surely, they would leave and head back to whatever quarters they'd found for themselves out here. Or even better, maybe they'd leave Wyoming Territory altogether. They couldn't want to stay out in this heat in their full dress suits. Where did they think they were? New York City? London? It was ridiculous to wear a top hat out to an excavation site, and yet here both of them were. Looking like they were ready to meet the king.

Miss Oppenheim was dressed just as extravagantly. Her dress alone probably cost as much as a year's worth of food for the Lakemans. And that hat and parasol. Heavens, what ridiculous frippery.

She winced. That wasn't kind. Besides, this man's money helped them to continue doing what they loved. Which was paramount.

"Miss Lakeman?" The elder Mr. Oppenheim had followed her. "If I could have a moment with you."

She quirked an eyebrow at him. "All right." She clasped her hands in front of her. "What can I help you with?"

He cleared his throat and puffed out his chest. "You see, I have my concerns about this project."

Concerns? "Oh?" How dare this man come out here and corner her like this. Hadn't he worked with her father before? But for now, she would hold her tongue and listen to what he had to say.

"Yes. With your father laid up, that changed everything. He is a well-respected paleontologist."

"Yes, sir. He is. And he is still involved. This is his find, after all." The man better not be pulling any stunts. The hairs on her neck stood up. She would not allow anyone to steal this discovery from her father. Nor would she allow any slander or sabotage.

He held up a hand. "I am not removing his name. He deserves the credit."

"Thank you." She released a breath.

"But I am concerned about a woman being in a supervisory position."

"I can't believe—"

"Miss Lakeman." He narrowed his eyes at her. "This is a project of unprecedented magnitude. This will change things for paleontology, and you know it. We cannot have any reason for anyone to doubt any part of this process. Thus, my suggestion is for my son, Albert, to become the supervisor on the project."

She clamped her lips together. He couldn't be serious!

"I also don't believe a woman should be the one to submit the official sketches for the scientific papers, magazines, and eventual books that will surely come of this incredible dinosaur find. My son has done several other projects for prestigious publications. I propose that he—"

"I'm sorry, Mr. Oppenheim." She mustered every bit of confidence within her to stand up to this man who thought she would cow under his authority. "I cannot allow you to continue. Your disrespect for me, my father, and *my* work is absolutely the most rude thing I've heard in all my life. My father has great respect for you and has had nothing but praise for you and your support of the scientific community. But this is unacceptable. If you would like to continue on this absurd path, I will have to liken you with Marsh and Cope and their underhanded dealings. If that is what you choose, I don't wish to have your name sully our field of science."

"I *say*, Miss Lakeman!" The man's jaw opened and closed.

"Sir, paleontology deserves better than that. This dig deserves better than that. I deserve better than that. If you'll excuse me, I have work to do."

twenty

"And the mind that searcheth findeth
More than it had ever thought
And thou go ever onward
Moving on from thought to thought."

~Earl Douglass

FRIDAY, JULY 5

"Dad, I was so furious. I can't believe that man. Why would you ever want to work with someone like that?" She stomped around her father's bed.

His jaw was open, eyes wide. "I had no idea he would ever pull anything like this."

"On top of everything else, his daughter, Rosemary, knows Joshua from Chicago, and she was fawning all over him the entire day. It was despicable." She placed her hands on her hips. "*Where* is Mr. Gilbert? I sent word over an hour ago."

"I came as soon as I could." Joshua's voice came from the doorway. "Sorry to intrude. Louise let me in."

Anna ran into his arms. "This is awful."

"Don't worry. Mr. Gilbert is on his way." He squeezed her shoulders and turned toward her father. "Do you have ideas on how to deal with this situation?"

Dad grimaced. "I'm afraid there are some things that are not in our favor. The biggest one is the fact that we only have our verbal agreement before my collapse. I'm hoping Mr. Gilbert can help us fix the problems."

A commotion outside the door made all of them turn. Mr. Gilbert appeared, hat and briefcase in hand, and a bit out of breath.

After they filled the lawyer in on the entire situation, he squinted and nodded. "The verbal agreement is still binding and the contracts were sent before Mr. Lakeman's illness. Mr. Lakeman is clearly in charge and the head of the find. He should have the right to choose who will work in his stead.

"As to the drawings, that is a bit more complicated. I'll need to speak to my friend in Green River, who is the judge for our area. I'll need his advice about how to proceed."

Not what she wanted to hear. Why couldn't the law move faster? "But what does that mean for us right now?"

"Mr. Oppenheim doesn't have the right to do anything until it's decided legally. He can make suggestions, but that is all. He invested so his name would be on the exhibit along with yours at the museum. He will also get paid a tidy sum from the museum, in addition to what they'll pay you. He wants recognition and I can handle that. My suggestion is that you proceed as usual and keep your chin up. I'll do everything in my power to see this is done accurately and legally." He scrunched up his face. "Perhaps they will leave in a day or two?"

"We can hope." Anna plopped down into a chair. She didn't care if she looked like a small child pitching a fit.

"Chin up, Anna." Dad pointed at her. "You are in charge. You are doing a wonderful job. My team knows exactly how to proceed. They have worked with me countless times before. No one can doubt their experience."

"But what about mine?"

He winced and put a hand to his chest.

"Dad? Are you all right?" She rushed to him.

He took several breaths with his eyes closed. "I'm . . . fine. Now, don't you worry about your reputation." He stabbed the bed with a finger. "I will not allow him—"

"Dad, there's no need for you to get worked up over this." With a shake of her head, she patted his hand. "As much as I love being a woman, this is one of those times when I wish there was a bit more help for the fairer sex. I'm not trying to take over the world." She sniffed. The tears wouldn't stay hidden. "I'm not even asking to dig in the dirt! I simply want to work in the field I love."

Dad lifted his hand again, reaching out to her.

She took it.

"Your drawings are the best I've ever seen and I'm not saying that because I'm your father." His voice was calmer. "It's a fact. You have been trained. You have been working in this field for a long time. We will fight for you, Anna. I promise."

Mr. Gilbert patted her shoulder. "I helped women gain the right to vote in Wyoming Territory a decade ago, Miss Lakeman. Believe me, I will ensure that you have every right that belongs to you." He slapped his hat on his head. "Now if you'll excuse me, I'm going back to my office and sending out several telegrams."

"Thank you for coming." Anna offered him a smile. Hopefully she hadn't whined and complained too much. He was a wonderful help to them. She'd just been so discouraged. Outraged. Offended.

The list could go on and on.

Joshua came to her side. "Maybe we can go for a walk and

stomp out some of this aggravated energy?" He wriggled his eyebrows at her.

Perhaps a walk would help her out of this awful, black mood. "Dad, do you mind?"

"Not at all." He leaned his head back on his pillow and released a long breath. "Let me spend some time praying. Will you ask Louise to give me a few minutes alone?"

"Sure." She tucked her hand in Joshua's and allowed him to lead her out of the room.

Once they were outside, she indeed stomped her way down the path. Joshua kept pace with her and held tight to her hand.

But her thoughts wouldn't calm. Her eyes burned with unshed tears. "What if they try to take it all way?"

"We've got to leave this in the Lord's hands, Anna."

"Easier said than done." She welcomed the black mood back. For now, it was more comfortable to wallow. Her strong father wasn't out there in charge of the dig. She was.

What if she failed?

SATURDAY, JULY 6

Julian had watched the goings-on at the dig with his field glasses. Whoever those rich people were who arrived yesterday, Anna didn't seem too pleased with them. If she didn't like them, Julian didn't like them either.

They came back this morning but left before lunchtime. At least they hadn't returned this afternoon.

But the frown etched on Anna's face told him all he needed to know.

His brother nudged him. "She needs some cheering up."

"Yeah." And he planned on doing it.

Damian paced. "I don't like all these new people coming around. Makes me uncomfortable."

"I know." A chill raced up his neck. "Wish we could get rid of them. For her."

"Well, there's still Ziegler to contend with. Seems like they patched things up."

"No!" The idea was like little bugs running up and down his spine. He wriggled his shoulders and back to get rid of the feeling. "Joshua had his chance."

"You're right. Anna needs *you*."

Just as much as he needed her. "I have an idea." He took off toward the house.

A few hours later, he watched Anna leave the dig. It was a little after four in the afternoon. Her workers didn't leave. They usually stayed until six. Sometimes later.

This was his chance.

He packed up his surprise for her in an old potato sack then went out to his garden and picked some of the beautiful blooms.

He couldn't wait until next year when his roses would really take off. They were his favorite. Though their thorns had made him bleed hundreds of times, it was worth it for the beauty and fragrance.

In the fall, he would plant hundreds of tulip and daffodil bulbs and expand his garden to cover the entire acre at the top of this bluff. All the way up to the treeline. It would be magnificent.

When he had a large handful of flowers, he tied some twine around them, grabbed his horse, and headed to the Lakemans' home.

After a quick knock on the door, it opened with a flourish.

Louise Bowden opened the door. "Why, Mr. Walker." But she didn't invite him in.

"Is Miss Lakeman here?"

"Yes, sir. Of course." She called over her shoulder, but kept the door partially closed. "Miss Lakeman."

He heard footsteps and then Anna appeared. "Julian. I wasn't expecting you."

"I brought you some surprises for your garden." He remembered the flowers in his other hand. "Oh, and these." Offering the bouquet from behind his back, he held them forward.

"Why, thank you." She smiled at him. "Do I need to change? Will we be digging?"

"No. You don't need to change. I can do the digging."

"Wonderful." She turned to Louise. "Will you tell Dad that I'll be outside his window if he needs anything?"

"Yes, miss."

Anna joined him outside and Louise closed the door. But not before he caught the look of wariness in the younger girl's eyes. Would people ever look at him differently?

He shook off the thoughts and walked with Anna toward the garden.

When they reached it, he gulped and ventured forth. "I noticed you haven't seemed too happy with the guests who arrived yesterday."

"Oh dear." She moaned. "I'm sorry. I should have told you about them."

She sat on a large rock that was on the perimeter of the little garden area. As she filled him in on the investors, Julian decided then and there he didn't like Mr. Oppen—whatever his name was. The more she talked, the more agitated she became. And then all of a sudden, great big tears were running down her face.

Julian blinked. How was he supposed to respond? Did he need to go hunt down this investor?

But she kept on talking.

About her dreams. About how she wanted to do this for her father. How he deserved this prestigious honor.

Julian shifted his weight from one foot to the other and listened.

Then her words stopped and she swiped at her cheeks. "I'm sorry. That was very rude of me to just blurt all of that out. But thank you for listening."

An idea formed. Perhaps he *could* be the one to save Anna from this mess. Then she would care for him even more. "Maybe this will get your mind off it." He held up the potato sack.

"Another lesson in gardening?" She lifted her chin and shoulders. "I'm all ears."

He dumped out the contents of the sack.

"Oh my." Her hand flew up to cover her nose and mouth.

Granted the three dead squirrels and five gutted fish weren't pleasant to look at—or smell for that matter—but wait until she understood. "One of the first things my mother taught me in the garden was how the circle of life fed all of us." She looked a little green. Did she think he intended this as food for her? "Don't worry, I didn't bring this for us to eat."

Keeping her hand in place, she muttered, "Good."

"You see, these dead things planted in the ground will make your garden even more beautiful and lush. Beauty comes from death. Don't you think that's poetic?"

"I'm trying not to smell it, but yes, I could see how that is poetic." Her voice sounded funny with her hand over her mouth.

He pulled out the hatchet he'd strapped to his waist and chopped up the squirrels and fish skin and bones.

"Uh . . ." She stood up. "Excuse me." Running over to a couple scraggly bushes, she retched.

"Are you not feeling well?" Maybe she was sick.

"Just tell me when you're done."

"With what? The chopping or the burying?"

"Um, yes." She paused. "Both." Her back was to him.

His mother had always chopped up animals and gutted fish in front of him. So it couldn't be indelicate. Maybe Anna had a queasy stomach?

So he talked the whole time he chopped. About how the animals decaying would nourish the ground. It would be so good for her blooms.

"That's wonderful." Her voice was weak. "Thank you so much for thinking of me."

"I'm excited for you to love gardening as I do." He couldn't keep the eagerness from his voice. Once he buried all the chunks, he stood up. "All done."

She turned and sent a smile his direction . . . but it didn't reach her eyes.

Yeah, she was probably getting sick.

All the more reason for him to help her feel better by dealing with her problem.

twenty-one

"How sweet to live in sympathy of kindred spirits, to work and live and love together in perfect sympathy . . ."

~Earl Douglass

At the ticket office in Green River, Joshua squeezed his nephew's shoulder. "Go ahead, Caleb."

The young boy shuddered under his hand and then took a step forward. "Sir, I hitched a ride on your train without payin' for a ticket. Could you please tell me how much I owe ya for a ticket to Cheyenne? 'Cause that's how far I rode without payin'. In fact, ya better charge me for the trip back too, sir."

The ticket agent stared for several seconds. Glanced at Joshua and then back at Caleb.

Caleb stepped closer. "Did ya hear me, sir?"

The man's mouth opened an inch, but nothing came out as he blinked and looked to Joshua for guidance.

He nodded. "Yes, sir. A round-trip ticket to Cheyenne. The boy wants to pay back what he stole."

The man found his voice. "Young man, this is the most admirable thing I've ever heard."

"Thank you, sir. But what I did was wrong." His bottom lip trembled.

The ticket agent nodded.

"We're travelin' to Cheyenne so I can pay back everyone, sir. So we're gonna need two of those round-trip tickets to ride the train today."

Joshua didn't miss the quiver in Caleb's voice, but he was so proud of him for speaking up and handling this. "Is it all right if we make several stops along the way? It might take us a day or two. Maybe more?"

"I'll mark your tickets as such." The man prepared some tickets.

"Thank you." Josh and Caleb chimed at the same time.

"Since you are on such a noble quest," the ticket agent leaned over the counter, "I believe some grace is in order. I will gladly accept your money for the two tickets today, but your debt is forgiven."

Caleb turned to Joshua and craned his neck to look up at him. "Is that okay, Uncle Josh?" His whisper wasn't all that quiet. "I don't know what *debt* means."

Josh worked to keep a stoic face and tousled Caleb's hair. "Just like Jesus paid for our debt of sin on the cross, this man is saying your debt to the railroad is forgiven."

"Oh, *thank* you, sir." Caleb's breath left him in a dramatic sigh as he turned back to the ticket window. "I promise I'll never do it again."

Once they were settled on the train, Caleb snuggled up next to Josh, placing his head on his shoulder. "Thanks again, Uncle Josh. And I'm real sorry."

"I know you are, Caleb. I'm very proud of you for being

honest and forthright. This won't be easy. Not everyone will be as forgiving as the ticket agent. But I will be with you every step of the way."

"I know. I expected that man to yell at me. I deserved it, I know. But Mama and Daddy prayed with me before we left and told me that Jesus would be with me." He yawned and pulled his knees up to his chest.

"Since we don't need to get off the train for a bit, why don't you take a nap so you'll be fresh for our next stop?" Joshua lifted his arm to put around the boy and it was all the coaxing he needed to lay his head in his uncle's lap.

Sunday morning dawned without a cloud in the sky. Joshua wasn't looking forward to the day. Not after several disappointing visits to vendors who had taken it upon themselves to scold young Caleb and charge an exorbitant price for the small items he stole.

Still, his nephew had held his head up even in the midst of tears. He'd apologized multiple times and handed over the money himself. Something he told Joshua he was determined to do.

The plan was to head to church after breakfast and then to the mercantile.

Caleb was quiet all through the meal, but at least he ate like the growing boy he was. At the church, he hesitated at the bottom of the steps. "Ya think the preacher will be like the people last night?"

"I hope not, son. But it's not our place to judge. We're here to apologize and pay off a debt." If he could take the pain for the young boy, he would. That's what love did. But his nephew was determined to continue.

They entered the church and Caleb strode right up to the preacher at the front. The service didn't start for a while so there were only a handful of people in the building. "Mr. Reverend, sir?"

Joshua followed and stayed a few paces back.

"Yes, son." The pastor held out a hand and took a seat on the front pew.

Caleb joined him. "I stole a dollar from the offering plate a few weeks ago. I don't live here. I ran away from home and hitched a ride on the train. But I'm paying back"—he looked over his shoulder at Josh a bit timid—"all my debts."

Pride filled Josh's chest. This man better do the right thing.

The pastor's face softened. "That's an amazing testimony, young man."

His nephew held out the dollar. "I'm sorry. I won't do it again. I was starvin', but that isn't any excuse. I got a lotta people in your town to apologize to."

"Do you know Jesus?"

"Sure do. He's been with me even when people aren't too nice about what I did."

Joshua took the chance to move forward and stand beside them.

"I have an idea." The pastor stood. "Are you two staying for the service?"

"Yes, sir." Caleb's little legs swung back and forth as he sat on the pew. "This is my Uncle Josh and I'm Caleb."

"Well then, young Caleb, would you be willing to share your testimony in front of the church? I have a feeling you just might receive a lot of grace in our community, and the people would love to hear your story."

Two hours later, Josh sat with Caleb on the outside steps of the church. "How do you feel?" He patted his nephew's back.

"Pretty good, all considerin'. The people were forgivin' and I'm glad I got to say I was sorry." His little shoulders lifted in a shrug.

"But . . . ?"

"I feel bad for not payin' everyone back."

Even though the boy was going to have to work hard to earn the money to pay back his parents for this trip, it was astounding to Joshua that he wanted to pay more than he had to. "Sometimes true forgiveness is hard to swallow. Seems like it would be easier for us to feel like the worst of the worst and punish ourselves over and over again because we deserve it, right?"

"Exactly."

He grinned at the boy. "Grace and mercy are beautiful things. Receiving them is just as much a sign of respect and honor as apologizing and paying the debt."

With a lift of his chin, Caleb stood. "I'm ready to go to the next stop, Uncle Josh. I have a lot more apologies to make."

"You got it."

Monday, July 8

Anna sketched the area around the skull. From what she could surmise, the fossil was snout-down. Which would make the excavation a little easier at this top layer but didn't guarantee that all the parts would be intact. The jawbones and teeth were of most interest to her but were also the most fragile. Prayerfully it was all still there, but they wouldn't know until they worked through the layers of rock over time.

Time.

Something they didn't have a lot of. Especially with the way Mr. Oppenheim was acting.

At least he and his family hadn't shown up this morning. It was unnerving to have someone peering over their shoulders about everything. Made it almost impossible to work.

"That looks great, Anna." Tom stuck a brush between his teeth as he climbed back up to his perch.

"Thanks." Her crew was always encouraging. Respectful. Like brothers she never had.

What she wouldn't give to have Dad here with her right now. If he were in charge, they wouldn't be dealing with this mess. So it was *her* fault. Ugh. What an awful thought. With Josh gone, she was just going to have knuckle down and get the job done. He would be back soon enough. Which would be wonderful.

It didn't solve her current problems, though.

If she didn't resolve this soon, every dinosaur hunter in the country would be on Julian's doorstep demanding he give them rights too.

The only good thing about it was that he was in her corner. They'd signed contracts. But that didn't mean he wouldn't allow someone to dig somewhere else in the gulley. Money was a powerful bargaining chip.

"Uh-oh. Heads up." Zach shimmied his way down the rock wall. "Two riders coming this way."

Anna turned. A frilly parasol. Great. "Oh boy. Well, I guess I better go meet them." Not ready for another showdown with Mr. Oppenheim, she walked back over to her table and tucked all of her drawings away. After the man's nerve to suggest that his son would be better than her at the sketches, she didn't need any comments on her adequacy.

Why had she allowed these people to get under her skin?

No matter. It was her duty to deal with this.

Anna walked out and folded her hands in front of her. She could at least greet them with a smile. But then the male rider split away from Miss Oppenheim.

The clip-clop of the horse's hooves on the ground was the only sound.

"Good day, Miss Oppenheim." She really did *try* to mean it.

"Good day to you, Miss Lakeman." The lady hesitated and cleared her throat.

Zach was the closest and caught the hint. He hurried over and helped her dismount. Then, just as quickly, he headed back to his hammer and chisel.

Anna kept the corners of her mouth upturned even though it took work. "What can I do for you? We're quite busy, as you can see."

"I asked my brother to accompany me out here so that I might speak with you."

"Oh? And where is your brother going?"

"He's on an errand for my father."

Curious. Exactly what kind of errand would take the man north on Julian's property? Anna narrowed her eyes as she watched the man ride up the gulley. Scouting for bones no doubt. She wanted to growl but maintained her composure. Did people like that just think they could run over everyone else?

"I heard in town this morning that you and Mr. Ziegler are engaged."

It was a small town, so that shouldn't surprise her, but why would that bring frilly Miss Oppenheim out here? "Yes. Thank you."

"You don't deserve him, you know." The woman stared off into the distance.

What did she say? "I beg your pardon."

Then the beautiful woman turned an icy glare toward her. "You don't deserve it. There *is* no pardon for the way you've treated such a wonderful man." She held Anna's gaze. "And you know it."

A wonderful man, was he? And how exactly did this woman know *her* Josh so well? She lifted her chin and matched the woman's glare. "You don't know what you're talking abou—"

Rosemary Oppenheim's smug smile silenced Anna. "Oh, but I do. You see, Joshua and I have had many conversations. About you. Your fight. The fact that you didn't write to him once in three long years. Who do you think was a listening ear for him? Who do you think helped him to shoulder the grief he bore?" She angled a look at her, letting those long, perfect lashes half lower over her stunning—yet chilling—eyes. "Poor form, dear Anna. Did you honestly expect to keep a man like Joshua by treating him with such disdain?"

"I . . . you . . ." Anna clamped her mouth shut. Was this woman—this *intruder*—saying what she seemed to be saying? Had Joshua pursued this all-too-appealing, entirely feminine, beautiful socialite while at school? And then he marched back into Anna's life?

How *dare* h—

No. No. No. Joshua wouldn't have done that. He'd also done his best to avoid the woman the other day. But was that only because Anna had been watching?

Oh, it was all too confusing.

"You might want to put on a hat, Miss Lakeman." The sugar all but dripped from Rosemary Oppenheim's perfect lips. "You look a bit . . . peaked."

She sashayed her way back to her horse. Instead of waiting for assistance, she mounted the large paint with ease. The smirk she sent Anna was like a challenge.

But how could she win any contest against the likes of Rosemary Oppenheim?

twenty-two

"They trusted Truth was safest—
That it could never die
But would conquer ghastly error
And triumph by and by."

> ~Earl Douglass, from his
> poem *Nature's Noblemen*

THURSDAY, JULY 11

Joshua rode up to the Lakemans' home. All he wanted was to see Anna.

What would he do when he returned to school? It'd been less than a week, and he was champing at the bit to tell her everything that had happened. To hold her hand and gaze into her eyes.

How could he go an entire year?

He knocked on the door.

It opened and Anna gasped. "Joshua! You're back!" She hugged him and then dragged him inside. Something indecipherable flashed in her eyes. "Are you hungry? We were about to eat dinner."

"I'm famished. Dinner would be wonderful. But I might have a bit too much road grime on me. Caleb and I just returned, and after I dropped him off at the ranch, I came straight here."

"Nonsense. No one in this house cares about a little dirt. We dig in the dirt every day, remember?"

He chuckled and followed her down the hallway to Mr. Lakeman's room.

"Dad, look who's here." She pointed Joshua to a chair. "Sit. I'll fetch another plate and we can have a wonderful dinner together."

After Anna returned with another plate of food, Mr. Lakeman asked the blessing over the food, and they all dug in.

"This smells so good, Louise." His stomach gave a loud rumble.

"Thank you." Her cheeks turned pink. "I love to cook."

"And we are so glad you do." Anna lifted her plate and fork. "So Joshua, tell us all about your trip."

He took a bite of mashed potatoes and swallowed. "Well, it was quite an adventure. We went to the train in Green River first and Caleb was so brave. He told the man at the ticket office what he'd done and asked how much a ticket to Cheyenne was so that he could pay it back. The man was so taken aback that he simply stared at the boy for several moments. Then he told him how admirable it was for him to come forward. He didn't charge him for the ticket.

"So then we traveled by train and went east. Stopping at each place Caleb had been. He tried to remember every place. Which was quite remarkable. Several establishments appreciated the apology and took the reimbursement, while others were shocked and amazed that we would travel back so Caleb could do the right thing. We had some wonderful conversations with people and Caleb shared how scared he'd been.

What it had been like to be hungry . . . starving. Then to be so ashamed that he didn't think he could come home."

"What brought him back?" Anna's eyes sparkled with tears.

"He remembered the story of the prodigal son in the Bible and he knew that his family loved him. As embarrassed as he was, he said that was nothing compared to his fear. So he started his way home."

"That's a long way for a little boy to travel all by himself." Louise appeared upset by the whole thing.

Joshua nodded. "I have to admit it opened my eyes to how many children are out there living on their own. How is it that we have become so blind to this problem?"

He shared a long glance with Anna. The thought of having their own children had been on his mind a lot. Especially after seeing the dirty and hungry children along the way. If he could have brought them all home, he would have. Anna had always had a soft spot for children too. Perhaps, in addition to their own children, they could take in some others? It was definitely a discussion that needed to be had.

"So catch me up on all that is happening out at the dig?" He took another bite of food.

Anna rolled her eyes. "Mr. Oppenheim insists on coming to the dig every day. Even though Mr. Gilbert has spoken to him several times about all the legalities."

"Since it took me longer with Caleb than I'd initially anticipated, I have to admit that I secretly hoped that they would be gone by now." His shoulders drooped. "No such luck, then?"

She put a hand to her chest. Why did she look so . . . relieved?

"No. Sorry. They're still here. We're waiting to hear official word from the judge that Mr. Gilbert contacted. Funny thing, Albert and Rosemary Oppenheim only returned once. They

haven't been back since and have stayed up in Green River."
Anna studied him.

"Huh. Well, that's fine with me. I'd prefer they all pack up and head back to Chicago."

Mr. Lakeman moved the conversation back to the dig and the work they were hoping to get done before Joshua had to head back to school. It was exciting to be part of something that could have such an impact on science.

After dinner, Joshua accompanied Anna down to the creek. Their nightly ritual was becoming one of his favorite parts of the day. The wind provided a cooling breeze after the heat of the day.

"Miss Oppenheim rode out to see me while you were gone." She kept her gaze forward and fidgeted with her handkerchief.

Every good feeling he had now plummeted like a giant boulder dragging him down to the bottom of a deep lake. "Oh?" He swallowed.

"Yes. She told me that you shared with her about our fight and the fact that I hadn't written to you even once."

If only he could take back all his conversations with Rosemary over the past three years. It had all been a huge mistake, but he hadn't seen it at the time. "Anna . . . I'm so sorr—"

She held up a hand and he clamped his mouth shut. "I have to admit, I was pretty upset with you after that conversation. But I've been praying about it and have calmed down."

So that must have been why she appeared hesitant earlier. He couldn't blame her. "Let me explain."

"I don't think I'm ready for that, Josh. She's a beautiful woman. Wealthy. Lives in Chicago. Her father could probably help you to be the greatest physician that city has ever seen."

The lump in his throat grew. "What are you saying?"

"I don't want to hold you back, Josh. I know you love me.

And I love you. I don't doubt that or your faithfulness to me. But . . ." She bit her lip and her eyes shimmered.

No. He couldn't allow her to walk away from him. Not now. "But . . . what?"

"She said I don't deserve you. And I'm beginning to think she's correct."

FRIDAY, JULY 12

It had to be almost one hundred degrees today. Anna wiped the sweat from her brow so it wouldn't drip onto the page of her latest sketch. If she caused the slightest smudge, all her hard work would have to be redone.

A horse approached from the north. Was that Mr. Gilbert?

She set everything aside and went out to greet him, praying for favorable results.

But as soon as she ventured out from under the canopy, the sun made the brutal heat that much more apparent. "Mr. Gilbert!" She waved.

He rode up next to her. "Let's get in the shade, shall we?"

"That would be much appreciated." She walked back over to the canopy.

He dismounted.

She tried to interpret his expression. "I hope you have come with some good news?"

He pursed his lips. "Yes, I believe it is for the most part. Would you like Mr. Ziegler to hear this as well?"

It wasn't a bad question. Josh was her betrothed after all. At least for now. They hadn't resolved anything last night other than stating their love for one another and saying goodnight without a hug or touch of any kind. "Joshua," she called down the gulley. Things were just . . . awkward. Because she wasn't convinced that he wanted to be here. Maybe once he went back to Chicago, he would change his mind? That would break her heart. Best to prepare herself for it now. "Would you come down here, please?"

When he had joined them, Mr. Gilbert laid some papers on the table. "The judge has ruled that the verbal agreement between your father and his investor stands, so Mr. Oppenheim is not allowed to supersede your father's decisions."

"That's wonderful news!" She clasped her hands together.

"But"—the lawyer tapped the papers—"my friend is not convinced that women belong in science of any kind. He also isn't sure that a female could produce better drawings than a man for publication."

"What? That's preposterous!" Of course the world she lived in was dominated by men, but the insult stung. Her drawings were better than any others she'd seen.

"Now hold on, he didn't say that he wouldn't allow it, just that he wasn't sure. So he proposed that we have someone with expertise compare a few different examples from each of you so the most accurate sketch may be chosen for official publication."

She swallowed. Dad believed that her drawings were the best, but what if they weren't? "All right. What does he require?"

"Drawings from both you and Albert Oppenheim. Of the exact same fossil. The impartial party will come and examine the specimen and the sketches. He won't know who has drawn which one and he will decide which is the most accurate." Mr. Gilbert shrugged. "That's the best I could do."

What choice did she have? She tucked her hair behind her ear and looked down at the table. "All right, then. You're sure it will be an expert in the field?"

"That's what the judge promised."

"Okay. How do we let the Oppenheims know?"

"I will go see them this afternoon." He pulled a document

out of his briefcase. "You'll need to sign this to indicate that you are in agreement with the terms. I think with that, the elder Mr. Oppenheim will be willing to sign the original contracts."

She blew out her breath through her lips. "The sooner this is over, the better. I can't allow someone to come in and trample all over my dad's find for the simple reason that they have money."

After signing the papers, she watched as Mr. Gilbert left. This wasn't over. Was she strong enough to deal with a decision that wasn't made in her favor?

"You okay?" Joshua put a hand on the small of her back.

"Sure. I'm fine." She clenched her jaw. "You know, I think I'll walk up the washout and see if there's anything else interesting to sketch."

"You're aggravated by all of this, aren't you?"

"How could you tell?" She didn't mean for her words to come out snippy. They just . . . did.

"Oh, I don't know. The way you look like you want to strangle the next person you see?"

"Exactly." She grabbed a sketchpad and some pencils. "I don't mean to take it out on you. I want to fix all of this. Who knows, maybe I'll find something else extraordinary to dig?" She faked a grin.

"All right. Well, don't go too far. That way you can holler if you need me."

Why was he always so sweet and encouraging?

Well, other than when he was infuriating her and arguing with her. Probably why they were such a good match. He could handle her temper and moods. "I'll bring one of the rifles with me. Just in case of snakes."

"Good."

Rosemary Oppenheim was right. She *didn't* deserve him. But how could she let him go—especially after she just got him back?

Stomping her way up the mini-canyon, she worked through her thoughts. There was a good chance Albert Oppenheim was skilled at sketching. What if he was as good as she? She'd simply have to trust in her own skill and ability. Do her best.

But what if the expert decided against her? Would that mean an end to her work in paleontology?

Without her work with her father . . . without Joshua . . . She would be lost.

twenty-three

"I have been inspired to rise above these little mean things like jealousy and resentment. I hope it is my privilege to live in a higher atmosphere."

~Earl Douglass

MONDAY, JULY 15

The Oppenheims were back at the dig this morning. And Joshua hadn't had a moment's peace.

Not only was Rosemary beside him every single moment, but she chattered on incessantly. Asking one question after another. Reciting facts she'd obviously memorized out of some book about fossilized bones.

It didn't help that every time he chanced a glance at Anna, she had that frustrated *V* in her brow. She had her own tag-along, too. Albert. Wherever she went, he went. Whatever she drew, he drew.

And watching every moment of it was Mr. Oswald Oppenheim.

The one good thing that had come of their visit was the

fact that he had signed the contracts. But now he seemed determined to get at least his son's name on the dig papers. Wasn't it enough that the Oppenheim name would be on the exhibit in the museum?

Rosemary seemed determined to annoy him. The woman would not leave him alone. After Anna shared about their little get-together the other day, he was more than a little concerned. But if he was downright rude to the daughter of the investor, that could spell disaster of another sort for the Lakemans.

To make matters worse, Walker had come to see Anna twice during the day since Joshua returned. Had the man come to see her while he was gone?

The thought wasn't a pleasant one.

But it wasn't like he could tell the man what to do. They were on his property after all.

If he spoke with Anna about it at lunch, would she get upset with him?

Probably.

Rosemary was droning on about something she'd read. But he hadn't been listening for a while now.

He glanced up to see Walker headed toward them.

Great. The man was coming to see Anna.

Again.

Well, this time, he'd be in the middle of it. It was a good time for a break anyway. He slid down to the ground. "Excuse me, Miss Oppenheim."

He strode toward the canopy where Anna was working, only to hear footsteps behind him. Rosemary was following. Of course she was.

He went straight for the water and then grabbed a sandwich. He reached Anna before Walker did. "How are things going today, boss?" He winked at her.

She blew some hair off her forehead and grimaced.

"That good, huh?" he whispered.

"It looks like you're having a lovely time." The words were sharp.

"Anna?" Walker had reached them.

She turned and looked at the other man. "Julian, how can I help you?"

The big man crossed his arms over his chest. "I've been speaking with my lawyer."

Uh-oh. Julian Walker resembled his father with the fierce look on his face.

"Gracious. Have I done something wrong?" She stepped toward him. "I'm so sorry, Julian."

"No," he ground out. And sent a sideways glance to the Oppenheims. "But I don't appreciate these other folks. They are not allowed on my property."

Mr. Oppenheim was quick to jump into the fray. "I beg your pardon, young man. It's *my* money that's financing this project."

"I don't care about your money." Walker spat. "It's my land. And my contract is with Miss Lakeman. Not you. Now kindly get off my property before I send for the sheriff."

"Do you have any idea who you're speaking to?" The older man's chest puffed out again.

"Sir. I'm sorry to interrupt." Joshua couldn't pass up this chance to get rid of the thorn in his side. Even if he was taking up sides with Walker. "But I don't think you realize who *you* are speaking to. This man happens to own the largest and most prosperous ranch in all of Wyoming Territory. I would respect his wishes."

Walker stepped closer to the older man. He towered over the investor.

Anna moved between them. "Mr. Oppenheim. I think it's best if you leave. I'll clear this up with Mr. Walker."

"I have never been treated in such a manner!" Mr. Oppenheim sputtered.

"I'm sorry. I'll do my best to find a way we can all work together amicably." Anna held out a hand to their conveyance.

"Get off my land." Walker stepped closer.

"Daddy, I think we better leave." Rosemary scurried to the wagon.

After the three Oppenheims piled into the wagon and left, Anna turned to Walker. "Thank you. That was genius." She patted his arm.

Well, she didn't need to go touching the man.

Walker grinned. "I thought of it the other day but had to ask Mr. Gilbert if it would actually work. I don't mind being the bad guy if it keeps them from annoying you."

Anna hugged him.

It took everything in Joshua to keep from lunging forward and pulling them apart.

"Will you come see some of my new blooms? I think you'll like them." Walker's expression had transformed back to congenial.

Joshua touched Anna's arm, but she spoke before he could say anything. "Of course. I'll take a break in a few minutes and come up. Is that all right?"

"Wonderful." Walker took long strides back toward his house.

Once he was a good distance away, Joshua lowered his voice. "You need to be careful."

"Whatever do you mean?" Hands on her hips, she pointed her narrowed eyes at him. So much for appreciating her fiancé's concern.

"My gut is telling me that something isn't right about how Julian acts around you. I think he's a bit infatuated."

"Honestly, Josh. Haven't we been over this enough?"

No. They hadn't. Because she wasn't seeing things clearly. "You know that I feel something is off with him. I don't want anything to happen to you."

"You don't have anything to worry about. Julian is harmless. He's been nothing but kind to me. Everyone should be given grace, right?"

He shook his head. "I don't think you should spend so much time with him. It will make him think you care about him."

"I do." She stalked to her table and straightened some papers. "Shouldn't we *all* care about him?"

"You know what I mean, Anna."

The fire in her eyes told him he should tread carefully. "Yes, I do. And I think it's silly. But I don't want to argue with you right now. The men are watching."

"Fine. But I'm not done discussing this."

Why couldn't he let it go? "You can discuss it all you want. Just not with me." She turned on her heel and stomped away with her sketchpad.

On the way home, Joshua allowed his horse to plod along. It had been a long day. And Anna was still mad at him.

He deserved it. His jealousy had reared its ugly head once again. Then there was the conundrum with Rosemary. He didn't even know how to approach that. Anna was adamant about how much she loved him but didn't deserve him.

If Rosemary had wanted to drive a wedge between them, she was definitely accomplishing it.

Needing to relieve himself, he pulled on the reins. "Whoa."

Climbing down, he walked over to a tree, but something caught his eye.

What on earth? He walked back over in front of his horse. A bunch of branches and leaves were in a pile. Had someone wanted to start a fire and then gave up? It was a mess. Why would anyone leave a pile of debris like this?

He kicked one of the branches with the toe of his boot.

The whole pile collapsed and fell.

Peering down into the hole, Joshua's stomach sank.

A trap.

Was it for him?

A blast in the distance made him drop down to the ground and he scrambled behind a fat tree.

Another shot rang out and bark flew around him.

Guess that answered his question.

Lowering himself into the brush as quietly as he could, he put his hands over his head and held his breath.

Someone moved closer. A twig snapped. Then the rustle of branches.

A rock lay under his face, so Joshua picked it up and threw it as far as he could. Maybe whoever it was would head in that direction.

Another shot.

Then footsteps.

But instead of going away, they came closer.

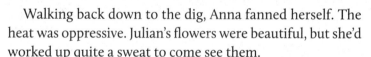

Walking back down to the dig, Anna fanned herself. The heat was oppressive. Julian's flowers were beautiful, but she'd worked up quite a sweat to come see them.

The walk had calmed her, which was good because Joshua's words had gotten to her. Julian was different. And yes, he was a bit infatuated with her. But it wasn't any different from that horrid Miss Oppenheim who couldn't seem to go two seconds without being right next to Joshua.

Anna was in debt to Julian for his quick thinking. Now if only she could keep the Oppenheims away with this excuse forever. But that wasn't fair. Albert Oppenheim had to be given the opportunity to draw the same fossil that she drew.

But it was nice to be rid of them for a little bit. She would revel in the reprieve for a few days. At least.

The thought made her smile.

She hated seeing how that rich woman flaunted time with

her fiancé by tossing a look Anna's direction every so often. What did she hope to prove?

She'd made it very clear that Anna shouldn't have Joshua. There were times she'd begun to believe it. Even though she loved him more each day. But she didn't have peace about anything right now. Nothing in her life was on solid ground. If she wanted grace, she had to extend grace.

She should probably apologize to Joshua. He had to get home this evening to help out with some things at home, but tomorrow night they could have a long chat.

She'd work on how she handled Julian. And would do her best to respect Joshua's feelings.

And she'd ask her fiancé if Miss Rosemary Oppenheim had ever been anything more than a friend to him.

⌇

Julian stood outside the Lakemans' front door. Mr. Lakeman had invited him, but he'd never had an invitation before.

It was awkward. He wanted to see the man again. To see if there really were fathers that cared about their children.

Anna was nice. She seemed to love her father. Why would she love him and do things for him if he was mean?

Taking a deep breath, he knocked.

Anna opened the door. "Hi, Julian. You're here to see Dad? He told me he invited you."

"Yes." He swallowed. Didn't know what else to say.

She led him down a hallway. "Here you go." She held an arm out toward the open door. "Go on in. You two can talk while I get us some of Louise's fresh pie."

"All right." He took a reluctant step into the room and held his hat in his hands. "Good evening, Mr. Lakeman."

"Call me Peter. How are you today, Julian?"

"I'm fine."

"Come on in and sit. Make yourself at home."

He sat in a chair and stared at the man.

Mr. Lakeman asked him questions about his ranch. The weather. His garden.

Why was this man being nice to him? It seemed odd considering how the rest of Walker Creek treated him. He didn't know what to ask the man. But shouldn't he do the same and ask questions?

Then he remembered the rock he'd put in his pocket. "I have something I'd like to show you. Could you tell me if it is a fossil or a rock?"

"Sure. I'd love to see it."

Julian pulled out the rock. But two faded blue ribbons came out with it.

They fell onto Mr. Lakeman's bed.

Julian snatched them up and shoved them back in his pocket.

He handed the rock to Mr. Lakeman. "Is this . . . is this a fossil?" He cleared his throat.

The older man's eyes were full of questions.

He'd seen.

twenty-four

"I was full of courage and the highest hopes. . . ."

~Earl Douglass

The days were beginning to wear on her. They'd had record-breaking heat for almost a week now and Anna was finding it hard to keep up with everything. Between the dig and all the watering of her garden at home, and spending time with Dad and Joshua—which she loved . . .

One of these days, she needed to go home and go to bed. Get some rest. It might help her to see things clearer.

She and Joshua had settled into a comfortable rhythm and routine. He'd flat-out told her that he wasn't the least bit interested in Rosemary. Never was. Never would be. He didn't want to stay in Chicago. He wanted to be here.

At the time, she'd been too tired to voice every doubt and question she had. She loved him. Needed him. And desperately needed to rely on his strength right now. Otherwise, she might not make it through.

Julian had asked her to see some more flowers today, and she'd gone. Because he'd been so sweet and had kept the Oppenheims away.

She owed him her gratitude for that one. It had been nice to work in peace. But she'd have to allow them back soon. She had promised to work it out with Julian, after all. Maybe she could wait until Mr. Gilbert knew that their expert was coming.

That could be weeks though. Could she keep them away that long?

What if Mr. Oppenheim decided to not give them any more funding? They'd have a difficult time finding people to work for free, that was for sure.

But the fire she'd seen on Joshua's face when she told him she was walking up to Julian's to see the flowers hadn't been pleasant. She tried not to get upset with him. She could understand, to an extent. He was jealous. That was all.

But he had nothing to fear. She'd simply have to make sure she let him know that this evening.

Joshua had gone straight to her house, and she'd promised she would soon follow.

So she gathered up all of her things and made sure everything else was locked up tight. With a wave to Zach, Luke, and Tom, she climbed on Misty and turned her toward home.

As soon as she walked in the door, she went straight back to Dad's room. She should just forget about all the other stuff and look forward to spending a quiet evening with the two men she loved. All this worrying was getting her nowhere.

But when she rounded the corner into Dad's room, he and Josh both wore frowns. "What's going on?"

Joshua's arms were crossed over his chest. "I don't think you should visit Julian unaccompanied anymore."

"I agree." Dad waved her over. "Please come sit. I have something to tell you."

Blinking several times, she took a breath and did as he asked. "All right. What is it?"

"When Julian was here the other night he pulled a rock out that he wanted me to examine. And two blue ribbons fell out of his pocket."

"And?" Why were the two men she loved most so paranoid?

"What is a grown man doing with ribbons?"

She looked between her father and Joshua. "He uses all manner of things to tie flowers to stakes. I've seen some old ribbons in his garden, twine, rope, torn shirts, all sorts of things."

"But sweetheart, they were blue." Dad sighed.

"What are you getting at?" She narrowed her eyes.

Joshua and her father shared a glance. "The ribbons Mary wore the day she disappeared were blue."

He couldn't be saying . . . She stood up. "Isn't that a bit farfetched? Why would he carry around ribbons for *ten years?* Isn't it more logical that he had them in his pocket so that he could work in his garden? His mother had plenty of ribbon, I'm sure."

Her father sighed. "They were faded blue. With white stripes."

Joshua's eyes were full of sadness. "Mary's ribbons were blue with white stripes. To match the dress she wore that day."

Dad cleared his throat. "I understand that you want to be nice to him, Anna. And I wanted to reach out to him as well, but I agree with Joshua—based on what he's told me has happened out at the dig—I think Julian Walker is becoming obsessed with you."

She snapped her gaze back and forth between the two. So

the ribbons were similar to Mary's. That had nothing to do with *her*. "Really? Both of you? Can't you see that Julian simply needs a friend?" She shook her head. "You know, I talked about him when I was a kid. Because he was odd. And his father was mean. But Mary taught me to believe the best in people. I always wished I had her courage to do that. Once she was gone, I vowed that I would be more like her. She showed love to everyone."

Her dad looked at her with such a sober countenance. "Yes, but what does that kind of love look like? Mary was a child. All of ten years old. Completely untainted by the world and all the horrors it contains."

How could she respond? The two men she loved were questioning her judgment. They thought Julian was a threat. It was absurd. "But don't you think that love can change a person? I believe that Mary had a wonderful impact on Julian. Just like his mother had. He was different before his mother left. Don't you remember?"

"Isn't it dangerous to believe and rely on love changing a person here on this earth?" Dad shook his head. "The only love that can truly change anything or anyone is God's love. His is supernatural. Our love here on earth fails. It falters. It isn't enough. We shouldn't love someone based on the idea that they will change. That's wrong thinking." He leaned back against the pillows. "I didn't love your mother so that I could change her. She wasn't perfect by any means, but she was wonderful. Just as she was. We prayed together that the good Lord would mold us, prune our hearts and lives. It had to be of Him. Not of ourselves."

Joshua leaned forward and put his elbows on his knees. "Is there something you wish you could change in me? That you're hoping your love can cure?"

"Of course not." She winced. Well, maybe the whole fact that he'd shared about their fight with a beautiful woman.

No. This wasn't about that. Why were they ganging up on her? "I know you have flaws. As do I. I'm thinking that we love and forgive. Give second chances. Give those who haven't been loved unconditionally a sense of what God's love is."

"That's an awfully tall order, Anna." Her father leaned his head back on his pillows. "How many times do you forgive?"

"Jesus said seventy times seven." She lifted her chin. "What has Julian done that needs to be forgiven? Have you two convicted him of some heinous crime?"

Joshua's voice was low and sounded full of grit. "I don't have any proof. I have a feeling in my stomach that makes me wary. It's the way he looks at you."

"What about it?" She swallowed and put a hand to her waist. When she stared deep into his eyes, she didn't like what she saw there. It almost looked like . . .

Fear.

For her.

Joshua's voice, though, was firm. "It reminds me of the way he looked at Mary."

───※───

Joshua leaned back, his heart heavy. But after hearing what Peter had to say about his visit with Julian, he knew his instincts were correct. "I don't want to say anything else that sounds condemning of Julian, all right?"

Anna studied him for several moments and then her shoulders relaxed a bit. "All right."

"But my hackles have been up after watching him with you. Yes, I'm jealous. You're my fiancée. I can't wait to marry you. I want to protect you from anyone that might hurt you." How could he convince her that Julian might be dangerous? Maybe if he told her that someone shot at him, but then she'd really think he'd lost his mind.

"Who says that he's going to hurt me?" She stiffened again, her lips in a thin line.

He held up a hand. "I'm saying that he might hurt you emotionally. What if you can't help him like you hoped? What if he says something that breaks your heart? And what if—hear me out—what if you find out that he has done something terrible? How will that affect you?"

She gazed at him. Then shifted her glance to her father. "I appreciate the fact that you both want to protect me. But didn't you see how Julian came to my—our—rescue with the Oppenheims? That has brought me so much relief. We wouldn't be able to even do this dig without his permission. Another thing to be grateful to him for. He's been patient and taught me about gardening. All so I could bring you something beautiful, Dad. Doesn't all of that count for something?"

Peter speared Joshua with a look. They weren't going to convince her of anything. Not today. Maybe not for a long while. He'd said nothing to Anna yet of his suspicions of Walker with the rope that had sent him careening, the trap on the trail that he used, and then the gunshots. But he'd shared them with her father.

The simple fact that Julian Walker carried those ribbons around in his pocket should have been enough to convince Anna. But no. For some reason, she was digging her heels in. If they told her about their other suspicions now, she'd probably blame it on the Oppenheims. There was no winning because she was blind to the whole situation. Which made Joshua more than a little afraid for her.

"Anna." He breathed deep as he peered down at his shoes. "I need to ask you something, and as the man you love and have agreed to marry, I'm hoping you will respect my opinion. And your father's."

Her lips moved into a thin line. "Yes?"

"Will you please—for me and your father—not go over to Julian's anymore without someone else with you?"

Shaking her head, she glared from him to her father and back to him. "I can't believe you two!"

"Don't look at me like that!" Mr. Lakeman's voice boomed.

Anna jumped back, her eyes wide. "Dad—"

"No. No more." Red suffused his cheeks. "I forbid it. Plain and simple."

twenty-five

"It is hard when a man has toiled all his life with unflagging energy and enthusiasm to be cut off when he had gotten where he could make his efforts count, yet the loss is not his. It is the loss to his family and to science."

~Earl Douglass

THURSDAY, JULY 18

Staring off into the distance, Anna couldn't believe it was already past mid-July. Joshua was leaving at the end of the month. What would she do when he went back to school? She wouldn't see him for a year. Would they be able to make it with just letters? Every time she thought about it, her stomach tied up in knots. The past three years didn't give her a lot of confidence.

With a lift of her chin, she forced herself to be positive. They'd patched things up. Shared from their hearts. They would be fine.

Just fine.

But last night's discussion with him and Dad had not gone

as she expected. Of course, they both wanted to protect her. They loved her. But they couldn't see what she could see.

Julian needed someone to help him.

Still . . . Dad hadn't raised his voice at her like that in years. So she'd promised and let the whole thing drop. But deep down, her conviction was still there. She would not neglect Julian again as she had after Mary disappeared.

With no best friend encouraging her to speak to him at school, she'd stopped trying.

He came to school and left.

Then didn't return one day.

Then he was gone from Walker Creek completely.

No one had been invited out to the Walker property since Mrs. Walker left. Except Mary.

Then there was Damian.

Stories had flown through the community over the years that he must be worse than his old man since Mrs. Walker kept him hidden away.

Anna shivered. It didn't matter. This was her chance to do something in honor of Mary. And Julian had been nothing but kind and generous to her.

A rumble of a wagon in the distance made her steel herself. She'd sent word last night to the Oppenheims via Mr. Gilbert. After seeing Julian's new flowers yesterday, she'd asked him for permission to have the investor and his family come once a week out to the dig site. Surely her team could deal with the inconvenience one day a week. It should also appease the man who so graciously poured out a lot of his money to fund the dig.

Regardless of his motivation.

As she turned to greet the wagon, she pasted on a smile and willed herself to be nice. She could do this. For her father.

Mr. Oppenheim nodded at her from his seat. "Miss Lakeman."

"Mr. Oppenheim. It's good to see you today. Miss Oppenheim, Mr. Oppenheim." She made sure to meet the gaze of each family member.

Albert jumped down from the wagon. "I need to see the fossils that you have chosen for us to draw." His nose lifted in the air. As he came closer, he brushed up against her shoulder and bumped her. "I have studied at the finest schools in the nation. You won't win."

"What was that, Albert?" Mr. Oppenheim asked as he helped Rosemary down from the wagon seat. She held another frilly parasol that matched her outfit.

"Nothing, Father." Albert smirked at Anna.

She wouldn't stoop to his level. She wouldn't. So she kept that fake smile attached and complimented each one of them on their extraordinary choices throughout the morning.

Oh, why had she promised Dad, as she left the house this morning, that she would do her best not to argue with anyone today?

Rosemary headed straight to Joshua and acted like it was her right to be glued to his side. Mr. Oppenheim kept saying that his daughter was fascinated with the work of digging for the fossils. Even though it was unseemly for a gentlewoman like herself to be digging in the dirt, she had asked about going to college for science. Mr. Oppenheim said that if his daughter put her mind to it, he wouldn't deny her the possibility. The Oppenheim name could be attached to many significant digs, and he would be happy about that.

So it wasn't okay for a woman of lesser status to be a paleontologist, but if a woman from a wealthy family wanted to do it, that was acceptable?

The gall of the man.

With all the people around, she'd barely gotten to say two words to Joshua at lunch. Then the afternoon rolled around, and Mr. Oppenheim tried to take over. He wanted the team digging for one of the large rib bones.

No matter how many times she explained to him that it was too dangerous to remove a bone lower in the slab because of the cracks and the layers in the rock, he kept insisting. Telling her guys what to do.

Finally, Zach came down off the wall and got in Mr. Oppenheim's face. "I take direction from *Miss Lakeman*. No one else, sir. She's been doing this for fifteen years. You would do well to listen to her expertise."

Joshua walked up at that moment with Rosemary, who had her hands on her hips. She looked at Zach. "Don't you dare speak to my father that way!"

Joshua glared down at her. "Miss Oppenheim, you have no authority here."

She gave an undignified gasp and marched away.

Anna turned to Mr. Oppenheim one more time. "You must remember, sir, that I know what's best for this dig. And I also have my father's experience and wisdom behind what we're doing and how we're doing it. Every night I go over every inch of the site in detail with him. He pores over all the sketches and studies every fracture in the structure. I listen to him because he knows what he's talking about. I would ask that you do the same for me."

"Fine." The man lifted that chin again, which told her he wasn't pleased.

Would the day never end? Whose idea was it anyway to invite them back?

If she could turn back the clock, she would. And change her mind on that.

She whipped around and stormed back to her table—then frowned. Where . . . ? She checked the ground . . . her satchel . . . even the crates.

Someone had stolen her pencils. Every last one of them.

FRIDAY, JULY 19

Julian and Damian watched Anna and Joshua across the gulley. Julian lifted the field glasses to get a closer look.

"Not what you wanted to see, is it, brother? I told you he was trouble." Damian's voice barked at him.

A low growl escaped his lips as Joshua leaned in to hug Anna. "No . . . she's mine." He groaned the words.

"I told you. Now let me take care of it."

Julian bristled. *He* wanted Anna. No . . . he needed her. She was the one left who could fix him.

"Well?" Damian's impatience grew with every second that passed.

"Let me think, will you?" His brother's attempts to remove Joshua with an accident had failed. And then he'd gotten so angry that he'd shot at Ziegler. Not that Julian didn't want the other man gone, but his brother had missed, and Julian noticed the way Ziegler now looked at him.

"There's nothing to think about. He needs to be gone. That's the only way you'll have Anna and you know it."

Julian lowered the field glasses. He couldn't watch any more. It hurt. The light and dark inside him warred with one another. "But Joshua Ziegler has been kind and respectful to me."

"Oh really? What about lately? Does he look like he trusts you? Do you really think he would be nice to you if Anna chose you over him?"

"Well, no."

"See? I'll take care of it." .

Julian stared across the gulley at the couple. "Fine."

"What about her father?"

"What about him?" That wasn't part of the plan. What did Damian care about Anna's father?

"You said yourself that he saw the ribbons."

He clenched his fists. "Don't you dare hurt Mr. Lakeman. I won't stand for it. Anna loves him."

His brother grunted. "You don't know what's good for you."

"Oh, and you do?" Damian *always* thought he knew best.

"As a matter of fact, I do. You'd do well to remember that. Who takes care of you? Who makes sure that you are safe and protected? The town doesn't hate you. They hate *me*. Because they hated our father. Well, I don't mind being the one everybody fears. Somebody has to stand up and take care of things and you're too soft."

The words stung. "Just promise me you won't hurt Mr. Lakeman."

Silence stretched for several seconds. "I promise."

Julian released his breath.

"For now . . ."

twenty-six

"They found the leaves were scattered,
With here and there a page;
And some were being written
And some were dim with age."

~Earl Douglass,
from his poem *Nature's Noblemen*

SATURDAY, JULY 20

They were making great progress on the bones from the spine. Well, progress for a small, five-person team on a paleontological dig where everything moved at a snail's pace because of the tedious nature of their work. But Anna couldn't be more pleased.

And not just with the dig.

The Oppenheims weren't underfoot every day. Joshua convinced her he never cared for Rosemary and never would. Dad was discovering something new each night when she showed him her sketches.

Now she had a detailed plan in front of her, with each item numbered in order of how it should be removed from the rock.

The larger bones appeared intact from the surface, but she and her team didn't know what to expect underneath. That was the most difficult part, using great care with the removal using delicate tools to ensure they didn't have anything crumble or break off in the rock. Even though the bones were fossilized, they were still fragile.

She darted a glance across the washout. Julian's garden bloomed in a vast array of color. It drew her eye often—a welcome sight after staring at rock and dirt all day long.

As she'd promised Joshua and her father, she hadn't gone to see Julian without someone else along. The big man probably felt like something was off, that she didn't trust him—which wasn't true—but hopefully he wouldn't go back in his shell. They'd made so much progress. Mary would be so happy to see Julian smiling.

Anna had almost gotten him to laugh. Almost. Hopefully one day.

Losing a mother was so hard. She'd gone through that herself. But having a violent father must have made everything that much worse for Julian and his brother.

The men who worked for Walker Ranch all these years had plenty to say about how Randall Walker had done things. How his temper was brutal.

Everyone suspected he'd treated his family much worse than anyone else. Especially since no one ever saw Julian's mom. At least not on a regular basis.

Anna had seen her maybe twice.

She was a lovely woman with a warm smile. But there was always a bit of a haunting in her eyes. It made Anna feel sad as a child.

The sound of a horse's hooves echoed through their little canyon.

Anna lifted her face from the drawing she'd been working on. All the guys were busy digging. Who was that?

Then the top hat became all too visible.

Albert Oppenheim.

Now what was he doing here? She wasn't expecting any of that family again until Thursday.

She set her pencil down and let out a grunt. She did *not* have time for this today. Neither did she have any desire to deal with this arrogant man.

He rode up and dismounted, a swagger in his step as he approached her.

"Good morning, Mr. Oppenheim."

"Good morning to you, Miss Lakeman."

She waited for him to state his business.

"Would you perhaps pour me a cup of coffee?"

Huh? He came out here for coffee? "Um . . . of course." She went to serve her guest.

When she returned, he was leaning over her sketches. What was he up to? "Here you go." She handed him the cup and scooched her way to her table, hoping he would take the hint and move away from her work.

He barely stepped to the side. "You surprise me, Miss Lakeman."

"Why is that?"

"You are indeed good at the details."

His compliment took her back. "Thank you."

"My father heard from Mr. Gilbert that our expert will be here next week."

"Oh?" She hadn't heard that but wouldn't put any weight behind Albert's words. Not until she checked with Mr. Gilbert herself.

He sipped his coffee. "I wanted to take another look at the fossils before returning on Thursday to do my drawings."

She went to the crate where they kept them locked up and opened it up.

"Oh my goodness, I'm so sorry."

Her head snapped back to him.

His cup lay on its side. The contents spreading over several of her sketches.

She rushed to the table, but it was too late. The coffee had spread over the three most important sketches. The ones she'd worked on for the judge. Hours of work were gone.

With a glance at Albert, she couldn't even register any words.

The smug smile he sent her as he shrugged lit a fire in her belly.

"You did that on purpose!" Her yell would certainly draw the attention of the men, but she didn't care. She stepped closer to her adversary and narrowed her eyes. "You horrible, conniving man. Leave. Leave now. Before Mr. Walker catches sight of you here."

The smile didn't diminish. It grew. "I've heard enough rumors in town to know that you must have put Mr. Walker up to his demands. Now who's the conniving one?"

A shiver ran up her spine. The evil look in his eyes made her stomach quiver.

"Is everything okay, Anna?" Joshua was at her side in a few quick steps, followed by the others.

"Mr. Oppenheim was just leaving." She glared at the man.

"It was a simple accident. I came here to see the fossils." Albert dipped his head.

She stomped over to the crate. "Forget it." She closed and locked it. "Not after that little stunt."

"Fine." He smacked his lips. "I'll see you on Thursday."

As she watched him walk to his horse, the anger burned inside her throat. If only she knew how to spit properly. As unladylike as that was, she'd love to spit in his face.

What a horrid thought.

"Are you all right?" Joshua touched her elbow.

"No. I'm not all right." She pointed to the table. "Look."

Joshua stole another glance at the woman he loved. Albert Oppenheim had ruined several of her sketches on purpose.

But after her initial outburst, where she'd called the man a slimy cheater and shattered the coffee cup on the ground, she'd been silent.

Too silent.

Giving her a bit of space was the best thing right now. For how long though, he wasn't sure. Because her temper was sure to get the best of her sooner or later.

A deep rumble sounded above his head. Oh no. Dark storm clouds were heading their way. "Zach! Look!"

The team leader looked up. "Quick! Get the tarps in place."

As they rushed around to cover the exposed fossils they'd been working on, he glanced at Anna. Rain was rare out here in the summer, but they were always prepared.

"Anna! Storm!"

Her head snapped up and she rushed into motion, packing the fossils in the crates and preparing them to be loaded on the wagon. Just in case.

Prayerfully this wouldn't cause another flash flood. But if it did, they had to be prepared for it.

Thunder grew in the distance and the day darkened.

Walker ran across the washout. "How can I help?"

Zach shouted directions to all of them and they packed as if they were being chased by the devil himself.

They loaded crates in the wagon, along with Anna's satchel. The canopy and makeshift table were taken down and loaded.

Anna's gaze was frantic as she peered around. The rain started coming down in massive sheets of water.

In a matter of seconds, they were all drenched.

"We've got to go now, Anna. We can't get caught in this gulley if it floods." Joshua tugged on her arm. The other guys mounted their horses. Walker ran back across the washout to his home.

"Do you think it will all be okay?" She bit her lip and wouldn't move.

"It's out of our hands. But we've protected it the best that we could." He pulled her toward the wagon.

The telltale roar in the distance spurred him into action.

Joshua swept her up in his arms and dashed to the wagon. He practically threw her up onto the seat and then jumped up beside her.

"Go!"

The horses flew into action.

Anna gripped his arm and kept her gaze over her shoulder. "I don't see anything yet."

"We've got to get out of this washout and onto higher ground as soon as possible. Keep an eye out for me, okay?" He flicked the reins again. "Yah! Faster, boys."

As dangerous as it was to race along the rocky, uneven gulley in the wagon, they didn't have much choice. Time wasn't on their side and it would be much worse to get caught up in a flash flood. The roar behind them grew.

It was coming.

"Twice in one summer. That hasn't happened since we've lived here, has it?" Joshua steered the horses toward the north side, where the rise of wall decreased. If he could get them up safely before the water reached them, that was all that mattered.

"Dad said that he was warned by the Indians he worked with on a small dig up near Casper. But I don't remember anything like this. The occasional flash flood when a storm came through, but nothing of the magnitude of the last one."

"Maybe this one won't be as bad." He spotted a grassy slope they might be able to make it up. As long as the horses kept their footing.

"Are you headed for that?" She pointed exactly where he'd hoped to gain higher ground.

"Yeah. Think it'll work?"

"It's not as steep. I think it's our only chance." Her grip on his arm tightened. "Oh no . . . *hurry!*"

He risked a glance over his shoulder.

Water rushed down the washout. He whipped his head forward and snapped the reins several times.

They were almost there.

"Come on, boys, you can do it!" He had to yell over the rumble behind them.

The team surged forward. *God, give them traction.*

They reached the grassy slope, and he leaned forward and whistled his encouragement.

Everything slowed around him as he watched the bobbing of the horses' necks as they strained to get the wagon up to higher ground.

twenty-seven

"They went through wildernesses
Where no man's feet had trod
To find out Nature's secrets—
The unfound way to God."

~Earl Douglass,
from his poem *Nature's Noblemen*

SUNDAY, JULY 21

Julian looked out on the washed-out gulley. The waters were taking longer to recede this time. Which meant Anna wouldn't be back to work on her dig for another day or two.

He didn't like that.

Walking out to his garden, he placed his hands on his hips. Most of the blooms were gone. Many of the flowers had been pelted to the ground with the torrential rain. But as things dried out, some of them might perk back up as long as the stalks weren't completely broken off.

He surveyed the damage and shook his head. Everything was still soaked. His boots were sucked into the mud with each step. Perhaps tomorrow things would be a bit drier and he could work in the garden while he waited for Anna's return.

The sound of horse's hooves made him turn on his heel. "Anna?"

Out of instinct, the name slipped out. No one else came to visit him.

Except for his foreman.

Huh. It was the reverend, sitting atop his horse and smiling down at him.

"Good afternoon, Julian." He got down, removed his hat, and strode toward him.

"Good afternoon." What did *he* want?

"I'm out checking on my parishioners after the storm. Wanted to see how you were doing."

"I'm fine." He stood stiff.

"It's been a while since your father passed. Are you handling your grief okay? It's normal to feel sad and unsure about things. You've got a lot to deal with out here." The man's concern seemed sincere.

What was expected of him? Should he invite the man in? "I'm adjusting."

"Good to hear." The man watched him for several seconds. "Your beautiful garden took quite a beating, didn't it?"

Beating . . . He flinched. "I'll take care of it."

"I've heard amazing things about what beautiful flowers you grow."

Julian shrugged. Why wouldn't the man leave?

"I'd love to meet your brother. Is he around?"

"No."

"Well, all right then." The reverend replaced his hat. "I guess I'll be off to check on others now." He climbed back up on his horse. "Just wanted to make sure nothing was wrong here."

Wrong. That word didn't settle well either. "Thanks for stopping by."

The reverend rode away and Julian watched the man's back.

The preacher wanted to make sure nothing was wrong.

Julian pulled the two faded blue ribbons out of his pocket.

Mary.

He'd cried for hours the other day.

Something he never did.

Yes, something was wrong here. With him.

His thoughts turned to Anna.

She was his only hope.

Monday, July 22

Everything was a mess. Anna thought almost being caught again in a flash flood was the worst of it, but now they faced an overwhelming task. A layer of mud covered everything. It had taken all morning to get this far. How much more time would they lose? So much water covered the ground, but at least they could now get to the wall of fossils.

Anna heaved a small log out of the way so she could set up her little worktable. The men were moving the bigger pieces of debris left in the floodwater's wake. The only good out of all of this was the fact that more ground had been moved, exposing rock layers beneath. Maybe there were more fossils to dig. The thought was exciting.

The earth was an amazing canvas that always changed. Over decades and centuries, the land changed by dirt that was brought in by windstorms. Rain. Things got compacted down. Then earthquakes split the ground or floods washed through and exposed what had been buried underneath for long periods of time.

Volcanoes, earthquakes, tornadoes, hurricanes, tsunamis,

floods, and landslides . . . the list was endless of the earth's growing pangs, as Dad called them. Different natural disasters exposing the earth's buried history.

Movement across the washout caught her attention. Julian was in his garden piling up debris. Poor man. That beautiful garden was now a mess.

Wait a minute . . .

She looked closer. A part of the bluff created by the first flood—where Julian's home and garden sat—had been eaten away by this last flood. Thankfully, it didn't appear like it took a portion of the garden. But there was a clear delineation now of dark soil sitting atop the white rock layer. Like God had come through and sliced off the edge of the hill.

She should sketch that side of the gulley later. Julian wouldn't mind. If she found something there, she'd have to tread carefully. Because the ranch house sat a mere eighty feet or so back from the edge.

Would Julian allow them to excavate on this side? He might think it could put his home in danger, and she didn't want that. Then there was the garden. She'd hate to disturb something so precious to him.

The day passed in lots of hard work putting everything back in place. The men were finally back to their digging. She'd sketched two of the fossils again and was working on bringing out all the details. It took a good deal of time to get each drawing accurate with all the fine minutiae.

But every time she glanced toward the Walker home, she had the itching to sketch that other wall. It would be fun to bring the sketch to Dad and see if his keen eye could pick up any fossils in the wall.

Julian stopped by after lunch and told her he was headed up to Green River. He needed some supplies to work in his garden.

She'd given him a smile and said she'd watch out for things at his place.

With a wave, he'd left.

Just the opportunity she needed.

She grabbed her supplies and headed over to the other side of the washout. Finding a large boulder to plop herself onto, she sat down and studied the layers of the wall.

Starting from the top where the soil of Julian's garden covered the first several feet of ground, she began her sketch. The dark rich soil lightened in color after the first few feet and then the line of the white rock layer began.

Below it about six feet was another layer a bit darker. Reddish in color.

Fascinating.

And in each layer, there were several darker lines. Their shape wasn't indicative of bones, but a lot of times those darker lines were fossils. What they were, she'd leave up to Dad to determine. If it would be worth them digging.

If they didn't need to disturb this side, she wouldn't ask Julian.

That evening, she handed her sketch to Dad. "The other side of the gulley had more wash away in the flood. I thought you might like to take a look at it and see if there's anything we should investigate."

His eyes perked up. "How much of it washed out?"

"Several feet of dirt? The rock wall is fully exposed underneath the garden." She pointed.

"This is incredible." Dad grabbed his spectacles and brought the paper closer to his face.

For thirty minutes, he didn't say a word. Just examined her sketch with an occasional "hmm" and a pucker of his brow.

Joshua's arrival gave her a wonderful reprieve. "I'm so glad you're here." She kissed him on the cheek.

"Why do you look relieved?" He scratched at the stubble on his jaw.

She slumped and leaned her head back with a groan. "Dad hasn't said a word to me since I showed him the sketch I did today. I'm dying to find out what he's thinking."

"Ah, you spotted something on the other side? I saw you over there drawing earlier. I had a feeling."

"Come on." She tugged at his hand. "Let's have dinner with him and see if he'll share what's on his mind."

Joshua followed her lead and they joined Dad by his bed. During dinner, Josh regaled her father with stories of the day clearing the site.

"How are the fossils?"

"The tarps seem to have kept the majority of debris from damaging anything. Plus the water wasn't as high this time. Only time will tell once we get in there with the fine tools."

Josh wiped his mouth with his napkin and leaned back in his chair. "Did you find anything of interest across the gulley?" He pointed to her drawing.

Finally. She sat a little straighter, trying not to bounce up and down on her chair.

"Anna, would you excuse us for a moment?" Dad sent her a lopsided smile.

What was going on? Why did he seem so . . . hesitant? Was he not feeling well?

"Don't worry, my dear. I'm fine. Getting stronger every day. Doc's herbal remedies and the tea have done wonders."

Almost like he could read her mind. A bit of relief washed through her, but something was in his eyes. She couldn't decipher it. But she wouldn't ignore his request. "All right." She stood, picked up their dishes, and headed for the kitchen. "As long as you don't talk about the sketch without me." She sent him a wide grin.

He waved her off but didn't respond.

Maybe Dad simply wanted to speak man-to-man with his future son-in-law.

That had to be it.

twenty-eight

"It seems that the moral foundation on which society rests is like loose, unstable sand. Men are losing their morality as fast as they are gaining in the arts, invention, and science."

~Earl Douglass

TUESDAY, JULY 23

Joshua headed out to the Walker property an hour before he would normally head to work.

The air was dry after days of scorching sun. Amazing how much water could get soaked up in such a short amount of time. But the territory was normally so arid. Except for the areas right around the river, the grass turned brown after June. The cattle still munched on the dried-out vegetation, but they congregated around the banks of the river and its offshoot creeks and streams.

Anna's sketch of the other side of the washout hadn't been in great detail—or so she'd said—but Peter had seen something

278

that upset him. He'd asked Joshua last night to check into something.

And he wasn't too excited about what he might find.

He dragged some scaffolding over to the side of the gulley directly below Julian Walker's home. Once he had it built high enough, he climbed to the top and looked above the white layer of rock. Several feet of dirt were built up for the garden.

Anna had told him what Julian said he did to create the lush soil for his garden. Layers and layers of dirt. Manure. River-bottom soil . . .

There. A small white spot stood out against the dark earth.

Not more than a couple inches across, it was amazing that Anna had picked up on the detail in her sketch. But that was how extraordinary her eye was. Probably without even thinking about it.

Using a brush, Joshua gently wiped at the spot and around it. Hoping and praying it wasn't what Mr. Lakeman thought it was. But the more he brushed, and the more the compacted dirt fell away, the more the round object indeed looked like . . .

Dirt tumbled down into the washout. Joshua drew in a breath. He didn't want to risk collapsing any of the garden by tugging the object out, but even with it embedded in dirt, he knew what he was looking at.

He brushed gently on the left and in a little. The dirt was deep and packed down from the years. Just a little more . . .

Then he saw it.

The opening for a left eye socket.

Mr. Lakeman was right. It was a skull.

His heart picked up its pace and cold sweat prickled his neck and brow.

Scrambling down the scaffolding, he broke it down and rushed it back across the gulley. He put his brush away and snuck another glance to Walker's home. No movement. Hopefully the man wouldn't return from Green River for another day or two.

But that didn't calm his nerves. He checked his pocket watch. Not much time before the rest of the team arrived. Maybe he should leave a note for Anna.

He scribbled something down and left it under a rock on her table and then grabbed his horse to head to the Lakemans'. He might even pass her on the way.

What would he tell her?

It didn't matter. He needed to see her father, and fast.

All the way there, he battled one horrific question . . .

Who was buried in Julian's garden?

Pounding hooves sounded outside.

Anna rushed to the door. Who could that be at this hour? She opened it and frowned. "Joshua?" She eyed him. Questions swirled around in her mind. Was everyone all right?

He grabbed her arm and dragged her to her father's room. "I'm glad you're still here. We've got to speak with your father right now."

"What is this about?"

They entered her dad's room.

"Mr. Lakeman." Joshua removed his hat. "I did what you asked."

Dad straightened his shoulders. "And?"

Joshua grabbed the drawing she'd made for her father yesterday. "This spot right here?" He pointed to it so she could see.

"Yes?"

"It's a human skull."

What? She put a hand to her mouth and shook her head. "It's just a white dot."

"I asked Joshua to go take a closer look this morning while Julian was in Green River."

She'd never heard Dad's voice so grim. She pierced Joshua with her gaze. "What did you do?"

For a moment he looked taken aback. "I used a small brush to get a closer look and I found the top of a skull. I've examined enough skeletons in my medical training to know a skull when I see one."

"But you didn't see the whole thing?" She crossed her arms over her chest.

"Anna"—he reached for her—"I brushed enough away to see the left eye socket."

No. It couldn't be. A chill raced up her spine. Mean ol' Walker had been a horrible man . . . but she'd never suspected this.

"Honey, don't you understand?" Dad appeared so sad. Defeated. Was it because something like this could ruin their historic dig? "This is why we've been worried about you. Someone is buried in that garden."

"Julian's father was a bad man. How do we know *he's* not the one responsible for . . . whoever . . ." She swallowed back the bile that threatened. "Whoever is there."

Joshua wrapped an arm around her shoulders, but she remained stiff. "We don't know. I'm sorry to be the bearer of this news, but we need to tread carefully. I've had a feeling—"

She yanked out of his grasp. "Don't you *dare* say it! I don't want to hear one more time how you think something is off with Julian." Even though deep down, she wasn't feeling too comfortable, she hated being wrong. Ever since she was young, she never wanted to admit it. This was a noble cause, right? She wanted to honor Mary. She wanted to help Julian. Surely he wasn't capable of . . .

She shook her head. "He's been nothing but patient and kind with me. With *us*. I don't believe it. Whatever is there . . . it must be from his father."

"Anna, you need to listen to reason." Dad tried to move forward but fell back against the pillows instead.

Why wouldn't they listen to her? Didn't they comprehend all she'd shared with them? Men. Always ready to storm the castle without getting all the facts. "Reason? I don't understand how any of this proves that Julian is a bad person." Her head wagged back and forth. It couldn't be true.

"We don't have proof." Dad's brow furrowed and his face settled into a deep frown. "But you need to understand that we are protecting you."

"I've heard all I want to hear right now." She marched out of the room, knowing full well that wasn't fair. Her father couldn't follow her. But Joshua sure could. And she heard his footsteps thudding behind her.

It made her want to turn on him and snarl.

Once they were outside, she spun on her heel. "Don't even start."

"Do you not realize—even the tiniest bit—that there is logic and reasoning behind what your father and I are trying to say?" He took a tentative step toward her, reaching out with his hands. His eyes held so much pain, it looked like he was about to cry.

No. She couldn't give in. Couldn't admit that the two men in her life had logic behind them. There *had* to be some other explanation. Julian's brother perhaps. "No one else is willing to stand up for Julian Walker. So I will."

"I'm not accusing him of anything yet."

"Exactly. Not *yet*."

His shoulders stiffened and his jaw clenched. "You're being ridiculous, Anna. You're so fired up about being correct that you're unwilling to listen. This is exactly what happened before I left for medical school. You took what I said and twisted it. You were convinced that I was against you working out at the digs. You didn't even listen to what my concerns were. Just like now. You're *unwilling* to listen."

His words cut through her like a knife.

"I think you should leave."

"What?" He studied her.

"You need to leave. Right now, Joshua Ziegler." She hated the sound of her own voice. But her temper had won the day.

"Fine."

Without another word, he was gone.

twenty-nine

"I want to get at the real significance of things and help my fellow man to arise and come into the light of freedom and truth."

~Earl Douglass

WEDNESDAY, JULY 24

Sleep hadn't been easy to come by last night. Joshua had tossed and turned, worrying about Anna and their relationship, until his dad had knocked on the door and told him that his flopping around like a fish wasn't helping. So they'd talked for a few minutes and his father, in his usual succinct manner, reminded Joshua that Philippians was clear they weren't to be anxious, but to bring everything to God.

When Joshua went back to his room, he'd read the epistle by the soft glow of the lantern. Convicted of his own lack of faith, he asked the Lord to guide him, to remove the worry, and to protect Anna.

He'd finally gone to sleep.

This morning, Mom asked him to run a few errands for her in town since she was still laid up and Martha was so busy with the ranch. He needed the time to himself anyway and wanted to give Anna her space.

He spent the quiet ride into town praying because it was far too easy for him to fall right back into the same pattern. Like he handed over the reins to God but then kept trying to yank them back. If anyone could keep him on the right path, it was the Almighty. Why was he trying to take control? Did he think he could actually steer this crazy ship himself? Ludicrous.

In Walker Creek, he tied his horse to the hitching post at the mercantile and pulled out Mom's list. Dad probably told her about their chat last night and she was doing her best to help him keep his mind off the problem.

The thought made him chuckle as he walked in the door.

"Why, what has you so amused this fine morning, Mr. Ziegler?" Rosemary's smooth voice washed over him as soon as he was over the threshold.

He shrugged and removed his hat. *Be nice.* "Just happy about life, I guess."

"That's lovely to hear."

"Nice to see you, Miss Oppenheim." Stepping forward, he approached the counter hoping that she would go on about her day.

"What has you in town? I thought you were working out at the dig every day?"

Guess it didn't work. With his back to her, he shuttered his eyes and clenched his jaw. "Lots of errands for the ranch this morning." It was rude to keep his back to her, but he handed the list over to the young man behind the counter. "Good morning." He nodded. "I'm Joshua Ziegler. My mother requested these items. Could you fill a box for me, and I'll return in a little while?"

"Of course, sir. I know your mother well." With that, the kid was off, leaving Joshua alone with Rosemary.

Again.

Nope. Not this time.

He headed to the door. "Have a good day." He slapped his

hat back on his head and walked out as if there was a fire chasing him.

But out on the boardwalk, the fast clip-clop of steps alerted him that he hadn't escaped.

"Mr. Ziegler," Rosemary called. "Mr. Ziegler, please!"

Joshua stopped and turned, waiting for her to reach him. "Did you need something? I apologize, but I'm in quite a hurry."

She put a hand to her throat while the other held tight to her parasol. "I'll only take a moment of your time."

"All right." *Be nice, be nice, be nice.* The chant resounded in his brain.

With a tiny step closer, she cleared her throat. "We've shared a lot, Joshua, and it would be remiss of me as your friend to not speak my mind." Her voice softened as she spoke. "After watching you and Miss Lakeman together, I fear for you. I really d—"

"Whatever for?" It was rude for him to interrupt her when she clearly wasn't finished, but his patience was wearing thin.

Her eyes snapped to life. "I'm not trying to be mean. Truly. But my father raised me to speak my mind with my friends. You'd be a fool to hold onto a woman who treats you so ill. Especially when there's someone else right here willing to love and support you and help make all of your dreams come true." She straightened with those last words and stared at him.

"Miss Oppenheim . . ." What on earth could he say to that?

"Rosemary, please." She smiled up at him. A lovely woman, truly, but *not* the woman for him.

He lowered his voice. "Rosemary. I appreciate your friendship more than I can express in words. But I love Anna. We are going to be married." He touched her elbow. "I don't wish to hurt you—"

"Stop." She pulled away. "I don't need to hear any more. I won't trouble you again, Mr. Ziegler. Not without an invitation to do so." With a jut of her chin, she spun around and walked away.

Julian wandered down to the dig site. Where was everyone? He hadn't seen anyone since he returned from Green River.

He looked around the work area. All the crates were locked up. No tools were lying around.

That was odd. They must be working on something else.

He turned back to his house, but the closer he got to his side of the washout, his heart pounded. The flash flood had washed away a good deal. . . .

No!

He ran the rest of the way.

With a glance over his shoulder, he winced. Maybe he could fix it before they came back to dig.

He scurried around. Grabbed the tall ladder. Filled a burlap sack full of garden soil. Then he picked up one of his larger trowels.

Once he was back down in the washout, he scanned the horizon in all directions to make sure no one was coming. That no one was watching.

He climbed the ladder and looked at the exposed grave. Was it . . . Mother?

Tears rushed to his eyes and he couldn't see. He swiped the sleeve of his shirt over his eyes to clear his blurry vision. For a moment he was frozen. How could he hide this?

Damian's whisper washed over him. "If you pull the skeleton out—even if you could—the ground above it will collapse."

He was right. What had he been thinking? He couldn't pull it out and then fill it back in. That wouldn't work.

He gazed down at the bag of soil he'd brought with him.

"The only choice you have is to get rid of what's sticking out. Just pull out the skull. Fill it in with dirt. No one will know."

Looking at it made him queasy.

"Get it over with," Damian hissed.

Using the trowel, Julian dug around the skull and tugged. It wouldn't budge. He stabbed at the dirt. Got his hand over the top of the skull and stabbed the dirt again.

Again and again.

The skull moved toward him.

He stabbed the trowel at whatever was holding the skull in place. Over and over.

It finally came out. The dirt above it sagged.

Julian shoved his arm into the hole while placing the skull down into the sack. Then he used the trowel to scoop dirt from the sack back into the hole before the earth above it crumbled too much more. The more dirt he packed in, the better it felt. So he kept shoving dirt, pushing it in with the trowel, until the sack was empty except for the skull.

Drenched with sweat and breathing heavy, he worked his way down the tall ladder. It shook with each step until he was down on the ground. He looked up at his work. No one would be able to tell where it had been.

As long as no one saw it, he was safe.

He dragged the ladder back up to his shed and put it away. Then he buried the skull in a different corner of his garden.

His heart hurt. Mother was the only one who had been able to help him when things were bleak. But she wasn't here. Fear of people finding out mixed with fury that his father had done this to him and made his mind swim. He didn't know what to do.

Anna.

She would know what to do.

He needed Anna. With him.

Forever.

THURSDAY, JULY 25

Joshua sat at the breakfast table with his family listening to all the goings-on from the ranch. It had been nice to stay home yesterday with his family, though he wasn't happy with how he'd left things with Anna.

Give her time. She would come around.

When she'd sent a note to him, and presumably the rest of the team, yesterday that they wouldn't be digging today, he wasn't sure if it was because she was still mad at him and her father, or if she'd come to her senses and needed some time to think through what she was going to do.

Or perhaps she needed to speak to Mr. Gilbert?

The possibilities had swirled in his mind all day. He'd spent a good deal of time praying for his fiancée and her father. The whole situation was a nightmare.

He'd said nothing to his family about his suspicions of Julian in Mary's disappearance. He could barely swallow the thought himself, but what if it ended up being true? What if Julian did have something to do with Mary?

A knock sounded at the door.

Martha went to it and came back to the table. "Joshua—" her eyes were wide—"It's a telegram for you."

"Thank you." He took it and opened it at the table even though all eyes were on him.

Unfolding the paper, he read:

> *Haven't received response from you. Pre-term examinations have been moved up. You must return by July 31 or forfeit your position.*
>
> *Professor Wright*

His heart thrummed as he reread the missive. He looked at the calendar Mom kept in the kitchen. The one way to ensure he returned in time was if he left . . . tomorrow.

"What is it?"

Joshua looked at his father and laid the paper on the table. "I need to leave tomorrow."

His family all spoke at once, but there was only one person he wanted to see and speak to right now. "I'm sorry. I need to go see Anna."

He ran out the door, jumped on his horse, and raced to the Lakemans', hoping and praying he could catch her before she left for the dig site.

At her home, he pounded on the door.

Louise answered. "Mr. Ziegler. Is everything all right?"

"Is Anna here?"

"Yes. She's with her father."

He didn't wait for an invitation, he headed down the hall.

"Anna?" He called before he even reached her father's bedroom.

"What is it?" She waited at the door for him.

He took a deep breath and gathered his thoughts. This was not how he wanted to leave. And what if she and her father were in danger?

He greeted Mr. Lakeman and told them about the telegram.

"Oh, son. I'm so sorry. But we understand you must leave. Your schooling is too important."

"Thank you, sir." He turned to Anna. "I don't want to leave on bad terms. Again."

Her shoulders were stiff. "Everything is fine. Don't worry. Dad and I had a long discussion this morning."

He looked over her head, but the worry in her father's face didn't bring Joshua any comfort.

"I promise I'll write and fill you in on everything at the dig. That is, if I'm allowed to return to it." She sent a look to her father.

Oh boy. What had transpired between father and daughter? She was clearly not happy.

What would happen if he stayed? He could spend so much more time with Anna. They could get married *now*. But if he gave up this opportunity, would he ever be able to finish his schooling?

He swallowed. God had given him the gift through the benefactor. Would he squander it if he stayed? Or would it be like a godly sacrifice?

He didn't want to leave Anna, but he had made a commitment to his benefactor. To his school. He needed to fulfill that. Mr. Bricker had paid a lot of money for him over the years.

Mr. Bricker! Did he know to set up Joshua's ticket early? He'd have to race to the train station too—

Anna placed a hand on his arm. "I can see you have a million thoughts going through your mind right now. I'm sure there's a great deal you need to do. Let's say our goodbyes now. I'll write you tonight. And I promise to write every week."

There wasn't enough time for them to right all the wrongs between them. Especially not in a rush. How could he leave?

His feet seemed frozen to the floor.

"It's okay." Anna's eyes softened. "Go. I love you."

First, he went to her father's bedside and leaned over to give the man a hug. "Sir, thank you for everything. Thank you for the job this summer. And thank you for lending me your wisdom. You've taught me a lot."

"You are welcome. I look forward to your return. I want to walk my daughter down the aisle to you." He reached out and gripped Joshua's hand. Strong and firm.

"I look forward to that as well." Joshua turned back to Anna and walked her out the front of her home.

"Anna—"

"Joshua—"

He raised an eyebrow. "You go first."

"I'll miss you. And I promise to write." But her words were stiff. They matched her posture.

Somehow, he had to break down the wall. "I'll miss you too. I love you, Anna." He touched her cheek.

"I love you, too." She looked down at her feet and sniffed. "Are we okay?"

A smile lifted her lips, but it was forced. "Of course." She reached up on tiptoe and kissed him.

Short and sweet. But he would hold onto it all year. "I hate to leave you."

"You have to go, Josh. Go be a doctor." She ducked her head, went inside her home, and closed the door.

Out at the dig site, Anna wandered around. She'd sent word to the Oppenheims not to come today because the team wasn't working. Then she sent the other guys home.

It wasn't right. Nothing was. Not the dig. Not the mess with the investor. Not her father's suspicions. Nor her fight with Josh.

Joshua.

With him gone, what was she going to do? Especially after how she'd treated him.

Her dreadful temper. Every time, it got her into trouble. Because she couldn't stand to be wrong.

Something in her made her gaze back over at the other side of the gulley. What if Dad and Joshua were right? Could Julian have hurt people? Could he have hurt . . .

She shook her head. No, it wasn't possible. The man who brought Mary flowers every day at school? The man who had never stood up to one bully at school? He'd never raised a fist to anyone who said hateful things about him. He certainly wouldn't hurt someone he cared about.

"Anna?"

She about jumped out of her shoes. She whirled and put a hand to her chest. "Julian. You scared me."

"I'm sorry." He smiled at her. "Come. You need to see this. My brand-new roses are beginning to bud."

Her breath wouldn't calm down. "All right. I need to catch my breath. You gave me quite a start." Everything was fine. He just wanted to show her some flowers.

She followed him up the bluff to his garden.

"Look. It's a pink one. Don't you love pink?" His earnest expression toward her increased as he stepped closer and his eyes widened.

"Pink is beautiful." Her promise to Joshua and her father came barreling back to her. She shouldn't be here. She was breaking her word. "I need to get back."

"No. Not yet."

A chill rose the hair on her arms and neck. No? Did he think he could tell her what to do? She started to turn, but he grabbed her hand and pulled her toward the house.

"Julian!"

"I need to tell you everything." His face turned grim. The pressure of his hand on hers increased.

"Ow. That hurts." What was he talking about? "I really need to get back, Julian."

"Not yet." He squeezed tighter.

He all but dragged her into the house and sat her down at the table. "Here's some water. And pie. I bought it in Green River."

"Oh, how nice. But I'm not hungry."

He slammed down two blue ribbons on the table. Then two of her pencils. Then her sketchpad.

"What are you doing?" Her throat was dry as she swallowed. What would he do to her? Why hadn't she listened to Dad and Joshua?

"Eat your pie, Anna." Julian set another glass of water and plate of pie on the other side of the table and took his seat. "I've been waiting to share my heart with you."

The look in his eyes . . . it was so cold. Even his features were different. Hard. And his tone was harsh.

If she didn't know better, she'd think this wasn't Julian at all. "Your heart?" She swallowed, then reached for her glass of water. Took a small sip. But her hand trembled.

He dove into his piece of pie. "Julian wanted apple, but cherry is better. It's my favorite."

What was he saying? Her insides shook. "*Julian* wanted apple?"

He didn't even look at her. Just kept eating his pie. "Don't worry. Anna. You're the only one left."

Was that a threat? "Julian, what do you mean?"

He stared at her. His eyes dark. Lifeless. "You're the only one left who can fix him."

She searched every corner of her brain. Why . . . How . . . ? "Fix him? Fix whom? Fix you? How?"

He frowned. "Don't be stupid. I don't need fixing. *Julian* does."

His eyes changed, softened.

Julian.

This was Julian. But a moment ago . . . it wasn't.

"I'm sorry, Anna. I told him to be nice to you. You can help me defeat the darkness."

Blinking, she gulped. Told *him* . . . "Told who to be nice to me, Julian?"

He shrugged. "Damian."

Dear God in heaven . . . She began to shiver uncontrollably. The brother everyone feared. "Is Damian . . . the darkness?"

Julian's nod was quick, as though he didn't want anyone to see it.

Dad was right. Joshua was right.

Julian offered a weak smile. "Mother helped me. Until she was gone. My father killed her, you know."

She put a hand to her mouth. *God . . . O God . . . help me. . . .*

Julian's smile turned . . . wrong. Evil. "When he told me, I killed *him*. Julian couldn't do it, so I did." A sick laugh escaped his mouth. "Dad hated Julian's garden. But that's where he is."

"I thought . . . I thought he was buried in the cemetery?"

That hateful laugh again. "He didn't deserve any such thing."

She felt the blood drain from her face and took a deep breath. She had to stay alert. Had to find a way out.

Julian's eyes softened, and he offered her a shy smile. "Mary was so nice to me. I loved her. She was going to help me." He stood up and went to the window.

"Help you?" Her voice squeaked.

"Yes. But now it's up to you."

She watched him for several seconds, frozen in her seat. "Do you know what happened to Mary?" It didn't matter what he did to her right now, she had to know.

He nodded. "She's out in the garden."

"No." The whispered word fell from her lips. Her stomach lurched.

He snapped his gaze back to her. Studied her. His eyes darkening with every step he took toward her. Julian, but not Julian. Her Julian was gone. In his place was . . .

The other.

thirty

"There have been months and years of suspense and waiting and hoping and disappointment. There have been times when the heavens looked dark."

~Earl Douglass

Anna couldn't stop shaking.

Huddled in a corner of Julian's basement, she hadn't moved since he'd carried her down here, told her to be quiet, and then bolted the door. The click of the lock had echoed around her like thunder.

God, I don't know what to do. Please . . . please don't let him kill anyone else. Moans overtook her. Where had he gone? Nothing but silence kept her company in the house. What if he went after Joshua or her father?

She wasn't sure what would be worse, the silence or hearing the floorboards creak overhead making his presence known.

The shivers worsened until she couldn't keep her teeth from chattering. She pulled her knees up to her chest, wrapped her arms around them, buried her face, and cried.

Long, soul-searching sobs erupted from the deepest well within her. This was all her fault. Every last bit of it.

She hadn't listened to Josh and Dad. Hadn't helped Julian.

Now what would happen to her? Fear clawed its way up her back.

Her mind froze. Words wouldn't come. It was like she was paralyzed and couldn't move.

Father . . . help me.

All of a sudden, she relaxed. The shaking stopped.

Her mind cleared.

Julian had endured more than she could imagine at his father's hands. His life had been in a prison with no escape. Could he have been so desperate and lonely . . . so terrified that his mind created a brother? A brother the whole town believed was real, although now that she thought about it, no one had ever seen him. Oh, some people said they'd seen him. Just to tell stories, no doubt. Rumors had swirled around about Damian Walker. How awful he was. Even more awful than their dad.

They'd all believed them. And felt sorry for Julian.

But no one had cared enough about the man to find out what was really going on. No one . . .

Except Mary.

Anna closed her eyes. Had Mary faced this . . . other Julian? Was that what happened to her?

Mary had risked everything to help Julian. Even—though she probably didn't know it—her life.

Sitting up a little straighter, Anna peered into the darkness around her.

If he returned, her life would be on the line too.

Was she willing to lay down her life?

Oh, God. Help me. I'm so scared.

She closed her eyes as tight as she could, willing the tears to go away. Why couldn't she be as brave and bold and loving as Mary?

My child . . . you belong to Me. Just like Mary.

The words in her heart brought warmth to her limbs. That's where her best friend's strength had come from. The love. The boldness to reach out. And ultimately lay down her life . . .

God was in control. She belonged to Him. She might not be able to help Julian or anyone else, but God could.

The hard question was no longer if she would live another day.

No. The question now was what would she be willing to do to save Julian from his prison?

Things had not gone as planned. Anna looked at him with such . . .

Horror.

Well, not him, but Damian. Even so, it hurt. After Damian locked Anna in the basement, Julian had gone back to his garden and cried himself to sleep.

When he awoke, his head ached. Mary's ribbons were clutched in his hand.

He sat up and put his hands over his eyes. Great big sobs shook his shoulders. Why had he done it? Why? What was wrong with him?

Mary had been wonderful to him. She'd been his friend. He hated that she was no longer here. They'd been destined to be together.

But that day . . .

Oh, that day.

Mary had never touched another boy at school. Never. He'd watched her.

Then little Evan's dad died. He'd cried all day at school after the funeral. Mary sat by him on the steps of the school. All during recess. At one point, she even shared her lunch with Evan.

And then?

He fought against Damian's fury, refused to let him out, but he couldn't stop his brother's mockery.

"She wrapped an arm around that other boy and allowed him to cry on her shoulder! She betrayed you!"

Something inside Julian had snapped.

He invited Mary to look at some flowers in his garden. She did love his flowers. He brought her some every day.

But when they arrived at the garden, he left her. With Damian. His brother asked her why she hugged Evan.

Her eyes grew wide at the rage in Damian's voice.

The Walker boys had always been larger than everyone else. Just like their giant of a father. But he'd never raised his voice with Mary. Not once.

Damian did that day.

Mary never went home after that.

And Julian was never the same.

The darkness had come to stay.

The bustle of the train station in Green River did little to keep Josh's mind on the task at hand. What he wouldn't give to be done with medical school *now* so he could marry Anna and start their lives together. He didn't want to leave.

To make it worse, things weren't the best between them. Again.

But he had to return to school or forfeit everything he'd worked for all these years. Was he doing the right thing?

Last night he'd hashed it out with Dad. This was clearly the Lord's will for his life. God had provided in miraculous ways and had given him the extra time with Anna this summer to reconcile.

It was beautiful. So there was a little more time apart ahead. They could handle it. Their love would survive.

299

God's will . . .

The words had rolled around in his mind like a tumbleweed blown by the Wyoming wind. All his life, he'd wanted to be a doctor. The doors hadn't opened for a long time, so when they did, God's provision was clear. In the most unexpected ways. It was time to stop being selfish. If he left Anna and their relationship in God's hands, all would be fine. God had brought them together. He would sustain them.

He pulled his pocket watch out and checked the time. Still another thirty minutes before his train.

"Joshua!" A deep voice rose over the crowd.

Turning around, he searched the sea of faces on the platform.

"Over here!" Zach waved his hat as he ran toward him.

What was he doing all the way up here?

The expression on his face made Joshua's stomach plummet. "What's happened?"

"Anna is missing. She didn't come home last night and her father is sick with worry. He sent me up here since we knew you were leaving today." The words spilled out in one rush of breath.

"What? No." It couldn't be. Not Anna.

"The sheriff is putting together a posse because they think she's at Walker's ranch. Somewhere." Zach pulled his arm. "I brought a horse for you."

Walker. A fire started in his gut. He raced to the ticket window. "I need you to hold my things. I have an emergency."

The ticket agent nodded. "Bring them in here, sir." He went around his counter and opened the lower half of the Dutch door.

After Josh deposited his things, he looked to Zach. "Bring the horses to the telegraph office." Without waiting for an answer, he ran around the corner.

Inside, he composed a short message to Mr. Bricker, praying

that the generous man would understand the urgency of the situation. But it didn't matter what the response was.

Anna was more important than anything else.

As Josh exited the tiny building, Zach was already on his horse and held out the reins to the other.

In one swift move, Josh was astride his mount and prodding the animal into motion. Once they were out of town, they rode as fast as the horses could manage.

Oh, God. Please let us find her alive and unharmed. Please.

His appeals to the Almighty repeated with the rhythm of the horse's hooves. Again and again.

What would he do if he lost her? The thought was torture.

Leave her in My hands, Joshua.

He shook off the words and as he rode, his anger toward Julian grew. If he harmed one hair on her head . . .

Creaking above her made Anna sit up.

Julian was back. At least . . . she hoped it was him.

She held her breath.

The metallic click of the lock made her freeze.

What would he do to her?

"Anna?" The soft voice of shy Julian spoke to her.

Give me the words to say, Lord. She braced herself for his footsteps on the stairs. Closing her eyes, she listened to his slow footfalls.

"I don't want to hurt you. I promise."

She released her breath and swallowed. "I know. But what about Damian?" Would the brother make an appearance?

"Now why'd you have to go and ruin it?" The vicious voice trailed down the stairs.

And then . . .

Julian stood in front of her.

Strength swept over her. She knew what to do. "God, I need

Your strength. Please save my friend from the darkness." Had those calm words really come from her mouth?

"Stop it!"

Damian. He was almost shrieking.

"Or I'll shut you up. Permanently! Maybe *you* belong in the garden. Along with Mary and our stupid father."

Anna had never seen such hatred. Such . . . evil. "You speak out of fear, Damian."

"Shut up!" He grabbed her hand and squeezed so hard that she let out a wail—but then he released her and yelled at the ceiling. "Go away! I want to hear what Anna has to say!"

Julian stilled and an eerie silence took over.

She watched him but didn't dare move. Would she face Julian or Damian when he came out of whatever daze he was in? *Speak through me, Lord. Use me as You will.*

When the man turned his gaze back to her, his face was once again soft. The Julian she knew. How long would it last?

"It's just us. My brother left. Now"—he sat on the basement floor in front of her—"we can talk about how you can fix me. You're the only one who can."

Rather than fear, she felt compassion toward him. That could only come by supernatural means. "I can't fix you, Julian. I can't fix myself. Only God can do that."

"But you don't need to be fixed."

"Oh, yes, I do. I have so many flaws. I've sinned so many times. You know, I started out being nice to you because Mary reminded me that we were commanded to love one another. I wanted to be your friend so I could do her memory proud. But now I understand things a bit differently."

"What do you mean?" At least he was listening. For now.

"You don't need kindness—although that's nice, isn't it? You don't even need a friend. But you do need to see God's love. He's the only one who can restore you."

He blinked several times.

Her time with the brother she no longer feared was limited, that much was certain. So, with a deep breath, she shared her simple understanding of the gospel. "We can't do anything to save or fix ourselves, Julian. Only God can do that." She closed her eyes and bowed her head. "Heavenly Father, I ask for You to touch Julian's heart. Draw him close to You so that he understands Your unconditional love and forgiveness. Help him to see clearly—"

"Stop!" Julian put his hands over his ears.

But she wouldn't. "God, please. Save him!"

An animal-like scream erupted from the man's mouth and he raced up the stairs, locking the door behind him.

She wilted against the wall, trembling. Like she had climbed a mountain and exhausted every bit of strength and energy within her.

But she was at peace.

All the worries about the dig, the sketches, the scientific papers. None of it mattered. She would probably die down here. They would bury her in the garden. But she'd shared the Truth with Julian.

And she could love him now, because Christ loved her first.

thirty-one

"I can't seem to quench my thirst to solve the greatest problems."

~Earl Douglass

There had to be some way to convince Anna that he wasn't a monster. The look in her eyes when Damian told her Mary was in the garden.

She'd screamed at him.

He didn't want to hurt Anna. He just wanted her to fix him.

Julian hated it when Damian took over. It wasn't who he wanted to be. But he couldn't undo what his brother did. Pacing the garden, he couldn't get her words out of his mind. Could God really love him? Forgive him for all he'd done?

"No!" Damian's hate-filled voice pounded at him. "How can a God who created a man like our father fix anything? God *caused* our pain, you simpleton! Let *Him* come ask *our* forgiveness."

"Go away." Julian didn't shout. He didn't scream. Exhaustion seeped out of every pore of his body. "I don't want you here anymore. Go. Away." He closed his eyes and sat in the dirt.

The warmth of the sun made him tilt his face up. The light was so much better than the darkness. He longed to soak it in.

So many thoughts warred with each other. But one kept coming back. God loved him.

Was it true?

The thought of a Savior sacrificing Himself for him—even though he was a horrible person—lifted the corners of his lips. His heart felt lighter. Someone *could* fix him.

The sound of horse's hooves forced him to open his eyes.

Men riding at breakneck speed. They were coming for Anna. For . . . him.

He smiled. It didn't matter. He couldn't see the darkness. Couldn't feel it.

Damian wasn't around.

Six horses rode up in front of Julian.

Six others rushed in behind him. Into his house.

"Mr. Walker." The sheriff dismounted. His face stern.

"Sheriff Lewis." What should he do with his hands? He didn't want to seem angry, so he shoved them in his pockets.

"Have you seen Miss Lakeman?"

He stared. Started to answer, but . . .

"No. They can't take Anna away."

So Damian hadn't really left.

"Julian?"

Damian's fury built. The kind that couldn't be stopped. He answered the sheriff in a roar. "No."

"Mr. Walker. We need your cooperation." Two more men stepped up behind the sheriff. Then the other three joined them.

"You take the sheriff. I'll take the others."

Julian frowned at Damian. "He'll hear you."

"Who will hear me, Julian?" The sheriff inched closer.

He shook his head. "No one." What was happening to him?

"Miss Lakeman has been missing since yesterday. I'm asking you again, have you seen her?"

"Stand your ground, Julian. Be tough."

Julian nodded and met the sheriff's gaze. "You need to leave. You can't have her. Not yet."

All three men in front of him drew their guns.

"Where is she?" The sheriff's voice brooked no argument.

"Get out of my way, Julian! I'll teach them to come here and make demands!"

"No—"

But there was no stopping Damian. "You can't have her!"

More horses arrived. Men with shovels. He counted five.

The sheriff called over his shoulder. "Dig every last inch of it up."

His garden! *"No!"* Julian lunged at the man.

Shots rang in the air.

The darkness seeped out of him as he lay on the ground, staring at the blue sky. Anna. He couldn't let anything happen to Anna.

Why was it so cold?

She heard the voices outside. Then gunshots.

Anna pounded on the door. "Help! I'm down here!"

She pounded again. Her arm would surely be bruised after this, but she didn't care.

"Anna? Anna? Are you all right?" Joshua's voice was the sweetest thing she'd ever heard. They'd found her!

"I'm here. Please . . . just get me out." She leaned her forehead against the door. What she wouldn't give to jump into his arms right now.

"Oh, thank God! We'll get you out right away."

"Step back, Joshua." Another voice rang out. "Miss Lakeman, we have to shoot the lock off so move away from the door!"

"All right." She rushed down the stairs and hid as far away from the door as she could.

Another shot rang out. Then the explosive sound of boots on wooden stairs. A lot of boots.

"Anna!"

Joshua's was the first face she saw. She dashed straight to his arms. For several moments, he held her as she cried.

"Miss Lakeman?"

She brought her head up. It was the sheriff.

"Are you hurt?" He approached her.

Her head wagged back and forth. "No. He didn't hurt me. Just locked me down here."

"Let's go upstairs and you can tell me what happened." The sheriff led her up the stairs. Sat her down at the same table where her pie and water glass still sat.

Flies swarmed it.

She closed her eyes. "Please. Take it away."

"It's gone." Another man spoke.

Then it hit her. The gunshots she'd heard earlier. "Where's . . . Julian? Did you shoot him?"

No one answered, but heads lowered.

She jerked out of Joshua's grasp and raced out to the garden.

"Wait, Anna—"

What if he didn't know God? Her heart tore in two.

When she reached him, she stopped short and had to put a hand to her mouth. Blood oozed from several wounds on Julian's chest and stomach, and a pool of it grew underneath him. Bile burned her throat and she swallowed against it.

He coughed and sputtered. "Mama, I was a good boy. I stopped the darkness."

Joshua wrapped an arm around her shoulders and she reached up to squeeze his hand. With a pleading glance to him, she took a tiny step closer and knelt beside the dying man.

"Oh, Julian, I'm so sorry. . . ."

"If we don't stop the bleeding. . . ." Josh's voice was strangled beside her. "I need to find something—"

"No. It's too late. . . ." Julian lifted a hand and it fell back at his side. "You prayed for God to save me . . . even after . . . I did . . . this. . . ." He choked and closed his eyes. "Why?"

She couldn't speak. Tears clogged her throat. None of them, not even she, knew what horrors this man lived with. The horrors visited on him all his childhood. The horrors of what he'd done. What he might have done to . . . her.

"Because"—Joshua's arm around Anna tightened as he spoke—"God loves you, Julian." He knelt beside Anna. "He sent His Son to be the sacrifice to fix all of us."

Tears pooled in the dying man's eyes as he glanced back and forth between Anna and Josh. He reached out again. "Forgive me?"

"Yes." No matter what he'd done, she could freely give it. Because *she'd* been forgiven. *Thank You, God.*

Joshua reached forward and gripped Julian's outstretched hand. "I forgive you."

Julian's eyes closed.

And didn't reopen.

Strong arms beside her helped her to stand. They walked back over to the house and waited outside.

The sheriff and his deputy joined Anna and Joshua. "I know this is difficult, but I need you to start from the beginning. Your father said there was a skull in Julian's garden."

"First, you need to know that there is more than one body out there." The words came out stronger than she expected even though she was pretty certain her stomach wouldn't co-operate for long.

The sheriff's shoulders drooped. "I was afraid of that. Go on."

She told them her story and tried not to look at the garden as the men flung dirt over their shoulders. When she got to

Julian's confessions at the end, she couldn't take it anymore. She ran over to the bluff and retched in the dirt.

Had she contributed to Julian's issues by being so stubborn? The thought had turned over and over in her mind the last day. If only she'd listened to the men who loved her and wanted to protect her.

It wasn't Mary's fault for being kind to him either. Anna wouldn't want to change her sweet friend's spirit for anything in the world. They needed more people like her. People willing to love the unlovable.

If only they'd been able to reach Julian sooner.

But she doubted much could have been done. The man who sat across from her last night was not the Julian she knew. That frightened her. How long had his mind been . . . divided . . . like that?

Once it was all out, the sheriff looked down at his notes. "So Damian Walker isn't real?"

She shook her head. "Something was wrong with Julian's mind. But I think it was how he survived. He told me that Damian always helped him deal with the beatings from his father. I never *saw* Damian until yesterday, and I know how strange this sounds, but he was inside Julian. What he called . . . the darkness. His eyes changed. His voice changed." The haunting memory made her shiver.

Josh practically held her up with his arm around her waist. "I think Anna's been through enough. Is it all right if I take her home now? Her father has been very worried."

"Go ahead. I'll come by later and update you on what we find." The sheriff walked over to the garden.

Josh led her to his horse and lifted her into the saddle. He climbed up behind her and took hold of the reins. "I'm so sorry, Anna. For this. For everything. I hate that you had to endure—"

"*I'm* the one who should be apologizing." She leaned back

against him, relishing the warmth of his arm around her waist. "I'm so sorry about Mary too. How will your family deal with this?"

"I don't know." The words against her ear broke her heart. His family had endured so much.

She touched his arm. "Would you stop for a minute?"

He pulled on the reins. "Whoa."

Shifting in the saddle, she turned to where she could at least see him. "I love you, Josh. And I never want anything like this to ever come between us again."

"I love you too." He leaned down and kissed her. The soft, sweet kiss of reunion and relief.

The sight of her home coming into view sent gratitude washing over her. She might never have seen it, or her father, again. Anna sat up a little straighter. "I'm so glad to be back, but I hate to have to tell him all that happened."

"It'll be all right. Take it one step at a time. Your father will be relieved you're unharmed." He slowed the horse in front of her house. "I need to get home and tell my family. It's going to be a hard day, but I don't want to leave you if you need me." He hopped down and gazed up at her.

"No. I understand. I plan on resting most of the day and just soaking in my father's presence." She gasped as he helped her off the horse. "You were supposed to leave today!"

"Yeah. Zach caught me at the station, and I left my things up there. Don't worry about it."

"But what about your schooling? Your funding?" She gripped his arms.

Josh kissed her forehead. "I sent a telegram. I'll go into town later and see if there's any response. I'll probably need to leave tomorrow." He closed the distance between them. "I can't imagine leaving you though."

She laid her head on his chest. "We'll make it through. As much as I hate the thought of you going away, I know that's the only way you'll get back here for good."

"Well, I'll come back tonight. It will probably be late, but I have to see you one more time."

Lifting her head, she welcomed his kiss. "I'll wait up for you."

Joshua rode off and Anna went inside.

Louise wrapped her in a big hug and then Anna ran to her father's bedroom and threw herself into his arms.

"My sweet girl." Her dad cried against her hair. "I was so worried."

"You were right, Dad. I'm so sorry I didn't listen."

"Your heart wanted to help him. I know that." He held on tight with his right arm. "I'm praising God that you weren't harmed."

She pulled back and wiped at her face.

"Tell me, Anna." Tears slipped down her father's face. "Was it Julian who . . . ?" His Adam's apple bobbed as he gulped.

She closed her eyes against the pain as the truth sank deeper into her heart. "Mary was buried in the garden." The tears flowed now. She sucked in against great sobs. "Along with Julian's mother—she never left, his father went into a rage and took her life—*and* his father. When Mr. Walker told his son what he'd done to his wife, Julian killed him too."

After she'd shared everything with Dad, she went to the window and gazed out. Beautiful plants, their lush greenery and blooms in the garden plot, caused her to reflect.

She looked over her shoulder at her father. He'd had such a hard time being stuck in bed, physically unable to do what he loved. But his mind still flourished.

Then there was Julian. Physically, he was tall and strong. He could grow beautiful things. But his mind and soul had been riddled with the ugliness—the rottenness—of death.

The juxtaposition wasn't lost on her. And the difference had been a relationship with Jesus Christ.

The garden before her would be a constant reminder of that. And the challenge to share His unconditional love with a lost and dying world.

Joshua reached the telegraph office in Walker Creek and prayed there would be favorable news. But if there wasn't, he was still at peace. God had brought him this far. Even if he had to find a way to pay for the rest of his schooling or change universities, he would make the sacrifice.

"Ziegler!" Mr. Mavery held up a telegram. "I was about to send someone out to your ranch with this. It's marked urgent, so I knew you'd want to see it right away." The smile on the man's face was a good sign.

"Thank you, sir." Josh took the paper and walked back to his horse. It was a lengthy note that must have cost a small fortune to send.

He began to read:

Joshua,

I pray all is well with your fiancée. Please send news. I will have tickets ready for you as soon as you are available to return.

Rest assured all will be waiting for you at school. The university will not argue with me on this matter. If you will be delayed longer than two weeks, I will have to pull some strings, but don't worry.

Son, it's time I let you know who I am. You know me as Mr. Bricker, but I am your grandfather. Matthew Ziegler.

Foolishly, I disowned your father when he was determined to follow his dreams and go west. In my old age, I realized my mistake.

*I would like to come see you in Chicago as soon as you
are back.*

Perhaps one day, I can reconcile with your father.

> *My prayers are with you,*
> *Your grandfather*

Josh had to read it several times. His grandfather? Would
wonders never cease? He let out a chuckle as he headed back
into the office to send a response. Ziegler in German meant
brick layer. No wonder he'd chosen Bricker as his alias.

His parents had taken the news of Mary quite hard. Perhaps this news could bring a bit of joy back to the family.
Dad often spoke of his regret in how he left, but he'd never
felt comfortable reaching out to his parents. Not after being
disowned.

It took Josh thirty minutes to take care of business in town.
He sent a telegram to his grandfather and received another
with more information in return. Tomorrow he'd have to leave
again. But so much had changed.

God was good.

It was almost nine o'clock by the time he reached the Lakeman home again.

Anna ran out the door to meet him.

He pulled her into his arms. "Oh, I don't want to say goodbye to you."

"Then don't. Let's just write as often as we can and never
say goodbye." She pulled his hand and tugged him along with
her toward the creek. "It's late and Dad's asleep, but he wanted
me to tell you that he'll be praying for you and he's always here
if you want to write to him, too."

"I will. He's been wonderful to me. And I hope that he con-
tinues to recover."

Stopping in the middle of the path, she faced him. "My hope—and his—is that he will be able to walk me down the aisle at our wedding."

"That's good motivation."

"I know you need to get home, and the longer we put this off, the harder it will be." She bit her lip.

"Let me tell you something amazing that happened today, and then I'll head home."

"Oh?" She bounced on her toes and held onto both of his hands.

As he told her about his grandfather being his mysterious benefactor, her eyes sparkled.

"Josh, that's incredible! And you'll get to see him?"

"When I return, yes. He's even offering to pay for Mom, Dad, Martha, Alan, Caleb, and *you* to travel out for my graduation."

She squeezed his hands. "That's so generous!"

"And he wants to come to the wedding."

thirty-two

"I have accomplished some things but there is ten times
as much that I wish to accomplish."

~Earl Douglass

Monday, August 12

"Mr. Oppenheim, Albert, Miss Oppenheim." Anna cleared her
throat. "Thank you for meeting me here today." She stood at
the head of a table in a room at Mr. Gilbert's law office.

The elder Mr. Oppenheim tapped his fingers on the table.
"You said there was news?"

"Yes, sir." She turned to the lawyer.

Mr. Gilbert opened up an envelope and read, "'First, the ad-
judication process has taken place and the drawings that were
chosen to be the most accurate belong to Miss Lakeman.'"

Praise God! She could finally breathe. What a relief!
Wouldn't Dad be overjoyed.

Albert jumped out of his seat and stormed out of the room.
His father didn't appear too fazed. Simply lifted his brows.
"And second?"

"'With the death of Mr. Walker . . .'" Mr. Gilbert pulled out another envelope, this one much larger.

Anna inhaled and held her breath for a moment. It didn't matter that she'd been awarded the privilege to do the drawings if the new owner of the Walker Ranch wanted to get rid of the contracts they had with Julian. Mr. Gilbert had warned them that because of the extenuating circumstances of Mr. Walker's death, a judge might very well award a clean slate for the new owners and let them determine if they wanted a paleontological dig on their property. But Mr. Gilbert hadn't been the lawyer for Julian Walker. So he didn't have access to the will.

Until now.

Gilbert opened the envelope and read the contents. His eyebrows shot up to his hairline. "This is unexpected." He grinned. "Mr. Julian Walker has left his entire estate to Anna Lakeman."

"*What?*" She stood up and bumped the table, knocking over her water glass.

Mr. Gilbert scrambled to clean up the mess.

She waved her hands in the air. "I don't understand. When did he do that?"

"This will is dated a couple days after his father's passing."

She sat down hard into the chair. "What does this mean?"

"It means . . . the most prosperous ranch in the territory is yours. You can certainly dig on your own land. And there's a great deal of it." Her lawyer sent her a big smile.

Mr. Oppenheim stood. Straightened his waistcoat. "Miss Lakeman, I don't wish to be rude, but if you aren't in need of my investment any longer, I wish to recind our contract."

"But . . . your name . . . the museum . . . ?"

"Your father has been a good investment for me over the years. My name is on plenty of discoveries. But you don't need me any longer and I wish to leave this territory and return home."

Now that she was a wealthy woman, she didn't need investors. The realization struck her stomach like a hammer on an anvil. It didn't seem right. Not at all. Not at the cost that had been paid. She swallowed. "I appreciate you, Mr. Oppenheim. Father and I both do. I'm sorry it hasn't been what you had hoped." She held out her hand, hoping he would agree to shake it.

He stared at it for a second and then shook it. "I'm certain Mr. Gilbert here can draw up the necessary paperwork."

"Yes, sir, I can. I'll get it done straightaway." Her lawyer nodded.

"Good. I'd like to return to Chicago as soon as possible." Mr. Oppenheim turned back to her and leaned in a bit. His voice lowered. "I must apologize on my son's behalf. His mother spoiled them both. I insisted he apologize for his childish and reckless behavior, but I'm assuming he hasn't?"

"No, sir. But I appreciate you telling me."

Two hours later, she left Mr. Gilbert's office with the feeling she could almost float home. So much tragedy and ugliness had happened at the Walkers', but perhaps she could bring a little beauty—in honor of Mary. And Julian.

Wait until she told Dad. He wouldn't believe it all.

And tomorrow? She would be back at the dig site—on her property!—releasing the bones to tell their tales.

EPILOGUE

"Above the firm foundation of the hills above the wooded glens, above what we call the realities of life, and in spite of the hard things we call facts, one feels that far off, somewhere, somehow, good and truth and love will conquer and there is peace."

~Earl Douglass

July 19, 1880 • Walker Creek

Dad held out his arm. "This is a proud day, sweetheart."

She beamed up at him through her veil. "I'm so excited." Taking his offered arm, she leaned into his strength. The past two years had seen Dad's full recovery, Joshua's thriving work with Doctor Walsh, and her name on a paleontological dig.

Once her beloved had come home to Walker Creek permanently, they decided to wait for her to finish the dig before marrying. It had been a joyous season with their community to welcome their new doctor back and for them to share their engagement with the families who'd known them their whole lives.

Thank You, God. For each and every little miracle. For how You've brought us to this day.

"Ready?"

"Ready." She nodded.

The next bit of time passed in a blur. Dad walked her down the aisle. She took Josh's hands. And the reverend spoke about love as he read from First Corinthians chapter thirteen.

But it all seemed like a dream. Was it really happening? Spots danced in front of her eyes, and she closed them.

"Anna." Where was Josh calling to her from? A strong squeeze to her hands made her open her eyes. "Are you all right?"

His whispered words brought her back to the moment.

"What happened?" she whispered back.

"Well, the reverend asked you a question. You swayed and didn't answer. I thought you might faint."

Nervous laughter bubbled up, but looking into his eyes steadied her. She took a deep breath and focused. "What was the question?"

A few soft chuckles came from the pews of their little church.

The reverend cleared his throat. "Do you take this man—"

"I do!"

The rest of the ceremony passed in joy, laughter, smiles, and oh, that kiss. Once she relaxed, she was able to relish the day.

And now . . . they were married.

"My beautiful wife." Joshua leaned in and kissed Anna one more time before helping her up to the train platform.

"Mr. Ziegler. You make me blush," she teased.

"Well, I have to admit that I have one more surprise for you."

"Oh? Isn't this lovely trip enough of a surprise?"

He handed her a newspaper from Washington, DC. "I asked my grandfather to do me a favor. Since he knows the owner of the paper, he spoke to him about doing a write-up on your Allosaurus."

She gasped and read the headline aloud. "'Paleontologist

and artist Anna Lakeman proudly shows off her father's find—the Lakeman Allosaurus—in southwest Wyoming Territory.'" The picture was from last month with the team of scientists who'd come to study the bones, and it filled the top of the front page.

"It says plenty about your father in there as well. I made sure of it. Grandfather promised me that it would be done accurately. No sensationalism."

Tears filled her eyes. This wonderful man. Oh, how she loved him. "This is amazing."

"You deserve it, Anna. After all your hard work." The sparkle in his eye was just for her. And she adored it.

"Thank you for believing in me. And thank you for giving me the opportunity to continue digging." The long gulley on their ranch had indeed been rich with dinosaur bones. They could dig for the next two decades and probably only reach a fraction of the fossils. But it was perfect. Because it gave her father what he loved, they were bringing beauty from death, and they would be able to raise their children with the knowledge of God's amazing creation. There was so much they didn't understand about dinosaurs yet, but they planned to learn.

Together.

One bone at a time.

NOTE FROM THE AUTHOR

The field of paleontology is fascinating, isn't it? Especially with the excruciating amount of time it often takes these scientists to recover the fossils from the rock and earth. My research—once again—for this series has been intense so far and I still have a lot to do. But if you know me, you know that I *love* research. The more I learn about this field, the more I want to get out there and dig myself. Although being an asthmatic, I probably wouldn't be able to handle all the dust. Or the heat for that matter.

The TREASURES OF THE EARTH series is very precious to me. Not only has it been a privilege to know and work with Earl Douglass's granddaughter on it, but my dad (who passed away in February) enjoyed it when I bounced ideas off of him. It was an area of science that he wasn't *as* familiar with (he was a chemistry professor a long time ago) but boy, did my father love learning. Even there at the end when dementia sometimes made him very confused, I could almost always get him back when I spoke of science or history. The Great Dinosaur Rush era definitely intrigued him.

Throughout this series, we will explore a bit more of the

happenings of the Bone Wars, and a lot more about women in paleontology.

To this day, it is difficult for women in this scientific field. It is also still an incredibly cutthroat field with finds and discoveries stolen. Hard to believe in this day and age. Granted it's not quite like it was back in the 1800s during the infamous Bone Wars, but shocking nonetheless.

Dr. Sue Ann Bilbey, a paleontologist, helped me during my research and even met me for breakfast with my research buddies. She has a wealth of information and knowledge and wanted to make sure that people understood the difficulties still present. She was also instrumental in helping to get Earl Douglass's biography (written by his son Gawin) into readers' hands. *Speak to the Earth and It Will Teach You* is an incredible read, full of Earl's diary entries, poetry, and insight into what he went through just to be able to dig for his beloved bones. I know he would be thrilled today to see Dinosaur National Monument and to know that people are able to see the fossils still in the rock—just like he always dreamed.

Be watching for *Set in Stone*, book two in the TREASURES OF THE EARTH series, releasing March 2024. I'd like to leave you with this poem of Earl's that I used in pieces throughout this story.

Until next time,

Kimberley

Nature's Noblemen (entire poem) - Earl Douglass

They went out into Nature;
They left the traveled way
To read her deepest secrets
In the open light of day.

They fled to wildernesses,
Away from the beaten road,
To search the pathless mazes
Afar from man's abode.

They went out into Nature
With firm and joyous tread
To read in Truth's great volume
Whatever there was said.

They found the leaves were scattered,
With here and there a page;
And some were being written
And some were dim with age.

And there were wondrous stories
That never had been told,
Printed in rocky tablets—
Tales of the days of old.

There were some who, starting, faltered,
Or went with cautious tread
When they heard the low-browed scoffers
Who jeered at what they said.

And some shrank back with terror
From pathless wastes unknown,
And vast, untraveled forests
And unsailed oceans, lone.

But these the unknown tempted;
The wastes they did not fear;
Where was even in the deserts
An unseen presence near.

And they went, fearless, forward,
For when they but looked back
They saw in the ways of error
Only a blood-stained track.

They trusted Truth was safest—
That it could never die
But would conquer ghastly error
And triumph by and by.

They went through wildernesses
Where no man's feet had trod
To find out Nature's secrets—
The unfound way to God.

And so they searched and labored
To find a way from night
And sin and pain and sorrow
To Truth's and Freedom's height.

ACKNOWLEDGMENTS

After 30-some-odd books, you might get tired of hearing me say that it takes a slew of people to get each story into your hands. Well, I need to say it again.

Huge thanks go to the team at Bethany House Publishing and Baker Publishing Group. They are the best, and I am privileged to be part of the BHP and BPG family.

Jessica Sharpe—thank you for getting so excited about dinosaurs with me.

Karen Ball—each book working with you, I find I learn more and more. Thank you. Thank you. Thank you. You are the best editor. Ever.

Diane Douglass Iverson—Earl Douglass's granddaughter—thank you for chatting with me and encouraging me. And most of all for allowing me the glimpse into your grandfather. Thank you for all the work you did to get *Speak to the Earth and It Will Teach You* out there. It is a treasure. You were very gracious to give me permission to use quotes from Earl in this series. Thank you. Thank you.

Dr. Sue Ann Bilbey—thank you for meeting with me, for answering so many questions about paleontology, giving me great connections, and for the emails back and forth. You are an incredible woman and scientist.

Carrie Kintz—I don't know what I would do without you. Seriously. I'm so thankful you are on my team. Thank you for all the pep talks. All the brainstorming. All the . . . everything. You are so dear to me, my friend.

Tracie Peterson—for all these years . . . thank you. As we head toward three decades of friendship, I'm in awe of what God has done. I love you more.

Becca the short and Jeni Koch—thanks for helping me to go through all of Earl Douglass's writings for quotes.

Jeni and Renette, for traveling with me and researching. Renette—you are a dear for driving all the way out there to help me and share all your knowledge of the area. Jeni—you just need to go with me everywhere I research because your wonder and excitement match my own. What fun we had!

Laura Flint—oh, my friend. Who knew that your little comment on Facebook would lead to this? I love it and am so thankful for you and your family. Give all the kiddos big hugs from me and tell them to practice.

To my precocious little grandson—oh, I love it that you now love dinosaurs and put up with Nana bringing you fun little stuffies. Dippy is still my favorite. Give him a hug from me.

Josh and Kayla (and Ruth and Steven)—my heart is so full. I'm blessed beyond measure to be called Mom.

Jeremy—oh, you knew I was weird when you first met me. But even though you thought it was just because I was a musician (and that ramped up when you found out I was a writer), I'm so thankful that you've spent the past thirty-two-plus years loving me, brainstorming with me, and enjoying the story with me. I love you, Superman.

My Lord and Savior—thank You. For the gift of story. The gift of life. And unconditional love.

To God be the Glory,

Kimberley

Kimberley Woodhouse (www.kimberleywoodhouse.com) is an award-winning, bestselling author of more than 30 fiction and nonfiction books. Kim and her incredible husband of 30-plus years live in Colorado, where they play golf together, spend time with their kids and grandbaby, and research all the history around them.

Sign Up for
Kimberley's Newsletter

Keep up to date with Kimberley's latest news on book releases and events by signing up for her email list at the link below.

FOLLOW KIMBERLEY ON SOCIAL MEDIA

Kimberley Woodhouse   @kimberleywoodhouse   @kimwoodhouse

KimberleyWoodhouse.com

More from Kimberley Woodhouse

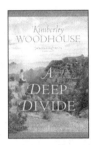

Kimberley Woodhouse presents a dramatic historical romance series set at the El Tovar Hotel, which overlooks the majesty of the Grand Canyon. Seamlessly combining adventure, romance, and faith in the Gilded Age era, you will be turning the pages until the very end.

SECRETS OF THE CANYON:
A Deep Divide, A Gem of Truth, A Mark of Grace

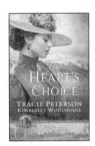

Rebecca Whitman is the first female court reporter in Montana. During a murder trial, she's convinced that the defendant is innocent, but no one except the handsome new Carnegie librarian, Mark Andrews, will listen to her. In a race against time, will they be able to find the evidence they need—and open their hearts to love—before it's too late?

The Heart's Choice
THE JEWELS OF KALISPELL #1

❧ BETHANYHOUSE

Bethany House Fiction

@bethanyhousefiction

@bethany_house

@bethanyhousefiction

Free exclusive resources for your book group at bethanyhouseopenbook.com

Sign up for our fiction newsletter today at bethanyhouse.com